CURSE OF THE RING

Loki glanced down at the dwarf, having forgotten him in the wonder and delight of the Rhinegold.

Andvari laughed bitterly. "Do not stare so! Remember that I held the gold for many years, and I have listened to its whisperings."

Loki looked annoyed, and raised his sword in a half-threatening gesture. "Begone! Crawl back into your hole. You have bought your freedom."

"Free? Am I truly free?" Andvari asked, and laughed harshly. "There is no freedom from the gold once it has been in your hands. Hear me well, thief . . . Thus do I curse the gold! While it has brought me wealth and happiness, let it now bring only death and betrayal to its bearer. Its bright gleam will bring no contentment or joy, only dark visions to trouble the thoughts and dreams. Fear and care will haunt the one who commands it, while it will awaken envy and greed in those about him. And in the end, it will turn upon the one who covets it, bringing deception and death. You have taken my treasure; now take my curse. Let it destroy every hand that holds it until it returns to me!"

Ace Books by Thorarinn Gunnarsson

SONG OF THE DWARVES
THE VALKYRIE *(Coming in August 1989)*

SONG OF THE DWARVES

Thorarinn Gunnarsson

ACE BOOKS, NEW YORK

This book is an Ace
original edition, and
has never been previously
published.

SONG OF THE DWARVES

An Ace Book/published by arrangement with
the author

PRINTING HISTORY
Ace edition/August 1988

ISBN: 0-441-72690-9

Ace Books are published by The Berkley Publishing Group,
200 Madison Avenue, New York, New York 10016.
The name ''Ace'' and the ''A''
logo are trademarks belonging to
Charter Communications, Inc.
PRINTED IN THE UNITED STATES OF AMERICA

10 9 8 7 6 5 4 3 2 1

Jotunheim

KULLTARS
ICE SHEET

YMIR MOUTH

SJÆLLBRYBOK

UTGARD

KLETTASTADUR

WORLD SERPENT

HROSKSJÆLLE

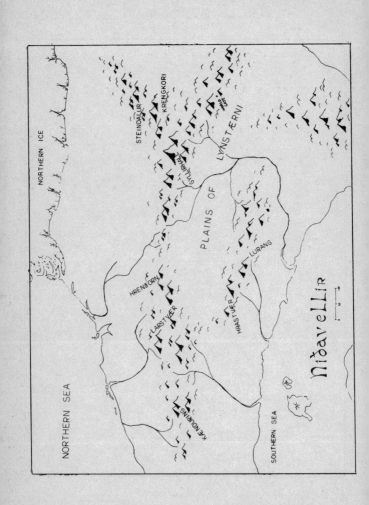

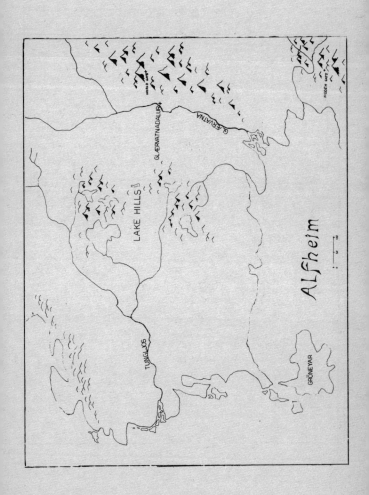

ALfheim

LAKE HILLS

GLERVATNADALURA

GLERVATNA

TUNGLJÓS

GRÓNEYAR

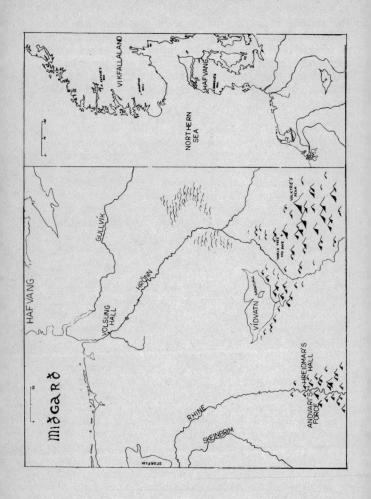

Pronunciation Guide

The spelling of names and places in this story has been adapted to reflect as closely as possible the pronunciation in the original Norse. For that reason, many of the names within may be unfamiliar to most readers. This is a guide to the approximate pronunciation of special sounds in modern Icelandic, the language which most closely resembles Old Norse.

A—Preceding one consonant, *a* as in h*a*t. The short *a*, preceding two consonants, has a briefer sound.

E—Preceding one consonant, *e* as in t*e*ll. Preceding two consonants, the short *e* is pronounced *e* as in g*e*t.

I—The long *i* has no true English equivalent. Either the long or the short *i* should be pronounced *i* as in p*i*n.

O—The long *o*, preceding one consonant, is most like the *a* in *a*ll. The short *o*, preceding two consonants, is pronounced *o* as in p*o*t.

U—The long *u* resembles *oo* as in m*oo*n. The short *u* has no true English equivalent.

ae—This is, in fact, one letter, æ, known in Old English as the *ash*. It is pronounced as the English *eye*.

ei or ey—resembles the English *a* in c*a*me. *Stein* is pronounced like the English *stain* rather than the German *stein*.

ð—This is a single sound which has long been represented by the two letters *th* in English. This sound occurs only within words and is the soft *th*, pronounced as the *th* in *th*en.

þ—This is also a single sound also spelled in English as *th*. It occurs only at the beginning of words and is the hard *th*, pronounced as the *th* in *th*ick. This character was once used in English but has since been mistaken for *y* as in the case of *ye*, a word which never existed in its own time but has always been *the*.

PART ONE

CHAPTER ONE

Of the Coming of the Aesir

Here begins the tale, and tells of ancient days and other worlds; of the Aesir and the Vanir, great beings who dared in their conceit to consider themselves gods. For gods they were not, and there were always those who contested their right to claim the nine worlds for their own and those who cherished and nurtured their own plans of claim and conquest. Herein lies the tale of that great conflict, the story of what once was and never should have been. Wars were fought and battles were lost and won, but in the end it was all for nothing.

The tale of this ancient universe began a very long time ago indeed, when all existence, all matter, time and space came into being in a single fiery instant. Of what came before perhaps not even the spirit of the living universe herself can say, if indeed there can be thought of a time before the beginning. The memory of that ancient, glorious beginning still echoes dimly through the star-realm, like the waves of some vast sea that knows no shore. Even the gods themselves do not recall that great beginning, or even if their own existence began then or long after.

The earliest memories of the gods are of themselves. In those days they were formless beings of light and energy. Whether they came into existence suddenly, in the heart of some awakening star or perhaps in the most ancient awakening, or whether they developed shape and intellect over a long period of evolution, they could not say. Their deepest and earliest memories told them only that they had lived and wandered the stars for a very long time. Slowly, one by one, they became aware of themselves as living, thinking beings. From that moment their memories began, and they began to observe the universe around them and direct their once aimless wanderings.

Thus did they begin to accumulate their vast store of learning and lore, although at that time their lore was only of the things they saw in their wanderings. Piece by piece they began to understand the workings of the universe. They probed the fiery hearts of stars and the immense dark clouds of the voids where stars formed and grew to blaze forth in sudden glory. Ageless themselves, they saw the life and death of stars and watched as the ash of old suns reformed into new, or into small, cold and solid forms. Worlds were new and interesting, and matters of special interest and excitement. They turned their attention from the vast to the minute, and discovered the form and shape of matter at its most elemental state.

And having discovered themselves and the secrets of the star-realm, they came in time to discover each other. The first such meeting was between the two who would later be called Odhinn and Frigg. Odhinn's delight was in the grandeur he saw in the star-realm, and he probed deep secrets and complex systems until he understood all parts of a given thing. But Frigg's interest was in small and often subtle things. She especially liked to see how forms changed with the passage of time, and when she saw the first humble stirrings of life on several of the small, dark worlds she found a lasting fascination for it. She was the first to understand the meaning of life, an existence that was so different in form from her own, and she was the first to recognize its great potential.

That first meeting was sudden and unexpected, for they had never thought nor had ever had reason to consider that others like themselves might exist. Nothing else that had befallen them had ever come as a greater shock, or a greater delight. They approached cautiously and with much apprehension, each uncertain until they found that they could understand one another's thoughts. So it was that they discovered speech, and they held it to be the greatest of gifts. Indeed they called it the Gift from that time on, for it was the one thing that Odhinn and Frigg gave to one another in their first meeting and which they later shared with others of their kind.

They remained together for many hundreds of turns of that dark ball of rock where they met, speaking and sharing their thoughts and memories. Speech allowed them to exchange thoughts and ideas and so increase their knowledge without the lengthy process of direct observation. And acquiring new knowledge, satisfying their insatiable but patient curiosities, was the only delight they knew, and the only thing that brought pleasure and purpose to their eternal and changeless existence. But all they knew at that time were things that they had seen, facts and theories they had inferred from their long observation of the workings of the star-realm, and so they found that the greatest part of their knowledge overlapped. They knew no histories other than their own, and they had not yet invented arts to amuse themselves.

And so they traveled for a time through the star-realm, Odhinn and Frigg together. They journeyed far and saw much, although in truth they learned little else of the workings of the universe. Indeed there was little that they did not already know, although it was to Odhinn's vast disappointment that he had in time to admit that knowledge itself did not give him any special powers of creation or command. In the earliest times, when he had still been alone, he had often thought that time and space, matter and energy would respond to his will if he only knew their secrets. Instead he had found laws, many that he could use to augment his own great powers but which he could never break. To break even one law, he found, would threaten the framework of the whole and risk the destruction of all existence. Perhaps it was only natural for him to have assumed that the universe was his alone, and it had displeased him to find it otherwise. The stars burned whether he willed it or not; worlds formed while he watched passively; and life arose and flourished while it was still beneath his notice.

Then came the moment when they suddenly felt a strange presence at the far limit of their senses, as if they heard a distant voice across the dark plains of the star-realm. Following that voice, they found a third of their kind, wandering as if lost through the far-flung remains of an exploded star. He was one of great powers, little interested in the learning of the secret ways except when it helped him to create and command even greater forces. Odhinn liked this one for his great powers; powers often greater than the ones even he possessed, although rough and sometimes unpredictable. The stranger joined them in their wanderings, and thus they became three.

Thereafter their numbers grew rapidly, for at Odhinn's direction they began to search out others of their kind. Three became six and later nine, and then they joined together with a second group of five. They shared their language and their knowledge with each new member, and so became a united body in speech and learning. Odhinn remained their leader, for none could match his wisdom and his abilities to reason and deduce. The powerful one became his second, and since he had little desire for close probing of the many things they saw, he served always to watch over the group and keep them from dangers. For there were dangers, although they most often brought perils upon themselves through lack of caution.

When their numbers grew to fourteen they decided that they must take names for themselves, as they had earlier given names to the many things of the universe. Just what their names meant in their own language was never known, for they allowed no one outside their own group to learn their speech. But they were always free with their own names, for they feared no one. They called themselves the Aesir. Odhinn was their leader, wise and powerful, and at his side was Frigg, the life-tender. The one of great strength was called Thor, and later known also as Thunor, the Thunderer, because he retained in his later days his ability to call forth great bolts of energy that he could direct at will. His special delights were in strife and conquest, although there was no evil in him. Rather was he a champion of the weak against any evil he found, and he would rage furiously at the slightest injustice.

Tyr was in many ways like Thor, except that the Thunderer

was always as exuberant in good humor and jest as he was in battle, while Tyr was forever grim and silent. But they were a pair, complementing one another, and there was no challenge that together they could not face. But there was also a very different Tyr that even the Aesir seldom saw, the gentle and sympathetic being who would later take pity on an unfortunate wolf cub.

Another of the great ones was Heimdall, who was called also the Guardian. His special powers lay in his unique senses, not just sight and sound but in others that mortals do not often possess. In those days all things lay open to his mind, and he could detect the least movement or trace the smallest source of any radiant energy. In the later days he retained a degree of his talent and so remained the Guardian of the Aesir, and they had little to fear as long as he guarded the entrance to their citadel. Little escaped his notice when he stood at guard, while in the chase he could track his prey by the sound of its steps even from far away or follow a trail from which all sign or trace of smell had faded.

Of equally great importance to the Aesir, at least in the later days, was Idhunn. She was, like Frigg, a life-tender, although her greatest talent lay not in the study of its form but its structure. She alone knew how to create life, and return the fullness of life to those who suffered injury or the slow decay of age, but those were secrets she guarded jealously. Her companion was Bragi, who first invented art for the Aesir by playing upon the wordings in the language they had invented, and called it poetry. He excelled in the arts thereafter, and elvish and mortal bards called upon him for inspiration.

There were others of the Aesir who joined with Odhinn in the days of wandering. There was Sif, the companion of Thor. If she had any special talent, it was her ability to keep Thor's exuberance in check and soothe his anger. And there was Hoenir, the Silent. Gefjun later left the Aesir to dwell as a queen among the mortals; while Thorgerda, the Radiant, went likewise among the elves. Mimir was called the wisest, but his wisdom failed him in the end. Five and sixty they were in number, although barely a score of them were ever known, even by name, among mortals. As many again chose not to remain with the Aesir but returned to their leisurely wandering of the star-realm. And at least five were destroyed in accidents, through playing with forces that they could not control.

After many long ages, the wanderings of the Aesir brought them to a small but green and lively world. Life had ascended there to such heights as they had never before seen. The seas teamed with weed and algae and a vast variety of creatures, fishes, worms and many small things that wore their skeletons on the outside. But what seized the interest of the Aesir lay above the waves. For here the sky was blue and clear and gentle winds shepherded clouds of the purest white, turning only occasionally to violent storms, while the single great mass of land lay beneath a carpet of green forest.

And in that forest dwelled creatures the likes of which the Aesir had never seen nor even imagined. Most were small and quick, darting about the shadowy underbrush in search of food. But some were vast and ponderous; immense grazers of the forests and the streams and bays, and the towering hunters who preyed upon them. And strangest of all was that these creatures thought—in a simple and highly reflexive manner to be sure, pondering no abstraction greater than where they might next find food—but they had minds enough that the Aesir could recognize rudimentary thoughts in their small, simple brains.

And so the Aesir descended to the surface of the world with the plan that they might dwell there investigating this new thing. It surprised and alarmed them that creatures of flesh could evolve along such paths that led to even a simple intelligence, for they had always considered things of matter and substance to be inanimate and unchanging, while only beings of energy like themselves could think and move according to their own desires. It led them to wonder if they had ever been like these beasts, simple minds without reason beyond the most basic functions, in those days before they could remember.

Frigg and Idhunn made the creatures of that world their special study, and they discovered a system of life and evolution vast beyond anything they had ever considered. They studied that matter at length and pondered its long development until they understood it as best they could. Then they called the others together in council and spoke of what they had found.

They explained that the creatures of that world were indeed beings somewhat like themselves, but of material form. Being of matter, and of a fragile sort that could repair but not renew itself, all living things grow old and eventually die. And then Idhunn spoke of her own beliefs, that life such as this could evolve into thinking beings in many ways like themselves, although that evolution would be through many long generations rather than within the life of a single individual as it had been with them. The others considered that a marvelous thing and wanted to see if it really could happen, but they were hesitant to stay on that one world for the millions of circuits it would make about its sun before that would happen. In the end they left the decision to Odhinn, as they had always followed him.

Odhinn did not know what he should do. He went alone into that strange world, to look upon the mountains and forests as he considered his choice. He did not desire to stay; indeed that thought frightened him as it had most of the others. Not to journey through the star-realm, searching forever for the heart of the universe and uncover its deepest secrets: Those things were the delight of the Aesir, and the only existence that they had ever known. There was a certain security in the old, familiar pattern, the eternal quest from which none of them had seriously deviated in all their long existence. It would take courage to give up their cherished life to remain in one place. But Idhunn promised results within one hundred million circuits of this world of blue and green; their memory stretched back a span a hundred times as long. It would be only a very short time by that comparison, and they could always abandon their wait whenever they wished.

Then he began to consider what manner of creature it might be, this intelligent being in animal form. He could imagine only something akin to the lesser predators, for they were quick in both movement and thought. Many treaded the land on two legs, and he had observed them using their forward limbs to grasp and hold. Could those keen eyes perceive the true form of all existence? Perhaps so, or perhaps such beings

would perceive a universe very different from the vast yet
familiar one of the Aesir.

In time he began to wander if such beings could be of some
use to him. They would be mortal, short-lived and, perhaps,
possessing no special powers at all. They would surely look
upon a being like himself, eternal and immensely powerful,
as their lord and master, if not a god. That thought began to
appeal to him, as he sat alone and brooded in the lofty peaks.
And why should it not be so? He was Odhinn, Lord of the
Aesir, and he and his fellows had the power to burn off this
poor, cold world in a sheet of flame or blast it to dust, or
cherish it and nurture it and make it into a grand and beautiful
thing. If there were more powerful beings, then Odhinn had
not seen their like in all the long ages of the wandering.

It pleased him, these thoughts and dreams of power. Power
had always been his special desire, power of his own making,
that he might create or destroy at will. Now he contemplated
another type of power, an abstract power based upon the
loyalty and obedience of some mortal race that would give
itself over willingly to his authority.

And so he returned to the Aesir and spoke of what he
would do. He related how he would guide and mold this
mortal race, teach them and cherish them, and the mortals
would return their care and love with honor and loyalty. But
the Aesir were divided in their thoughts. Many saw clearly
the image that Odhinn created for them and were pleased. But
many saw no use in such an experiment, not if it would
interrupt their wanderings for so long, and they had little or
no desire for such power as Odhinn spoke of. Three score and
five of the Aesir chose to remain with Odhinn, among them
Thor, Heimdall and Tyr, while as many elected for themselves a new leader and returned to their wanderings.

Now that the Aesir were bound to a single world, they
began to measure time for themselves according to its years.
And the years passed swiftly. The Aesir soon began a survey
of their new world, such as they had never before sought to
know any one thing. Idhunn and Frigg went out into the
forests, so that they might learn the shape and manner of
every smallest creature and plant and watch their development
through the long ages. Odhinn gathered together the most

powerful members of their group and went out into the world also, to seek out any hidden danger that might exist, although they hardly expected to find anything that might be a danger to such beings as themselves in that quiet, peaceful place.

They went in pairs, each with a separate area to explore. Odhinn went himself with Thor, while Tyr and Heimdall were sent to investigate that world's single moon. Bragi and Gefjun were sent to the polar seas, to seek answers to the riddle of why such vast sheets of ice should form there at certain times of the year. And Hoenir and Mimir went into the mountains to discover what vast forces could thrust the towering peaks so high.

Mimir was considered the wisest of the Aesir, for he had unraveled more of the deeper and more complex mysteries than any of the others. He cared little for that world or for the race of mortals that Odhinn spoke of, and no one had expected that he would remain. Indeed he intended only to rest from his wanderings for a short time and put his thoughts into order before returning to the star-realm. Hoenir was most often his companion and, some believed, nearly his equal in wisdom, except that he was remarkably silent, speaking seldom if ever to anyone except Odhinn and Mimir. It was never known just why he was so reluctant to speak, since he was also the most patient of listeners.

Some time had passed since their search had begun as they drifted slowly up the length of one great range of mountains and down the next. One day they came upon a wide valley, a grassy plain bordered on all sides by snow-crowned peaks. A rocky, barren plateau stood at its northern end, and it was here that they were led by some dim murmur of unknown power. They ascended to the top of the plateau and looked about for the source of that energy; as strong as it was, it was also shadowy and difficult to trace. They searched the vast expanse of the plateau's broken and rocky surface before they found it at last in one corner.

What they saw was a small black shape suspended a short distance above the ground. It changed shape constantly, revolving and flowing in upon itself, sometimes sending out misty black tendrils, then swirling faster and faster to become a black whirlpool. Even Mimir had not seen its like before, although he immediately guessed that it must be some hole or gateway into another place. It appeared to have no effect upon solid matter, but it drew all forms of energy into itself. Light seemed to bend toward it, and the curious vortex had drawn all heat from the surrounding rock for some distance about until it stood within a circle of barren, frozen ground.

Mimir was drawn to the thing. He looked at it from all sides before returning to Hoenir, who was watching from a safe distance.

"I am going up to it," he said. "I want to see if I can look through it, or at least determine what is on the other side."

"You will be drawn in," Hoenir warned. He was plainly disturbed, for it was not like him to venture even that much unbidden.

"I know that," Mimir replied impatiently. "But I will be careful. I will extend only a part of myself toward it, while the greatest part of my being will remain here firmly anchored to this rock. Its pull is not great, or it would have drawn all the heat from this world long ago."

But that was incorrect, as Mimir should have known. True, the range of the thing was very limited, but he should have guessed how great its pull was by the way it bent light toward itself. He was inattentive to such clues in his curiosity and excitement. He anchored himself to the immense slab of rock, encircling it like an envelope of golden light, and sent forth a slender tendril toward the black vortex.

Slowly and cautiously he approached it, and yet it seemed to take no notice of his presence but continued to spin and flow inward upon itself. He could feel its gentle tug, striving to steal the light and energy from his very being, but its hold was ever a slippery one. Satisfied that he was safe, he began to move toward it, peering into its shadowy depths, until he was barely a yard away.

The icey vortex convulsed suddenly and without warning, and sent out a black tentacle that engulfed Mimir's own extended tendril. He cried out as the thing ripped away his very substance and tried in vain to draw away. But he could not, for the cold grip of the thing was beyond his strength. In a desperate move he tried to free himself by breaking his own tendril of power, sacrificing a part of himself to gain his freedom, but he found that he was paralyzed. Then the thing jerked him suddenly inward with overwhelming strength. He disappeared shrieking into the vortex, and the huge stone, still locked in his grasp, came crashing down upon the thing like a cork in a bottle. Mimir had never released his hold upon it.

A terrible shudder ran through the world, moving outward from the plateau like a circular wave, passing itself and then a second time as it sent the planet swinging in its orbit. The oceans rose up from their beds and flooded the lower lands, so that vast areas of forest and coastal marshes were buried beneath the silt. The shuddering of the crust released earthquakes of tremendous scale; old volcanoes were shaken into life and new ones sprang forth. Skies darkened over large areas of the world; violent winds descended from every direction, and sheets of lightning arced back and forth between ground and sky.

The Aesir looked up wherever they were throughout the world, and as the world shook beneath them they prepared for flight. Then they heard a distant cry and paused in their retreat. Hoenir, always the silent, had this once sent forth a call for help that even Tyr and Heimdall heard on the moon. The Aesir hesitated a moment, caught between their desire to flee and the need of one of their own, but they responded one and all to Hoenir's single call and flew immediately to his aid, while it seemed that the world was destroying itself beneath them.

They found Hoenir alone atop the plateau. There was no indication that this was the site of some terrible blast that had shaken the entire world, but there was no doubt that something very strange and mysterious had happened there. They immediately noted the circle of ice-laden ground. An immense slab of rock lay in the very center of that ring, now broken into four even pieces. And in the very center, where all the cracks met, there stood a tall, slender tree. Although only a bare sapling in appearance, it was already more than a hundred feet in height and growing with visible speed. Its long, narrow leaves were over a foot in length.

Odhinn indicated for the others to keep their distance and approached cautiously until he stood beside Hoenir, who remained motionless, staring up at the tree not thirty yards away.

"Hoenir, what happened?" he demanded gently. "What is

that thing, that its mere presence could cause an entire world to tremble?''

"It is Mimir," Hoenir replied. And with that he grew even more unwilling to speak than ever before, and it was some time before Odhinn was able to get from him the story of what Mimir had done. Odhinn was very fearful by that time, for many scores of volcanoes had been awakened by the shaking; floods had devastated fully a third of the world, and some lands had submerged never to return. Idhunn fretted that the native life would not survive the destruction.

As the day turned to night the shaking slowly subsided and ceased, although the echo of it would continue to resound through the depths of the world for some time. Odhinn sent the others away to do what they could to halt the destruction, while he remained behind to watch the tree. He believed that something would surely happen before that strange tree reached its full height. Thor waited atop a snowy peak not far away, ready to lend his own great powers at need, while Heimdall cast about, using his own talents in an attempt to learn all that he could.

The terrible day passed into an uneasy night. A brisk wind came up from the south to chase away the dark, rolling clouds, revealing a clear, frosty sky full of stars which seemed to burn with unusual brightness, as if inviting the Aesir to leave that dreary place and return to their wanderings. Odhinn looked up at the stars, and he wondered if he had given up too much in his great plan. What was the use of being a god to a race of mortals when he could have been the uncontested lord of the star-realm? Mimir had trusted him, and Odhinn still did not know what had become of him.

"One comes," Heimdall warned suddenly. "From almost directly below you."

"One what?" Odhinn asked.

"That I cannot say," Heimdall replied. "One like ourselves in many ways, and yet unlike. Perhaps it is the spirit of this world, come to chase us away before we do any more damage."

"We will not be so easily removed," Odhinn declared contemptuously.

"Will we? This one has a subtle power even Thor would respect. If we stood up to this power, we would all be consumed."

"As Mimir was?"

"I do not know. Will you wait?"

"I will wait," Odhinn replied without hesitation. "There are questions that I must have answers to."

Heimdall said no more, although he was plainly uneasy. He sensed a far greater power than Odhinn anticipated, a hundredfold the power that all of the Aesir together could command. Always fearful of a fight he could not win, he withdrew to where Thor waited on the mountaintop and wondered if they would be able to get Odhinn away if there was trouble.

Odhinn drew back somewhat from the tree, withdrawing well beyond the edge of the bare rock from which the ice was slowly melting. Soon he too felt the power rising beneath him, growing steadily in strength until it surpassed anything that he had expected, and still it continued to grow like a star rising from the depths of the rock beneath him. And he was afraid, never suspecting that such spirits of energy dwelt within the hearts of worlds.

A pale blue light grew out of the darkness to bathe the plateau in its wan illumination, as if an unseen moon had suddenly shown through a break in dark clouds. A cold wind swept down from the north, carrying leaves and other debris, collecting into a small whirlwind halfway between Odhinn and the tree. It grew and shaped itself into a sphere that turned and twisted, while a small spark of blue flame in its center began to shine forth in increasing radiance. That core of light suddenly blazed like an exploding star, then steadied and held constant. The incomplete shell of leaves continued to turn about it, while a thick blue mist poured down and flowed across the rock.

Odhinn came forward a short distance and allowed his own golden light to shine, as if in answer to some challenge. He was encouraged, for this was a being in most ways like himself, a creature of light and energy without outward form. He could guess why it seemed to draw its substance from the heart of the world beneath it, if indeed this was the living, conscious spirit of this cold world. But he could not understand why it chose to clad itself in a shell of wind and leaves, unless the air itself added something to its being.

"I see you, Odhinn, and I know why you are here," she

said suddenly in the language of the Aesir. "I am called Jordh."

"I see you, Odhinn replied. "But I do not know who you are or why you are here, although I can well guess. I would prefer not to guess."

"Do you not know me?" Jordh asked, either in amusement or anger. Odhinn could not tell which. "I have listened to your words and watched your deeds since you first arrived, for I am all about you. I am Jordh, the world you thought to claim for your own."

"You are mistaken," Odhinn answered. "We make no claims upon this world. We belong to the star-realm, and we will return to our wanderings in time. We wish only to stay here for a while and observe. We did not mean to interfere."

"Do not tell me your lies, even if you believe them yourself!" Jordh snapped. "I know your mind, Odhinn. I have watched you; I am not easily deceived, and Mimir has told me much. You intend to watch until some group of my children has enough intelligence to learn some crude language and shape things to their own use. Then you intend to interfere in their affairs and order their small lives for them, play with them as if they were rude and simple copies of yourselves. Do I not speak correctly?"

"In some things I suppose you do," Odhinn admitted reluctantly. "But we do not intend to simply play with the lives of any creature of your world. We would cherish them. We would teach them and guide them, but their lives would remain their own. All we want from them is to see what manner of thoughts they might have, and what type of lives they would lead."

"Why do I doubt that? Why do I doubt that you could ever learn to respect life, as I hold dear every single growing thing and every creature that walks the forests and the plains, and flies through my skies? You hold life in secret contempt, because it grows old and dies while you do not. You destroy without thought. Look at what you have already done to me."

"What you have done to yourself, it seems to me," Odhinn countered. "If you would set traps for the Aesir, you should expect that we would struggle to free ourselves."

"Traps!" Jordh raged. She blazed in a fierce blue light,

and the shell of dried leaves and twigs that whirled about her burst into flames. "Would that I could trap you and destroy you all! But I dare not, for fear of the fragile life that still dwells within my realm. I was hoping that you would grow bored and depart to whatever disturbing place you came from, but no! You have all the tenacity of the small carrion feeders, digging and probing and caring nothing for what you disturb or destroy so long as you satisfy your own hunger for knowledge. If you are indeed here to learn, then you should know the foolishness of breaking something to discover what it is.

"As for your companion, I did nothing to him. I laid no traps, nor is it within my power to restore him to you. He now belongs in part to me, although the greatest part of his being belongs to other realms where I have little knowledge or power."

"What has become of him?" Odhinn asked.

"I will explain as fully as my understanding allows," she said, and paused a moment before she continued. "There are many other realms in which I have counterparts in form more or less similar to myself. I cannot say clearly, for my existence is tied to this world and to this level of existence, and I can no more than look into the other realms when the gate is open to its fullest. You see, my existence began with the formation of this world, and my development to my present state has been long and slow. And I will continue to exist only as long as this world does, until the day when the star above me burns itself out and consumes me in its final throes.

"I believe that it is because of the existence of my counterparts in the other levels that the gate came into being. It was as if we had stretched the fabric of space between us until it ripped at that one small point. I never bothered about it, for it was no threat to me or the creatures of my realm, but it is a deadly threat to the Aesir. I have looked within it often enough and without danger, for I have an entire world to hold me back and so I could not pass the gate if I wished. But Mimir had only that great slab of rock when he peered within, and it consumed him.

"But when he was drawn in, the gate sought to throw equal parts of his being into each of the counterpart worlds. But he still held to the rock and did not let go, and the rock could not pass. So it was that portions of his being were thrown into each of the different levels, and yet he remained intact but forever lodged within the gate. Then the tree began to grow. Its roots extend through the gate into all the worlds, and in five there are other trees identical to the one you see before you. That is Mimir.''

"How do you know these things?'' Odhinn asked.

"Because Mimir has told me. Part of his being is fused with my own, even as the great tree sends its roots into my substance. Did you not feel my struggles as I tried to draw away?''

"But what of the tree,'' Odhinn insisted. "Why should he take the form of some immense tree?''

"That I do not know for certain,'' Jordh replied. "Mimir believes that in one of the corresponding worlds, the world of undying life, there was the winged seed of some strange tree lying on the ground just below the gate. Such trees do not exist here. His being was somehow infused with the thing, and it began to grow. Not just in that world but in four others, as it is here, and all connected by their roots through the gate. All are Mimir.''

"Can he no longer speak with us?'' Odhinn asked.

"If he desired it, I suppose he could. For now, I know that he does not. Do not disturb him in his contemplation. His power and his wisdom have grown, and he could now tell you things that you would not want to know.''

With that it seemed that Jordh was prepared to depart. The light that shown from within her being began to fade, while the rebuilt shell of leaves and twigs began to dissipate. Odhinn was relieved, seeing that she did not intend to challenge him. But then he felt some guilt for the damage that had been done, and responsible for the acts and deeds of those who followed him.

"Wait! One moment more,'' he insisted. "What of you? We do regret the damage that has been done. . . .''

"What of me?'' Jordh interrupted. "All will be well, in time. Indeed, as much as I regret it, what has happened was likely for the better. The great beasts will not survive this, but they were doomed already. They have ruled the lands and the seas for a very long time now, and they have grown far more complicated in their forms and habits but no better. The world is changed from what it was, but perhaps the small, furry ones will make the most of it. Or the feathered ones.

"As for you, I do not suppose that there is anything that I can do about that. You are here. I could drive you away or destroy you, but I cannot afford the destruction that would cause. Make annoyances of yourselves and I may do so anyway. But if you behave yourselves and do not interfere, then I suppose that I might even enjoy the company. Just do not presume upon me in your schemes."

The blue light faded away and Jordh was gone, leaving the shell of debris to collapse and settle to the ground. Odhinn approached the tree and tried for some time to speak with Mimir, but without success. The great tree continued to grow for almost a year, until it stood over five miles in height and almost eight hundred feet across the base of its trunk. Then it ceased to grow, although it never aged or decayed. No storm or lightning could hurt it greatly, and the damage always repaired itself without a trace. Its long-bladed leaves turned golden in the winter and did not fall, and each spring it would shed its new foliage for a new cloak of green. The winds carried its winged seeds throughout the world so that it fathered a new race of trees, later to be called the ash, and the great tree itself was known as Yggdrasill.

The destruction was great, and the world thereafter was a changed place. As Jordh had predicted, most of the great beasts of the earlier world died quickly, and almost all of their lesser kindred disappeared also. The climate turned dry and cool, compared with what it had been, and it was to stay that way for all time. And yet life continued and thrived, a new, hardier breed of life. Now the furred ones came to dominate, and they seemed to do better in this new environment than they had in the great forests of the past. Their senses were sharper and their intelligence greater, and it seemed that Idhunn's prediction of a sentient animal would come true even sooner than expected.

In those days the Aesir took no place in the world for their own to dwell, but lived at will wherever they desired or wherever their explorations took them. But they always met beside the trunk of the great tree Yggdrasill. There Odhinn remained much of the time, listening to the tales of the others when they returned from their wanderings, and speaking with Jordh at those times when she would consent to conversation. But Mimir, if his being did indeed dwell within the world-tree, would never respond in any way. Then one day he did speak, suddenly and unbidden.

At first Odhinn was uncertain when he heard his name called as if from out of the lower branches of the tree, but the memories of the Aesir are complete and unfading and he knew that voice even if he had not heard it in sixty million years of the world. He looked up at the world-tree, then approached its vast trunk cautiously.

"Mimir, do you speak?" he asked, rising upward toward the lower branches where the voice seemed to have originated.

"It is I," Mimir answered.

"I have waited a very long time," Odhinn said. "And in all that time you have been more silent than Hoenir."

"It is not often that I can speak." The soundless words rose from within the trunk of the tree, but dim and echoing as if from a great distance. "In this realm I am free to speak only with Jordh, and she will not bear my messages. Listen well, while time remains.

"Jordh has spoken to you of what became of me when I was drawn within the rift in the universe. Parts of my being were fused with the spirits that inhabit several other worlds. Jordh you know of. Also there is Nidhavellir, who speaks with me almost as often. Most of the others are considerably more quiet. Also there is the tree, which gives me physical presence in the nine worlds I know. There are identical trees in five of those worlds, interconnected by their roots. I have the greatest awareness of the worlds where the trees exist, but roots of the trees extend into four additional worlds that I see only dimly.

"Listen well now, for time is short. There are many things that I could teach you; valuable lessons, which would be of very great use to you. But my time is short. One thing only will I be able to impart to you before this moment passes, and it will be a very long time before I might speak with you again. I can show you how you can open gates of your own; safe ones, which you can pass as you will. Then all nine of the corresponding worlds would be open to you, and eight other universes that you could explore at your leisure. Or I can tell you of these intelligent creatures that you have waited so long to see, for I believe that their thoughts and actions will be so different from your own that you will find them alien and incomprehensible. Choose quickly now which gift you would have, but choose well.''

Odhinn was silent only a moment, for he did not need long to decide. As for an understanding of the sentient animals, that was a task that Odhinn wanted to master for himself. But there was one thing that he had wanted since that day when Mimir had disappeared through the hole in the structure of the universe. Now he could ask for it.

''Tell me of the making of gates into the other worlds,'' he said.

It seemed that Mimir was pleased. ''It may well be that you have chosen wisely. If you were more interested in power and control, then you would have selected an understanding of your future subjects. Perhaps knowledge is indeed your main desire.''

Then Mimir spoke long and quickly, fearing that the strange shift in power between the corresponding worlds that allowed him to speak would return to its normal state and silence him too soon. Much of what he spoke of was beyond Odhinn's immediate understanding, as learned as the Lord of the Aesir was in such matters. So it is, that the understanding of one thing is dependent upon the understanding of others, until there is a long chain of facts and theories that leads to the comprehension of a single major concept. But Mimir was able to explain it all, and Odhinn needed no point repeated.

The late morning sun rose to its zenith and was sinking into the west, and still Mimir spoke, marveling that his gate had stayed open for so long. He imparted to Odhinn the knowledge that had been requested, and had time yet to speak of other, lesser things. As they spoke the others came and gathered about the great tree to listen, although none approached.

''Time is short now,'' Mimir said at last. ''Great powers are shifting; already the outer worlds have passed out of alignment, and my gate will close very quickly now. You have the knowledge you asked for. Use it wisely.''

Then he was gone, never again to speak from within the great tree. Odhinn sank back to the ground and considered for

a moment what he should do next. Mimir had spoken of other
worlds but his sight into each was limited, in some more than
others. And he had warned of dangers. Odhinn would be
cautious, but he had to see those worlds for himself. He
summoned those who would aid him: Thor, Tyr and Heimdall,
whose powers were the greatest, as well as Frigg and Idhunn,
whose powers were subtle yet firm and constant. And they
withdrew well away from the world-tree to insure that no
harm would come to it.

The first gate they opened well up in the air above the
northern seas, so that there would be little damage if matters
got out of hand. Odhinn gathered together Thor's and Tyr's
powers with his own and focused them into a single point,
opening a rift in the fabric of the universe. Heimdall watched
closely the flare and shift of energy, ready to give warning if
it began to wander beyond their control. Then Frigg and
Idhunn lent their own powers to the making of a ring of
force, which they set within the rift. Odhinn allowed the rift
to close about the ring of force, which held and so remained a
tunnel between the universes. Then Odhinn and Thor passed
alone through the newly opened gate.

What they found on the other side was a world remarkably
like the one they had left. The lands were not the same in
shape or size, and it was a world where forests and ice-clad
mountains dominated. But the life there was much the same,
although there was no indication that any native creature
might soon rise to true intelligence. And, in a place corresponding to its location in the world they knew, they found a
great plateau, three times the first in height and many times in
area. On its rocky surface they found a great tree identical to
the one that stood in their own world. Odhinn knew then that
the plateaus must have been created by the original rifts in the
universes, large blocks of stone pulled upward by unnatural
forces.

They looked about for several hours before returning to
their own level, where the others waited impatiently. Odhinn
declared it safe and allowed everyone to pass. For many days
they simply played and satisfied their curiosity about what it
was like to dwell in another universe. In those younger days
of the Aesir, they were all possessed by an overwhelming
curiosity. They wanted to open gates into all the worlds and

rush off to explore all eight of the corresponding universes as quickly as they could; a large order for barely three score beings who had yet to explore the entirety of their own dimension. But they were also more practical in those days.

Next they opened a gate into the second world above their own, and found the undying lands that Mimir had spoken of. Life there did not age or decay, either plant or animal, although it could be destroyed. And it was a twilit realm, where the sky was black and the stars shown brightly even in the pale glow of full daylight, which was never brighter than twilight on most other worlds. This realm proved to be Idhunn's special delight but also a trap for her own great curiosity, for she remained there long seeking to understand it.

Encouraged by their success, the Aesir decided to build a single vast gate that would open upon the same place in all nine of the corresponding worlds. It seemed that the plateau was a universal feature in all the realms, even if it was of a different size and shape in the various worlds. They chose to open the main gate before the edge of the immense plateau in the first level above their own. The plateau there seemed likely to be the highest, so that a gate opening from that level would always be well above the ground in the other realms.

Then it was that their troubles began, for as all things have their inexact equivalents in the other realms, so did the Aesir find their own. It happened in the third world above their own. They had just opened the gate into that level, and Odhinn, Thor and Frigg went ahead to explore the way. They came out upon a plateau so like the one they had just left that they wondered if the gate had failed them. They were even more confused when they saw a single being like themselves waiting near the base of the great tree. But then they saw that while this being was just like the Aesir in form, it was no member of their own group. It was even more startled by their own appearance, and seemed half inclined to flee. Then the stranger hesitated, and cautiously flew up a little way to meet them.

Thus Odhinn of the Aesir met with Njordh, leader of the Vanir. The Vanir were beings so like the Aesir that there was no difference to be found between the two, although the Vanir were fewer in number and, on the whole, possessed lesser powers than the Aesir. Little is known of them in later days, for they had little contact with mortal folk and seldom came into the mortal lands, staying for the most part in their own realm. Their first meeting was rather constrained, and trouble might have come of it if Odhinn had not kept his own people away from that realm for many years. But in time a strong link was forged between the two groups, and Njordh gladly relinquished his own leadership to Odhinn. From that time on the Aesir and the Vanir dwelled and worked as one, and as one they faced the doom that they had prepared for themselves.

For the time they had much to do, for five of the nine worlds were yet unexplored. Of the Vanir only Njordh possessed exceptional power and wisdom, and he now accompanied Odhinn and Thor into the newly found worlds. Moving downward from the first they found another realm much the same in form, except that it was a place of rugged mountains and great belts of towering ridges that bordered narrow seas. And yet it seemed that here too sentient life would soon arise. Below that was a second world of undying life, and like the first it was a realm of eternal night. But it was also a world of strange and terrible beasts; an evil place where the pure light of the sun was never seen, dominated by an unending night of fear and darkness.

Below that world they found yet another of eternal night and unending life, a world of broken, barren mountains and desolate plains. And yet it was here that they found the first sentient life, like in form to that which was developing on other worlds, yet creatures of vast size. But strangest of all was that while they were creatures of physical substance, they also commanded powers like those of the Aesir, if in a considerably lesser degree. Also they were of different forms, depending upon the powers they possessed. Some could command flames, others cold and ice, although most had no great powers but many lesser ones. The Jotnar they were called, or giants, and there also the Aesir found the first dragons, both the great firedrakes and lingworms and the small, quick icedrakes.

Odhinn found one, dwelling among the fire-Jotnar in the broken hills, who had not physical form but was in many ways like the Aesir, except that his essence did not shine with golden light but burned with an undying flame. He was Loki, spirit of flame, who had been dwelling among the fire-Jotnar because they were most like him in nature. But he most resembled the Aesir in form and power, and Odhinn soon came to cherish his shrewd mind and quick wit. After a time he followed the Aesir back through the gate to remain with them, and he proved invaluable whenever a quick, sharp tongue was needed. But he was perhaps more mischievous than helpful; he was out of favor with the others as often as in, and Frigg could never abide him. Loki was in temperament not unlike the flame that was his basic substance: always the friend who was just as likely to burn the one who was careless with him.

Below the world of the Jotnar they found yet another of the twilit realms, except that this one was cold and misty, and a thick, dense layer of clouds hung in the windless skies over all the land until it seemed to anyone on the surface that they were in some unimaginably vast cave rather than open land. Here too they found spirits of death who fed upon the life-energies of living things. The leader of these strange beings was Hel, who sent her many servants out to collect the lesser spirits of living beings when they were released at death and return them to her vast stronghold. These strange beings had one special power: They could reach through the barriers between the universes and draw spirits of the dead into their own realm. The Aesir did not remain there long, for that world was detrimental to them and drew energy from their very being. Odhinn had the single gate into that level blocked off, so that only the most powerful of the Aesir could open it and pass through.

That left only one last world that was yet unexplored, the one on the uppermost level just above the world of the Vanir. This time Loki asked to go on the initial expedition into this new world, since this was to be the last. Therefore he accompanied Odhinn and Thor as they set out through the final gate, and it was well that he went with them.

What they found was a land dominated by a fiery, merciless sun, a world that seemed one vast desert. There were no rivers or lakes and only small, bitter seas choked with salt, while all the land stood barren and lifeless, baked brown and hard beneath that cruel sun. There was life, but of a simple and hardy sort, and there was little enough of that. There

were wind-swept plains of dust and great ridges and mountains of naked rock, tall cones that poured forth fire and ash,
and great fountains and geysers, not of water but of flame.

Loki entered that world hesitantly when he saw it, and the
more he saw the greater his unease grew. It was like the dim
awakening of some long-forgotten memory, and yet he knew
nothing for certain except that there was danger here. Not for
himself, for this was like home for him, not for the Aesir,
who had the protection of their own great powers. Rather did
he sense that in this world there existed something that was a
danger to all other worlds, an evil that sought to destroy for
the sake of destruction. This was the realm of flame, a flame
that would consume all else and grow all the greater and more
powerful in doing so.

Thor halted at the same moment he did. "We are not
alone. This place is teaming with flame-spirits, and they are
watching us even now."

"Yes," Loki agreed. "Like myself, and yet unlike. They
are a flame that lives only for the destruction of what they
burn. Go carefully, and do not forget where we left the
gate."

They went on, but even more cautiously than before. Odhinn
was drawn by a strange presence far removed near the center
of what was surely the most desolate and blasted lands in that
entire world. Soon they saw that it was a single vast volcano,
as large as a continent, with a towering cone more than fifty
miles in height. Great fields of lava had poured outward for
thousands of miles, and there were vast regions completely
laid over with endless tubes of rock.

They came at last to its immense cone, and found on one
side near its base a wide shaft that bore directly into its fiery
heart. Following this tube inward, they found in the center of
the cone a vast chamber, circular in shape and two miles
across. The lower half of the chamber was filled with a lake
of molten rock that bubbled and hissed and sent forth great
tongues of flame. And on the many ledges and shelves of
rock that lined the upper portions of the shaft they saw
countless spirits of flame, tens if not hundreds of thousands in
number, flickering like jets of flame.

The lake of magma suddenly convulsed and a great column
of fire and smoke shot upward from its center. And from that

towering shaft of fire and vapor there arose a demon of flame, vast and burning with fierce heat like the heart of a star, yet surrounded by a cloak of darkness as if his flames consumed the very light about him. Loki drew back involuntarily, for here was a power vast in comparison with himself, which could claim him if it so desired. But the Aesir were unafraid, for their powers were still the greater.

"Who are you, and what do you desire here?" the flame-demon demanded in a terrible voice full of arrogance and malice. "This is my realm, and I suffer no intruders save those who serve me. I am Surtur, Lord of Flame."

"And I am Odhinn, leader of the Aesir and the Vanir. I seek dominion over none; therefore do I claim the right to go where I will."

"Do not trade claims with this one," Loki secretly warned his companions. "He seeks to delay you, for he means your destruction. He knows of the corresponding worlds and seeks to conquer them all, but he has never had the means. Now you have opened the gate for him, and he means to use it."

"And so I shall, foolish one," Surtur, overhearing what was not meant for him, blazed with arrogance. "I shall blast your prideful companions with undying flames, but I will command your will and make you the least of my slaves, cast into the fiery pits of my subterranean fortress. So will you see who is your rightful lord."

And with that he gathered his great powers of flame and heat to blast the Aesir, at the same instant calling down his countless slaves to attack the intruders should they escape his wrath. But before he could act, Thor suddenly exploded in a blaze of power and golden light. So great was that blast that the sides of the immense volcano exploded outward, and the massive cone crumbled and collapsed inward. As it fell Odhinn and Thor streaked up and out of the volcano's wide neck, while Loki weaved and bobbed closely behind.

Surtur's flame-demons were scattered and confused, but they were not destroyed, not even those trapped beneath the falling rock. At their lord's command they rose from the wreckage to pursue the three intruders, and many others came from throughout the fiery realm. For it was Surtur's hope that enough of his servants could force their way through the world-gate to prevent the Aesir from closing it behind them until he could come himself with his vast army.

Odhinn and Thor shot through the gate directly into the middle realm, startling those who had gathered to await their return. But Loki was by then some distance behind, and Odhinn was loath to leave him to his enemies. Thus the two Aesir waited to either side of the gate and made ready to close the opening into the fiery realm. A moment later Loki shot through with three of the fire-demons close behind him, and the gate collapsed upon a fourth that exploded in flames. Then Thor, Tyr and Heimdall hunted down the three who had come through and blasted them.

But that was not the end of the matter, as Odhinn already knew. While Surtur was forever trapped within his own universe, it was not long before Jordh arrived in a terrible rage. She had been unaware that Odhinn had been told of the making of world-gates, and she had already seen the trouble that had come of it. She was both angry and frightened, for there seemed to be no limit to what these beings would do in the name of learning. She wondered if that was how they entertained themselves, leaving whole worlds wrecked and cast aside in their path. This time she intended to be rid of them, whatever the cost.

Odhinn had anticipated this since Mimir had first instructed him in the making of the world-gates, and he was prepared. When Jordh appeared he was there to meet her, and he offered to withdraw with the Aesir and the Vanir through the gate to one of the corresponding worlds, to return only at need. Jordh accepted this, although she knew at the time that she was actually gaining very little. Indeed it was Odhinn who gained the most, for in withdrawing to an uninhabited world he and his kind could go forth whenever they desired, and yet hold the gate against all enemies. For he knew that Jordh's powers were restricted to her own realm, that she could not pass the gates or even reach through them.

And so it was that the Aesir and the Vanir withdrew from the world of Jordh and settled in the uninhabited realm immediately above. They came to dwell on the lofty plateau, whose grassy, windswept top was called the Plain of Ida, and from the edge of the plateau they built a great bridge in the form of a vast arch that reached up into the main world-gate and beyond into all of the seven worlds upon which it opened. The bridge was known as Bifrost and was made of the clearest crystal, and in the sunshine it appeared to burn with rippling flames or glow with the colors of a rainbow.

Upon the plateau they built great mansions for their own use. Odhinn built Valhalla, which he meant to be a meeting-place of the Aesir, and for himself the palace Vingolf. Frigg built a great mansion called Fensalir, which held a great library and was later a place of learning, and within whose court was the Garden of Idhunn. Thor dwelled in Bilskirnir, which had a different wing furnished to match whatever mood he might be in, and which was filled with the many things he made for himself or collected in his many journeys. And Heimdall built his hall Himinbjorg at the base of the bridge Bifrost, where he could look out through the world-gate and warn of approaching danger.

And so the long-awaited time drew near, and the Aesir now had not one but nine worlds to observe. Centermost was the world of Jordh and so was called Midhgardh, or Middle Earth, because it was in the very center of the sequence. Above this lay the realms of Asgardh, the world of the Aesir, and Alfheim, the elf-world, the undying land where it was forever night. Above these was Vanaheim, the world of the Vanir, and there several of their number made dwellings for themselves even after the founding of Asgardh. Uppermost of the sequence was Muspell, the fiery realm where Surtur ruled, and the one world where the bridge Bifrost did not extend. But there was at least one secret gate into that level, through which it was held that Odhinn occasionally sent spies.

Below Midhgardh was Nidhavellir, the mountainous land of the hardy Dvergar, or dwarves. Then there was Svartalfheim, the realm of the dark elves, who were immortal like the Alfar, but dark and often evil creatures who carved vast underground fortresses like those of the dwarves. Below that was Jotunheim, the land of the giants. They came, in time, to be the chief enemies of the Aesir, and their king Loki cherished long-laid plans to take the rule of the nine worlds from Odhinn. His fortress was Utgardh, and so he was often called Utgardh-Loki to distinguish him from Loki of the Flame. Finally there was Nifheim, or Nibelheim, the realm of the

dead, in which the death-maidens, or Nibelungs, reached up
into the other worlds to collect the spirits of the dead to bring
back to their queen, Hel. Bifrost extended there also, and a
single road ran from the base of the bridge to the gate of
Hel's great fortress.

It seemed that time passed more slowly now, although
there was so much to be done throughout the realms that the
Aesir and the Vanir were always busy. Then the long-awaited
time came at last, when Idhunn stood before the others in
Valhalla and said that the sentient animals had come. In
Midhgardh there were mortal men; in Nidhavellir the Dvergar;
the undying folk of Alfheim; and even the Svartalfar. For
they all now had languages of their own, had tamed fire and
made tools and weapons. But Idhunn was also dismayed, for
they were a more base and brutish folk than she had ever
imagined. Only for the Alfar did she have any hope, for they
never died and so their wisdom and learning grew and did not
pass away, and they developed more quickly than the others.

Then more than ever did the Aesir desire to take on physical form so that they could move more at ease with these new
folk. But while Idhunn could make for them any form they
desired, she could not make one that could long endure the
terrible stresses of housing such powerful spirits. With the
opening of the gates she had withdrawn often into the undying realm of Alfheim, for the idea of immortal life intrigued
her as nothing ever had. And, after long study, she finally
understood it to the extent that she could now prepare a
potion that would preserve the living forms they wished to
wear.

Idhunn brought back from the undying realm the saplings
of oaks, the mightiest and most enduring of all the trees of the
elf-world. In her own garden she nurtured them and tended
them with the greatest care, and they grew strong and tall and
bore much fruit; the nuts were called *eplir*, meaning acorns,
although later men took the word to mean apple. From the
nuts she extracted a clear liquid, which she made into a
special potion that could strengthen and preserve the living
forms of the Aesir, so long as it was given two or three times
each year.

Now the Aesir were free to take physical form, and Idhunn

made bodies for them to wear of a fashion to match their personalities. Odhinn took the form of a tall man, stern and majestic in appearance and neither young nor old. Thor was also tall and very powerful of build, with flaming red hair and matching beard. Loki was young in appearance, as thin and lithe as an elf and exceedingly handsome, for most ordered their appearance and Loki liked best to pass undetected among the Alfar and take part in their festivities and amusements. Two only, Aegin and Ran of the Aesir, chose not to take on physical form; their delight was in the seas of Midhgardh, and with Jordh's approval they went to dwell beneath the waves.

But they also gave up much to take physical form. For they had to suffer a second great reduction in their powers, as they had previously surrendered their greatest powers when they had left the star-realm. With that they also gave up much of their past mobility, their ability to pass through solids and to endure extreme conditions. Mostly, however, they placed their very existence in danger, for if their bodies were to die while they still inhabited them, then they would themselves be vastly reduced in powers and would wander the worlds forever as lesser spirits. But this concerned them little, for they believed that they would be able to shed their physical forms in an instant if danger threatened.

Others came like Loki to dwell in Asgardh, lesser spirits who took other shapes. Most noted of these included the ravens Huginn and Muninn, who served as the messengers of Asgardh and flew the skies of many worlds on Odhinn's errands. Also there were the great wolves Geri and Freki, who sat beside Odhinn's throne in Valhalla. But the most famous were the Nibelungs of Nifheim, death-maidens whom Odhinn brought to Asgardh and gave human form. They were afterward known as the Valkyries, Odhinn's personal warriors. In later days they brought the spirits of fallen heroes to serve as the guards of Asgardh, returned to immortal life by the talents of Idhunn.

When Jordh learned of these things she was greatly concerned; not angry, but dismayed and very worried. And so she called Odhinn down from Asgardh to meet with her beside the world-tree Yggdrasill. She was even more dismayed when she saw him there in human form, robed in white.

"Odhinn, what have you done?" she demanded in despair.

"Of what importance is that to you?" he asked in return, mistaking her agitation for anger. "This is what we have waited for, and while the time lasts we will wear their forms so that we might better understand these beings. When the time is past we will return to our true forms and be gone forever, and you can continue in peace until your sun destroys you."

"No, Odhinn, for now you have surely destroyed yourselves," she said. "Do you not see the mistake that you have made? As you dwell in this form, so will you become like these lowly creatures: greedy, proud and arrogant. Then you will leave yourselves open to your enemies, and they will overwhelm you. Do you think that you will be able to abandon this form at will? You will come to cherish it as your own, and think that it is indeed your life. That is how you have doomed yourselves."

"I cannot believe that you are so concerned for us," Odhinn replied coldly. "I think that your concern is rather for the people of your realm, whom you would keep to yourself and have them know and worship only you."

"My people? I renounce them, as they know and care nothing for me! I would rather that they had never come to be, and I hope that they will not thrive but falter and die. But the Aesir are eternal, and great beings in their own way." Then she paused, and was silent for a long moment. "Do you not see, with your own words, the doom that you have made for yourself. Worship only me? I require no worship, but it seems that you desire it. Part with that animal you wear, before it dominates and destroys you."

"I will not. I must understand this thing. Mimir once offered to explain it to me, but I chose instead to learn the making of the world-gates, and I still consider that to have been the wisest choice. But now I must learn this thing for myself."

"Would you speak with Mimir if you could?" Jordh asked. "Go then to Jotunheim into the hills of the frost-giants. There you will find an exposed root of the world-tree, and beneath it the spring of Mimir. The spring travels long through the cracks in the rocks that the root has made, and it is infused with the substance of the world-tree. Drink deeply of that water, and the substance of Mimir will become a part of your being and you will be free to speak with him. But beware! You may pay a price for drinking of that spring!''

Odhinn did as she directed, and went alone and secretly in Jotunheim. He drank of the spring and spoke long with Mimir, but nothing was ever known of what happened or was said. Odhinn was away for nine days and nine nights, and on the tenth day Thor found him in the wilds of Jotunheim. And he did indeed pay a terrible price, for he was nearly destroyed, and he was thereafter blind in one eye. The water of the spring had taken its sight.

Odhinn never spoke of what he saw and heard during those nine days and nights in the wilds of Jotunheim. But it can be guessed that Mimir spoke to him of the true meaning of authority, not the shadow of leadership that he had among the Aesir, but of what it meant to be a king of mortal and immortal folk, to face enemies from without and unrest from within. He had found life to be without clear unity and purpose, and it was his desire to guide the three major races to achieve their fullest potential. It was a worthy if impossible task, and if Mimir warned him against following such a foolish and dangerous path, then Odhinn did not heed that advice.

So it was that the last of the elder ages of the worlds had come to an end, and a new age began that was unlike any previous. For it was the age of men, and of the Alfar and the Dvergar. And all things that had existed before were changed, even the worlds themselves, which now became in a measure subject to the wills of the people they had given rise to. But the Aesir were changed most of all, and their memories of what they had been faded and were slowly lost. Their lives became tied to the worlds which they had meant only to visit for a time, and they forgot that it had ever been otherwise.

CHAPTER TWO

Of the Walling
of Asgardh

In the earliest days there was peace in Asgardh, in the short time before any of the Aesir, except perhaps Odhinn, knew that they had potential enemies in the eight worlds that were open to them. In that time Asgardh, still far from complete, was a great citadel of learning and not a fortress besieged by storm. The Aesir and the Vanir were only then beginning to go out into the inhabited worlds to teach the men and dwarves and elves of a higher learning and a better way of life than they had discovered for themselves. At first the Aesir considered this interference and contrary to their original reasons for staying worldbound. Then Odhinn saw how slowly the three races were to develop and how easily they regressed or turned to evil, and it seemed better to him that the three races should be guided in their development.

And so the Aesir began the opening of many lesser gates for their own convenience, and with the thought that there might one day be trade and travel between the worlds. But this soon proved ill, for many evil creatures then used the gates to invade new territories. Trolls spread out from Jotunheim into most of the other worlds, and tribes of Svartalfar raided and sometimes stayed in such places as Midhgardh and

Nidhavellir. Dragons were seen in places where they had not previously existed, the greatest of which was the great sea-dragon Jormungandh of Midhgardh. The rare times that he surfaced and was seen by men, only his broad back was ever seen, and so he was thought to be some unimaginably vast serpent. And the legend grew of the Midhgardh serpent, so long that it encircled the world.

Soon after there arose a great king of the Jotnar, Loki by name. He had built the great citadel and fortress of Utgardh, and from then on he was called Utgardh-Loki so not to be confused with Loki of the Flame. The giants declared themselves openly opposed to the Aesir and sworn to their destruction, and they raided into the other worlds and even assailed the bridge Bifrost. The Aesir were surprised and very confused by such events, for few of them yet understood what evil and greed and hate were. But they knew that they could not sit idle while the Jotnar plotted their destruction. Thor and Tyr began to go often into Jotunheim to discover what they could.

It was at this time that a Jotun appeared out of the wilderness and approached the base of the flaming bridge. He was not overly tall for his kind but heavily set and very broad of back, and he was leading one of the great, powerful horses that his people kept, twice the size of the biggest draft horse of Midhgardh. He called up to Heimdall, who could scarcely believe what he heard, that a Jotun of the hills should walk up to the world-gate and request entrance into Asgardh. Heimdall stepped out onto the bridge and looked down into Jotunheim at the stranger.

"What do you desire?" he called down.

"To speak to Odhinn," the giant responded. "I have a business proposition that he might be interested in."

Heimdall stood for a moment and shook his head in astonishment. He knew that the Jotun must be up to something, but Odhinn could best determine what. He bade the giant to ascend the bridge and ordered him to leave his horse and gear at the gatehouse. Then Heimdall called for the Valkyries to escort the giant to Valhalla, where the Aesir were already assembled in council.

The Jotun did not have to wait long for an audience, for the news of his coming brought all other matters to an immediate halt. He was brought into the hall and stood before Odhinn's high seat, while the Aesir and the Vanir stared in amazement.

"I would like to make a proposition," the Jotun began immediately and without introduction, speaking in a deep voice like the rumble of distant thunder. "You know that Utgardh-Loki has declared himself king of Jotunheim, and he has had a fortress built for himself. I should know, for I built it. Now he is going to be moving against you whenever he can, and he can throw every foul creature under his command at your gate and the walls of your plateau. So it seems to me that I should build a great wall around the outer edge of your plateau, and then you would be able to hold it against anything that walks or crawls. What is more, I can do it by the first day of spring."

Then the Aesir were even more amazed, for winter was then fast approaching. Odhinn sat back in his chair and laughed. "And what payment would you require for this marvelous deed?"

"A payment fitting the deed," the Jotun replied. "I want the sun and the moon, and Idhunn for my bride."

This time the Aesir were not amused, but sat in stony silence. It was well for this Jotun that Thor was away, or he would have learned quickly to regret such words. Instead he stood patiently awaiting his answer, as if he had asked a fair price for some small deed.

"Would you describe the type of work that you intend to construct," Loki said suddenly, remembering how giants conducted their business, and how they sought to defraud each other under the terms of a "legal" contract.

"A standard defensive barrier of solid stone blocks, each forty feet long by twenty wide and thick," the Jotun said in aggrieved tones, understanding exactly what Loki meant. "The stones will be laid in two rows, forming a wall forty feet high by twenty thick, and joined by interlocking grooves. You also get a gate with towers to either side, with an inner and outer set of double doors locked by iron crossbeams."

"And the stone?"

"Quality marble, of course! The remaining terms of the contract are that I do the work myself, using what tools I have and my horse Svadilfari. Starting tomorrow morning, I have one hundred and two days to finish, ending at midnight of the last day. Now, if you would like to discuss this among yourselves, I can wait outside until you call."

The giant bowed low before Odhinn and allowed himself to be led away. The Aesir remained silent until he was gone, all except Idhunn. She resented being included as part of the giant's required payment, and she had been silently fuming.

"That insolent, oversized idiot!" she hissed even before the door of the hall was closed. "My suggestion is that we throw him back into his miserable world without the benefit of the bridge."

"Oh, no! Quite to the contrary," Loki exclaimed. "This fine Jotun is not nearly as stupid as he may seem. He knows exactly what he can and cannot do. He must be here for a purpose other than the one he spoke of."

"So I thought," Odhinn agreed. "Do you know what that can be?"

"I think that he must be a spy. Consider this. He comes and proposes to do an impossible task, which we know he cannot accomplish. Therefore we invite him into Asgardh for one hundred and two days, and when the time is up he has failed and quietly returns to Jotunheim."

"But there is nothing here that he could learn to his advantage," Frigg protested.

"Yes, but Utgardh-Loki cannot know that until his spy returns. I suggest that we allow this Jotun to do his best. He should get a section of the wall built—which we will not have to pay for—and Utgardh-Loki will know that he cannot try such tricks with us. We can finish the wall later."

"And what if he does finish the wall?" Idhunn demanded. That was her only concern.

"It is simply impossible," Loki insisted. "Consider this. A wall around the edge of the plateau would be at least a hundred miles in length. That comes to over twenty-six thousand of those forty-foot blocks, which he would have to cut, transport and lay at the rate of a mile or more a day. It cannot be done."

"What does he want with the sun and the moon anyway?" Frigg asked.

"The Jotnar believe that the sun and the moon are the eyes of their mythical forebearer Ymir. They believe that Odhinn slew this huge giant and had his eyes removed and thrown into the sky. One, the moon, was blinded in flight, but the other still blazes with life," Loki explained. "You have to

remember that in Jotunheim the sun is only a glowing yellow
ball against a dark sky. Of course, there never was a Ymir,
and Odhinn certainly did not slay him.''

''But you want us to allow him to try this thing?'' Odhinn
asked. He trusted Loki's wisdom in this, for the affairs of the
Jotnar had been widely discussed in Asgardh of late and
Odhinn could seldom follow the logic that dictated their
thoughts and actions, especially their cut-throat legalities.

Loki shook his head. ''No. The only advice I have is that
you would be safe to make this agreement. If you do not want
this giant in Asgardh, that is for you to decide.''

The deliberations continued throughout the afternoon and
into the evening, for Idhunn resented making this agreement,
however safe it was. Heimdall, who came in later, liked the
idea of a wall, since it would help him to guard the bridge
more securely. Odhinn also liked the idea, and he liked even
more that the giant should do part of the work without wages.
The elves who served in Asgardh were not heavy laborers,
and a crew of their kind could hardly work faster than a single
giant. But he was also loath to enter into such a contract that
he had no intention of honoring, for fairness and honesty in
all dealings was one of the most important things that he
wished to teach the races of the nine worlds.

At last it was decided to accept the Jotun's contract, for
Loki insisted that it was safe. None denied that it was wise to
have the Asgardh plateau walled, now that evil things were
coming through the lesser gates into all the worlds. As a
group the Aesir feared the destruction of the undying oaks of
Idhunn's garden, and they hoped to keep secret the fact that
they were dependent upon Idhunn's potions to preserve their
physical forms. But, for that same reason, they feared to have
the giant in Asgardh, and many thought it more than coincidence that he named Idhunn for his price. Odhinn promised
that the giant would be guarded by the Valkyries every moment that he was on their side of the gate, and that settled the
argument.

With the very first light of dawn the giant was off, passing
over the bridge to collect his first load of stone. Some wondered if he would ever return, now that he had been within
Asgardh, and no one expected to see him again for some
time. So it was to everyone's surprise when he returned

within a quarter of an hour leading his horse. Then the Aesir were indeed alarmed, for the horse was one of the immense beasts of the Jotnar, forty hands or more in height, a solid black stallion named Svadilfari. Nor was he any ordinary horse of the Jotunheim breed, but was possessed of some spirit of power that gave him strength many times beyond even his great size. This single beast drew a train of ten great wagons, and each wagon held ten of the stone blocks that were to be used in the construction of the wall.

The giant himself pulled a strange machine, a large metal framework on wheels and rigged with various pulleys and levers. Using this strange device, he was able to lift the large stone blocks from the wagons and move them into place by himself with no more trouble than a stonemason would have laying bricks. First he took out a large ball of twine and laid out a long section of the wall. Then he brought forth another device, like a plow with a wide horizontal blade, and used it to cut a level foundation for the wall. So sharp was the blade and so strong was Svadilfari that it cut through dirt, root and even stone with ease. After that, the laying of the great stone blocks proceeded quickly, and he was off again for another load.

Then the Aesir were even more amazed and alarmed, for the giant continued to work on through the night. For this Loki had forgotten, that the Jotnar enjoy sleep and are prone to indulge their laziness, but they do not need it and can, at need, work tirelessly for weeks. By dawn of the next morning, the end of the first full day of work, the giant had built all of the gate and more than half a mile of the wall itself. The Aesir realized then that he must have a supply of stone already cut and waiting, and so they saw that they had entered into a contract that was less favorable then they had thought.

Obviously this Jotun was no fool, nor was he a spy. He had selected a seemingly impossible task and had devised a way that it could be done. By cutting the stone before, he had now only to lay it. The great strength of Svadilfari allowed him to transport the blocks quickly, and his machines moved them easily into place. Now it would be a race against time, and undoubtedly a very close one. It seemed that the giant could build about a mile's length of wall each day. If his rate was any less, or if the wall was too long, then he would not succeed. Otherwise the Aesir would have to consider how they might make the required payment.

That was one thing that worried the Aesir, for they had agreed upon a payment that they were not prepared to give. If the Jotun had asked for gold or silver they would have given that gladly, for they could get all they needed easily and did not value it greatly. But it was beyond even their former powers to give him the sun and the moon. Nor were they prepared to give Idhunn as payment, even if she did not hold the key to their physical existence. Thus there remained no question that they could not make the payment even if the giant fulfilled the contract.

And that made it Odhinn's problem, to either meet the terms of the contract or to break it. And it seemed to him that he had no choice at all, for he could not pay the giant's price and he could not afford to break his own promise. It was true, as Loki and many of the others were quick to point out, that the Jotun had asked for things that he could not have. They insisted that if he came to collect his payment, then he should receive only their scorn for his foolish belief that the sun and the moon were things that could be taken from the sky and given to him. But that was unacceptable to Odhinn, for he had made a promise. How fine it would be if the Aesir, he thought, who wished above all else to teach fairness and consideration, broke their promises with impunity. Then his authority and all that he stood for would be reduced to lies and hollow words.

But every day he could look out across the Plains of Ida and see the wall of white marble snaking its way slowly around the citadel of the Aesir. The days were passing, and still the giant held to his schedule. Never did he stop to rest, except perhaps a few minutes each day to eat and to stretch his aching arms. But still he showed no signs of tiring, nor did his pace ever falter. And the great horse Svadilfari was ever at his side, lending his supernatural strength and understanding far more than any simple beast could. The Valkyries, who guarded the Jotun and were never far from him, said that at times he would speak with the horse, and Svadilfari would reply in a deep, low voice. But what was said between them was never known, for the two were always secretive and the battle-maidens did not know the Jotun tongue.

So the time passed, and as the day drew near it became increasingly apparent that the giant would be very close to completing the wall on time. For the final two weeks Asgardh became a silent place as everyone forgot their tasks and watched. And so it was that the time came at last that the Aesir knew that they had lost, for three days remained and there was only two days of work left to be done. That night the Aesir gathered again in Valhalla to discuss what they would do, and Odhinn saw even before it began that the discussion might easily go against his will. This he considered long, and in it he saw how he might himself avoid all blame in the breaking of his promised word.

"My good people, this is simply ridiculous!" Idhunn began immediately. "We have simply sat here for the past one hundred days and allowed that giant to make fools of us."

"In all fairness, we have made fools of ourselves," Odhinn said. "Our most industrious friend only provided the means. We agreed to make a payment in goods that we knew we could not give, so the failing is ours. The first question is whether we could induce him to accept payment in some other form."

"I doubt it," Loki answered. "I imagine that he would defer all other payments if we just give him Idhunn. Indeed I rather suspect that he would have any bride from among our number, for with the powers of an Asynjur at his command he could depose Utgardh-Loki and become himself Lord of the Jotnar."

"That is out of the question!" Idhunn exclaimed.

"I was not suggesting it! We need no greater enemies than the ones we already have. I was only saying that we can rule out his accepting any other payment. This is one intelligent giant that we have, a genius among his kind, to conceive and carry out such a plan. But intelligence does not mean wisdom, or he would have had the foresight to know that we cannot make this payment."

"I will give him a payment he does not expect," Heimdall muttered.

"No, not that way," Odhinn said firmly. "I will not have it said that we will not do what we have promised, and certainly not that we will resort to such measures."

"What then?" Idhunn cried. "If that giant comes to collect

me as payment then I will blast him myself, even here before the council of the Aesir in Valhalla.''

"No, I do not wish others to see us take such actions, even the elves who serve us loyally," Odhinn replied. "I am bound by my promise. If the Jotun completes his task and comes before me here to collect his payment, then I will make amends as best I can. What the rest of you might do is your own affair. I only hope that you will be subtle."

"More subtle than yourself, perhaps?" Loki asked, and laughed. But the others were silent. Idhunn sat back in her chair for a moment, deep in thought. Then she smiled.

"I suppose," she said slowly, "that we might be fortunate enough that some terrible accident might befall our friend and prevent him from completing his work."

"Some subtle accident, no doubt?" Loki asked, enjoying the joke more than it was worth.

"Only so long as it is not obvious," Odhinn said, and smiled also.

Idhunn turned to look hard at Loki. "You were so certain that you had it all figured out. You advised us to accept his terms, saying that we could show Utgardh-Loki that he has nothing to gain by spying upon us and at the same time we would get a part of our wall built at his expense. Perhaps you wanted this giant in Asgardh. Did you want the Aesir to lose me and therefore their mortal forms? Were you doing the bidding of your true master in Utgardh?"

"That I will not accept!" Loki declared, rising in anger, and he spoke more harshly than they had ever before heard, since he usually ignored or made light of such things. "I do not desire to lose my mortal form any more than any of you. Nor do I serve Utgardh-Loki. My powers are still greater than his, and if I had any dealings with him then I would be the master."

That last part the Aesir knew to be true, for while Loki never desired authority and mastery over others he would suffer no one to be his master, and in all the nine realms he would obey only the word of Odhinn. But it hurt him to see Idhunn so angry with him, for she of all the Asynjur had been willing to teach him things of great knowledge and power. So it was that Loki was ashamed, one of the few times that ever happened, and he truly regretted that he was so vain and stubborn that he always desired to have his own way in all things and so did evil when he had intended only good. And that shame proved to be the spark that brought to life the small flame of true nobility that burned deep and most often hidden within him.

"Very well, then," he said, rising from his seat. "Loki got you into this trouble, and he will do his best to get you out of it. I should imagine that I am the most capable of contriving the type of subtle accident that is required. But I will need just a little help, if Idhunn is willing to give it. I fear that I will never be very good at her trick of shape-changing, and I need also one of her special potions."

Later that night the giant descended yet again from Asgardh into the rugged wastes of Jotunheim. Svadilfari followed dutifully behind, pulling the train of now empty wagons. They followed a path that was now deeply worn, and the many wheels of the wagons fell immediately into the tracks of the two deep ruts that would lead unerringly to their destination. Now at least the ground was frozen hard by the icy blast of a winter storm, that same storm that had blinded the pair with swirling snow throughout the previous day. But however deep the snows of winter, the way was always kept open by their constant passage.

They made their way swiftly along the winding path through the snow-covered hills, coming soon through the sheltered valley where rows of massive white shapes stood like the streets and buildings of some abandoned town. The Jotun paused a moment to consult the list of stone that he needed and led the way to a broad avenue of towering blocks, standing silent and gray in the night. There he slipped the heavy harness from Svardilfari's neck and pulled the rolling framework over to begin loading blocks onto the wide beds of the great wagons.

Svadilfari shook himself gratefully and trotted off in search of a quick drink. At the far end of the valley was a small spring, gently warmed by some underground heat, and the giant had laid a large stone trough to catch the trickling water. Svadilfari bent his long neck and drank deeply, chuckling to himself as its warmth filled him and the swirling steam thawed his frozen nose. There was some strange taste to the water this time, neither pleasant nor unpleasant and very faint. But the water was mineral-laden to begin with, so he took no real notice of it.

Suddenly he paused in his drinking and stood for a long moment with his nose in the water, for he was filled with a fiery, invigorating warmth such as he felt only at those times when he helped himself to his master's liquor. Then he lifted his head, grinning broadly and chuckling in an evil way. Thoughts came to him unbidden, of warm days and long-legged fillies running through high grass, and nature made a demand upon him that he could not refuse. He arched his neck and called loudly into the night, and it did not surprise him that his call was answered.

Following that call, he ran through the streets of stone until he came to the entrance of the valley, where there stood the trailing edge of one of the vast, dark forests that covered large areas of Jotunheim. There he saw a mare of his mighty race standing alone on a low hill before the shadowy eaves of the forest. She was young, tall and proud, solid white of coat, which was rare and highly esteemed among his kind. She had small ears that stood erect through a thick, flowing mane, and her sleek flanks were graced by a sweeping tail. Svadilfari paused when he saw her, and she looked upon him with large black eyes and smiled.

"Well, hello there!" he said, drawing himself up proudly. "What could a fine young thing like you be doing out here in the wild on a night like this?"

"And what would you like to do?" she asked suggestively. "Perhaps we could do it together."

"Indeed, for the game I have in mind requires two players."

The mare only laughed, a cute, horsy laugh, then turned and trotted off into the forest with a provocative swish of her lovely tail. Svadilfari started and leaped after her.

At that very moment the giant himself came running up. He had heard the calls of the two horses in the night and he had known in an instant what it meant. And he knew also his own danger, for without Svadilfari he could not move the stone and there was no time now to make up a day of lost work. He ran, knowing that if he did not catch the horse then he would lose his contract. But he arrived only in time to see the two turn and head off into the woods.

"Wait! Stop! Svadilfari, you oversized oat-burner, you'd better stop where you are or I'll tie you up and hang you by your tail!" the Jotun called, and began to run after the two horses. Svadilfari did not even look back. "You . . . you horseface! I'll make a gelding of you when I get hold of you!"

So the race began, and whenever Svadilfari increased his pace so that he might catch his prize the mare only ran faster. She never varied from her path, but headed as fast and as straight from the valley as she could. The great stallion never lost sight of her as she weaved her way among the trees of the forest, and somehow the giant stayed close behind them both. But he was still falling steadily farther behind while the hours of the night passed and their lead widened to a mile, then two and more. At length he realized that he would never catch them, and that dawn would come soon and find him many miles from both the valley and the world-gate. Then he knew that his only hope was to continue with what work he could do himself and wait for the horse to return.

Dawn came at last, or such dawn as there was, for the sun came up as a misty yellow ball in the eastern sky and the shadows became less deep, although the sky remained dark and full of stars. Even as the sun began to rise, the two horses left the woods and came out onto a vast snow-covered plain like the seas of the north that are frozen over and covered with frost. Then there was no danger that Svadilfari would lose sight of his prize. The white mare increased her pace just a little beyond that of her pursuer, thinking to widen the lead. He tried to match her speed and could not, but he still had one trick to use to his advantage.

With a mighty leap he took to the sky and ran along as if on some invisible bridge. But he was flying in truth, carried by some strange power that he possessed. Unsuspected, he overtook the mare and passed above her. Then he descended upon her abruptly, and so he caught her. She struggled desperately to free herself, but Svadilfari prevailed at last. For while she was light and had the advantage of speed, he could call upon the hidden strength of a hundred horses his size.

"Help! Stop! Help!" the mare called loudly, but in the language of the Aesir. "Help! Idhunn, get me out of this! Change me back! Odhinn . . . Oh my word!"

*   *   *

The giant returned to his valley by dawn, and sought out some way to move the massive stone blocks by himself. He took spare pulleys and used them to try to move the train of wagons, but it was not enough. Then he released the foremost wagon and spent half the morning inching it along the road to the gate. There he was stopped again, for the crystal bridge was too steep even for all of his pulleys. By now his strength was spent, for he had been three months in building the wall, and before that he had been a year cutting and assembling the stone, and he had come to that straight from the building of the mighty fortress of Utgardh. The long hours of the futile chase and the morning of harsh labor had taken the final toll, and he despaired of ever finishing his task after coming so close.

Then his mind turned to darker thoughts. It seemed to him more than coincidence that he had lost the aid of Svadilfari at the very moment when he would win or lose. He wondered if it might be the doing of the Aesir, and the more he thought about it the more certain he became. Suddenly he noticed that it was growing dark, for the sun was sinking into the west behind him. And he knew that he had lost, for a day's work remained and he had only until midnight of the following day to complete his task. Svadilfari had to return then or not at all.

The giant was seized with a terrible rage when he realized that, and he believed that the Aesir had intended from the first to cheat him and humiliate him. What wisdom he had departed from him, and he was possessed by the mad fury of his kind. Without weapon or thought he ran up the bridge to Asgardh, shouting and cursing loudly.

But Heimdall heard him coming and closed the gate securely. This the Aesir had not considered, that the giant would see through their ploy or turn to uncontrolled violence. It went against their purposes to have to fight him, but it seemed that they must. For the Jotun was beating upon the outer doors of the gate, shouting accusations and cursing the Aesir with terrible names, some they deserved but many they did not. Heimdall called upon the Valkyries to help him defend the wall, but soon had to consider leading an attack upon the indignant giant.

At that moment Thor and Tyr returned from the wilds of Jotunheim, and that proved most opportune. They had been away since before the giant had come to Valhalla to make his proposal, and so it came as a complete surprise to them, as they ascended Bifrost, to see Asgardh encircled by a wall of white stone, with towers standing to either side at the top of the bridge. But it was even more surprising to see a Jotun beating furiously upon the gold-plated doors of the new gate.

Thor was so surprised that he was beyond anger, and there was something about that sight that appealed to his odd sense of humor. Also he had had quite enough of Jotnar and their ways in the past few weeks. He came up quietly behind the giant and stood there watching for a short time, like some curious bystander.

"Is there some trouble, my friend?" he asked at last.

"These filthy, cheating Aesir!" the giant replied, giving the door a final kick. "I made a deal with them, and kept my part. And now they refuse to give me the payment they promised."

"Well, that is certainly no way to go about it. What if Thor heard you say such things? He might be offended."

"Thor is away, for all it matters," the giant said scornfully. "But even if he was here, I would hang him from a tree by that beard of his and show these oathbreakers to not try their tricks with me!"

"Is that a fact? Well, it so happens that Thor is here," he said, and drew the great sword that was his only weapon in those days. Then he paid the giant's wages, but not with the sun or the moon or any lady of the Asynjur. And the Aesir always held that they were guiltless in the breaking of their word, since Thor had not been present for its making. But truths cannot be changed with words, and the truth remained that the fortress of Asgardh was built by deceit and the builder received deceit and death in payment.

In the morning of the second day afterward the white mare ascended the bridge into Asgardh, followed closely by the great black stallion. Her head was hung low and she walked with leaden hooves, but Svadilfari pranced along with a broad grin quite pleased. The Aesir came out of their halls to greet them, and the white mare, seeing Idhunn in the crowd, looked up with blazing eyes and trotted purposefully over to her.

"You!" the mare declared. "Just how much of that potion did you give this overambitious stud? He is only now coming out of it."

"Then I gave him exactly as much as you requested," Idhunn replied. "You did say that he would have to chase you until the morning after the deadline, and here you are. Did he pursue you the entire time?"

"Pursue me?" the horse asked incredulously. "He caught me, and as often as it pleased him! No one warned me that amid all else he can fly. Now, if you will kindly help me back into my true form. . . ."

"Immediately," she said, and laying a hand to the horse's head she began the transformation. But nothing happened. Again she tried, but the shape-changing would not occur. Then she understood, and laughed aloud.

"I am sorry, but you will have to endure that form for a time yet," she said. "The transformation cannot be made. I cannot place the two of you in one body."

"What two of me?" Loki demanded.

But for once Thor's mind proved the quicker, and he roared with laughter. "Congratulations, Sly! You are going to be a mother!"

Svadilfari stayed in Asgardh and was loyal to the Aesir, and by his great strength the wall was completed. Then the wall was made higher yet, for they used the extra stone cut by the giant to add a third layer of blocks. Then the Aesir believed their citadel to be secure against all enemies, and they dwelled there long in peace and security.

Loki had to wear the form of the white mare for several weeks, until the colt he carried was born at last. Then Loki transferred quickly to his former shape, and he had nothing more to do with his unfortunate child. For the colt was strange in shape, blacker than night, and while he lacked much of his sire's height he had four pairs of legs. Sleipnir, son of Svadilfari, he was called, swifter than any steed of the nine realms either on the ground or in the sky. He had his father's gift of flight, although not his strength, and was even faster still. He became Odhinn's own mount when he came to his full growth, and although he was a monster in form he was wise and faithful.

In time both steeds came to father a new race of horses. Svadilfari's descendants were the larger, and many of the Aesir took these for their own. But Sleipnir's offspring were the swifter, and these became the mounts of the Valkyries, and they bore the battle-maidens on their errands through the nine realms. Glaerfaxi the shining-mane was of this breed, whom Brynhild rode, and Sigrune's Gullholnir. And so the Aesir, who had given up the power of flight to take physical form, now had steeds to carry them through the upper ways. And everyone was pleased except Loki, for the horses of Asgardh called him Hvitfaxi in jest, the white-coated mother of their race.

CHAPTER THREE

Of the Acorns
of Idhunn

I t was still in the early days of the world, just a few short
years since the Aesir had taken physical form, that they
learned that they had many enemies among the Jotnar.
Loki was of that world and related to the spirits of power that
dwelled within the fire-Jotnar, so that he was like them in
some ways but very unlike in others. The giants were very
learned in many things and yet very superstitious in many
others, and they were wise in certain ways but were ruled
most often by their emotions, particularly in their insatiable
greed for wealth and flattery and power. But for so long they
had been very disorganized and warring among themselves,
and the Aesir paid them little heed.

Then there came one of higher ambitions and possessing a
talent for leading and for laying skillful plots, who was
named Loki. When still young he came to be chieftain of his
tribe of hill-giants. Soon he began to gather many other tribes
of hill-giants under his banner and many also of the frost-
giants, and in time he came to be liegelord of most of the
tribes of Jotunheim. Then he proclaimed himself king and had
built his great fortress Utgardh, and from that time on he was
called Utgardh-Loki. And with the conquest of Jotunheim

behind him his attention turned in time to the Aesir, the last and greatest conquest. But he knew also that the Aesir were a power beyond him, if only because they controlled the world-gate.

Utgardh-Loki emptied the lands about the world-gate for many hundreds of miles around, and between the gate and his own fortress he established realms for his two mightiest captains and gave them great armies to protect their lands. Thjatsi was the wisest and most cunning, and his fortress was Thrymheim. The other was Thrym, the builder of Thrymheim, but he had abandoned that fortress to dwell with his army of rock-giants in Klettastadhur.

The Aesir knew that there was a unification of the Jotnar against them, but they knew little else of what form it took, of whom its leaders were or how great a strength of arms they could command. Therefore Thor and Tyr made several journeys into Jotunheim to learn what they could; indeed the walling of Asgardh took place during one such trip. But they learned little, for Thor and Tyr together were not subtle enough to be good spies. All that came of their journeys was Thor's lasting reputation as a giant-slayer, and the healthy respect the Jotnar were always to have for him.

But Odhinn was greatly disturbed after the ill deeds that befell during the walling of his citadel. Then he considered more trips into Jotunheim, and if Thor and Tyr were not subtle enough for the task then he would call upon the special talents of that greatest of sneaks, Loki himself, who also had some knowledge of Jotunheim from the days before. And he thought also to go himself. Therefore he called Loki and Thor, Tyr and Hoenir to him, and also the Valkyries Sigrune and Brynhild.

"I have decided that we must make yet another attempt to learn something of the affairs of Jotunheim," he said. "This time I have decided to go myself, with Loki and Hoenir, and we will try to pass within the walls of Utgardh and learn something of its strengths. Thor and Tyr will circle around to the north and the Valkyries to the south, to trace the perimeters of Utgardh-Loki's domain and determine its size. The ravens Huginn and Muninn and the wolves Geri and Freki will accompany them to spy out the lands."

With daybreak of the next morning they were off, descend-

ing the bridge to head west across the rolling plains that
bordered the wastelands. For a time they traveled together
and did not fly, but set their impatient horses to trot across the
empty lands. It was the spring of the year, even in the wastes
of Jotunheim, and the grass that covered the flowing expanse
of hills was deep and green. But the sky was hidden behind a
dark ceiling of gray clouds, as was almost always the case. At
least it seemed more like an overcast day on one of the
lighted worlds, if perhaps the deepest dark before some terrible storm; only in the elf-world was the eternal night a
peaceful one.

The party split when they came to the edge of the inhabited
lands, and Thor and Tyr went north while the Valkyries
headed south. But Loki led Hoenir and Odhinn straight into
the heart of the giant's realm, although even he had no clear
idea of where they were going and was only following the
directions that Thor had given him. They did know that they
were on the southeast border of the lands held by Thjatsi, and
were some two hundred miles from his great hall on the
shores of the northern sea.

That night they camped on the bank of a small river that
crossed their path. Hoenir had brought down a rabbit with a
single arrow, and he considered that no small trick, as the
rabbits of Jotunheim were as big as a wild boar. But when he
tried to light a fire to cook it, he was unable to set a flame to
even the smallest bit of kindling. That confused him, for the
wood was dry and he could produce a steady spark. It was
like trying to set fire to a stone, for none of the wood along
the bank would burn.

At last he gave up in frustration and called upon Loki to
try. Loki was a spirit of flame and boasted that he could make
even water burn; it was in fact a favorite trick of his. But that
night he had no better luck than Hoenir, even when he held
the kindling within an open flame he produced in mid-air. He
soon knew that there was something that prevented the wood
from burning, but it wounded his pride that anything could
keep him from striking a flame to a piece of wood when he
wished. At last he gathered together a handful of sticks and
summoned all of his power.

There was a flash and a violent explosion, and everyone
dived for cover as chips of wood shot in all directions. The

smoke parted to reveal Loki still holding the broken ends of a few sticks, his head down and his eyes tightly closed. After a moment he cautiously opened one eye and stared in amazement at the wood in his hands. There was not the slightest trace of flame. He threw the sticks down and stomped on them, then brushed his hands and turned to the others.

"Forget it," he said in a very matter of fact tone. "I suggest that we ignore the rabbit and see what we might have in our bags."

"Eat grass," Sleipnir suggested, and all the steeds gave a hearty horse-laugh.

"Well, I might try calling down a bolt of lightning," Odhinn teased, and even Hoenir was trying hard not to laugh. Loki liked a jest as well as anyone, even at his own expense, but he did not find this one at all amusing.

But someone did, for the sound of laughter came from the dark canopy of the great tree that stood above them. It was a curious laugh, shrill and cracking. A moment later there was a rustling of vast wings and an immense eagle dropped to the ground a few yards away. It was a huge bird, large even by the standards of Jotunheim, taller than any of the Aesir as it stood before them, and the spread of its wings was forty feet. But it stood now with folded wings and looked at them shrewdly.

"So, perhaps there is a problem?" the eagle asked in its shrill voice. "Those who creep about in unfamiliar places should not be surprised by such things. The wood will not burn, of course. Not unless you know the secret."

"And what secret would that be?" Odhinn asked.

"The secret known by those who are given the right to use this wood in fire," the great bird replied, striding forward and bending to look at the collected firewood. "This deal would I offer. I know the secret of making the wood burn, but I cannot strike a spark. You could make a fire if the wood would only burn. If I help you make a fire, will you give me a portion of your catch?"

"Yes, that is most agreeable," Odhinn said quickly before Loki could refuse indignantly. Something was up and this eagle was somehow the key to it all, and he wanted to find out what was really going on. The eagle simply bent over the firewood and, opening his hooked beak, breathed over the wood.

"Now it will light, if the Lord of Flame will honor us," he said. "But do be careful, for it will burn very easily now."

And so it did when Loki touched a spark to it. Now Odhinn did not believe for a moment that the eagle had made the wood burn simply by breathing on it, whatever he might have been drinking of late. That was a distraction, a shaman's poor trick, but employed to hide the use of real power such as the Aesir possessed. He had felt the magic, although he could not say just what had been done.

The meat was cooked, but even before it was taken from the spit Odhinn called the eagle forward and asked him what portion he would have. But the eagle helped himself; striking out as swift as lightning, he seized the entire rabbit and leaped away into the night. Loki proved almost as fast, and seizing a long, heavy stick he ran after the eagle as he flew low to the ground and beat his broad wings as if struggling to carry his prize skyward. Loki almost caught him, and was raising his club to strike when the eagle turned suddenly and dove straight at him, knocking him to the ground. The eagle seized Loki's wrists in his powerful claws and bore him skyward with ease, thus proving that his earlier trouble in getting airborne had been only a ruse.

"Do not fear, my little one," the eagle said, although not in any reassuring tone. "I will not harm you. I am taking you to show you something very pretty."

"And what might that be?" Loki asked.

"Oh, I will not lessen the surprise and joy of your first sight by giving you the least hint. But you might want it. Indeed you might be willing to pay very dearly for it."

It seemed to Loki that many long hours passed while he hung beneath the eagle, although he knew that it was not much more than an hour and a half before they began to descend. Far below was the dark shape of a great stone fortress, a massive structure with thick walls and squat towers surrounding a central keep that rose like the jagged cone of a sleeping volcano. The eagle dropped swiftly in a tight spiral, perhaps thinking that he should come down too swiftly for Loki to try some trick to escape. At last the huge bird circled wide about the inner keep and descended toward a broad terrace, dropping his passenger a couple of feet before coming to land a short distance away.

"Welcome to my humble nest," the eagle said as he folded his wings. Then his form shifted and seemed to melt, reforming into the shape of a giant.

"Does it alarm you that one of your enemies should have some of your cherished powers?" the giant asked, now in an appropriately deep voice. He was truly a lord of his kind, fifteen feet in height and lighter in build than most, surprisingly handsome even for a hill-giant. He still bore some resemblance to his eagle form, for he possessed an aquiline nose and a short, black beard that came to a sharp point below his chin.

"Magic is for those who possess it," Loki answered. "I have such powers myself, and a few others besides."

"No doubt," the giant replied. "But they say that your most potent power lies in your sharp tongue, which you will now use to our mutual advantage. I am Thjatsi, lord of this realm. And you are by your own word Loki, Lord of Flame."

"At your service," Loki said with mild sarcasm, and bowed. "My reputation precedes me. What service may Loki's sharp sword be to you, and what reward is he to have for his work?"

"What I have in mind is more a trade than a service."

The giant led the way into the heart of his great fortress. Its darkened halls were like vast caverns, or so it seemed to Loki, for the Jotnar built on a scale three times that of Asgardh. But even so it was an impressive structure, a mile across and a third as high. At the first corner four guards fell in behind them, warriors of the castle guard clad in black armor and carrying bared swords whose blades were nine feet in length. Loki feigned unconcern, trusting that Thjatsi did indeed have some deeper motive than just taking him prisoner.

Thjatsi stopped abruptly beside one door and turned quickly. "This is the chamber of my daughter Skadi. She is . . . entertaining a guest who has been staying with us."

"Anyone I know?" Loki asked.

"Someone you do know, although you have never looked upon her face," the giant said, and knocked softly.

A moment later the door was opened by a giantess, Thjatsi's own daughter by her looks. She was fully as tall as her father,

and she was beautiful indeed to look upon. She bowed her
head in respect to her father, but hardly took her eyes off
Loki, standing like a child between his towering guards.

"Skadi, this is Loki of the Flame," Thjatsi said. "He
would like to meet our other guest."

Skadi said nothing but drew back from the door, and Loki
entered. There were other giantesses in the room, frost-Jotnar,
and fully armed. But across the room he saw one of his own
size, and he stopped short.

"Sygyn!" he exclaimed, for he possessed senses that could
not be fooled. Within that mortal form dwelled Sygyn, a
flame-spirit and his companion through the long years before
the coming of the Aesir. He had not seen her since, but he
had thought of her often.

"Yes, that is Sygyn," Thjatsi said. "Go and speak with
her. But please do not consider fighting your way out. There
are nine frost-giants in this room now, and I am no small
power to deal with myself."

Loki ignored that, wondering briefly what great danger
there was in frost-giants. He crossed the room to where
Sygyn waited. Whoever had given her this form was to be
commended, for he was impressed. She was as beautiful as
any of the Asynjur.

"Sygyn, is that you indeed?" he asked.

"It is," she said. "Thjatsi has learned the secrets of shape-
changing and of making life, and he has been giving the
flame-spirits physical form these past years. I resisted, until it
seemed to me that I might go like you to dwell in Asgardh if I
had a body to wear. Thjatsi granted it to me, but he had other
plans thereafter."

"So I have noticed. Can you escape?"

Sygyn shook her head sadly. "No, not now. I gave up a
larger part of my powers than I had anticipated. At least five
frost-giants are around me at all times. If I even start to call
forth my powers, then they let me feel their ice."

"So that is what the old buzzard meant," Loki said to
himself before turning back to Thjatsi. "You have made half
of your bargain very clear. What do you want for our release?"

"What?" the giant asked incredulously. "I want nothing
for your release. In fact, with the dawn I intend to put on my
eagle shape and carry you back to your friends. I have no

choice if I am to get what I want. But for Sygyn's release, you must bring me something of equal value in trade.''

And then, even before the coming of dawn, Thjatsi returned to his eagle shape and carried Loki back to his companions. Loki did not know what he should do. For he wanted Sygyn delivered to him, even as she desired it herself. It was a pleasing thought, to have a companion of his own, when all the Asynjur shunned him. Sygyn had been devoted to him since ancient times, when he had been Lord of the Flame-Spirits and she his second. She was like himself, and in her company he would no longer be alone and wholly apart among the Aesir. But he knew also that the deed would have to be paid for when it was discovered.

Thjatsi set him down less than a mile from where Odhinn and Hoenir were camped and allowed him to return to his own. So it was that when Loki did return, he would say only that the eagle had carried him several miles before setting him down, and he had been the rest of the night walking back. If Odhinn was suspicious then he did not show it, but said that Loki got just what he deserved for being so impetuous. Hoenir, of course, said nothing.

Those were miserable days indeed for Loki, because of both his impatience to be reunited with Sygyn and his dread of what he was a part of. But there was no alternative that satisfied him. He did not believe that the Aesir would agree to rescue Sygyn. Odhinn might desire it, but he was forever mindful of his own authority and would not go against the will of the others. Perhaps in this Loki underestimated the Aesir, for nothing would aròuse their desire to help more swiftly than such a sad tale. He thought that he might not remain in Asgardh after Sygyn's release. There were other places, including his old, favorite haunts in the wilds of Jotunheim. And he could gather all the flame-spirits to him, founding a realm of his own. It displeased him that they would turn to Thjatsi for the physical forms they desired. That was also the second reason why he would have his revenge upon that proud Jotun.

The appointed time came and Loki, gathering his resolve, sought out Idhunn as she worked in her garden. Loki was always a traveler and explorer, and he often brought her new

things as payment for the learning that she had given him.
And so it was not strange that he came to her now.

"I would have come sooner," he said to her. "But for
these past two days I have been busy with Odhinn preparing
maps of Jotunheim. I want you to see this, for the longer I
have had it the more amazed I am."

He handed her what appeared to be a twig of some pine or
fir, but its needles were of a strange design and it bore a
single great flower like an orchid.

"There are two things about this which are quite strange,"
he explained. "For one thing, I broke it from its branch nine
days ago. And it has also lain that entire time in my pack and
was pressed completely flat, and yet you can see that it has
returned to its former shape."

Idhunn looked at it long and probed its structure with her
magic. "Life remains strong within it. Indeed it is almost as
if this small piece of wood was still on the tree. Hardy is the
life of Jotunheim, beyond that of even the other undying
realms, but this is almost beyond belief. If the giants build
their halls of this wood, then the beams and boards must
always be taking root and sprouting new growth!"

"There are many such trees in the forest north of the
world-gate in Jotunheim," Loki offered. "I had never before
thought them particularly strange."

"Can you take me there now?" Idhunn asked impatiently.

Loki laughed. "Yes, but we must hurry."

They passed the world-gate undetected, for Loki had known
that Heimdall would be away for some time, and descended
the bridge into Jotunheim. There it was a morning so bright
and clear that only a handful of the brightest stars would dare
the light and shine faintly in the violet sky, while the ascend-
ing sun awoke the rainbow within the crystal bridge. Such
were the delights of Idhunn, to see a morning in Jotunheim so
beautiful and peaceful that it was almost a mirror image of the
elf-world, or to see the crystal bridge glowing with an inner
light. Now she took little notice of such things in her eager-
ness to see the tree that would not die.

Loki led his horse north along the very road the giant had
made hauling stone for the building of Asgardh's wall. When
they came to the edge of the great forest he turned to the
northwest and proceeded on for more than a mile into the

woods. Soon they came upon a small tree that stood apart from the others in a tiny clearing. Its shape was that of a cone, perfect in symmetry, and it bore many of the white flowers on its branches. Except for the flowers it could have passed unnoticed as any of a dozen other pines and firs which existed in that world. Loki stopped a few yards back, and Idhunn slipped from the back of his horse to run up to the strange tree.

She did not see the dark shape rushing toward her from behind, nor did she hear the rustle of the wind through vast wings. As soon as she came within three yards of the tree she noticed a curious scent, not unpleasant, and thinking it to be the fragrance of the flowers she breathed deeply. The magic potion worked quickly, and even as she began to suspect that she was drugged she fell in a faint. The eagle was upon her immediately, and taking up her limp wrists in its great talons it bore her aloft.

"You have kept your part faithfully," the eagle called back to Loki as it circled once. "You will have your payment before nightfall."

That afternoon a maiden appeared before the bridge in Jotunheim, and calling out she requested admittance into Asgardh. Heimdall was amazed, for she was too small by half to be a giantess, and he guessed that she might be an elf who had been captured by the Jotnar and had escaped. For that reason he brought her quickly into Asgardh and took her immediately to Odhinn, who was alone with Loki in his great hall Vingolf. Loki had thought to pretend great surprise and delight at her arrival, but he did not. He had made his first payment to Thjatsi, now he would make his second and add no more guilt to that he already bore.

"Lord of Asgardh, I am Sygyn, a fire-spirit and a servant of Loki of the Flame, who is our lord," she proclaimed boldly, as she had been instructed by Thjatsi how to play this game. "I ask admittance into Asgardh so that I might remain with my lord."

"Answer for me one question, and I will grant it freely," Odhinn said. "I would know how you came to hold a mortal form."

This was one part of the tale that Thjatsi had forgotten, or

he never would have allowed her to depart from his fortress.
Sygyn could find no answer but the truth. Heimdall was
openly dismayed, while Odhinn himself sat back in his chair
and pondered that for a long moment. Loki saw that this news
had upset them both, although he could not understand why.

Odhinn shook his head pensively and looked up at Heimdall.
"You know then what must be done."

"Of course," Heimdall replied. "But where is our strength?
Thor and Tyr are in the wilderness of Jotunheim, and half of
the Valkyries as well."

"What then would you suggest?"

Heimdall shrugged. "If Thjatsi must be eliminated immediately, then I suggest a quick assault or a quiet assassination.
Jotunish tricks, but we are dealing with a Jotun. Otherwise
we need a month for our missing members to return and to
put together an army."

"But what is so urgent?" Loki asked, utterly confused.

"What urgency indeed?" Odhinn asked in return. "This
giant has powers that I trust only in the hands of Idhunn.
There are enough monsters in the nine worlds without Thjatsi
making more."

It was then that Loki saw the terrible mistake he had made,
and he dreaded it beyond the wrath of the Aesir. "Then it is
decided; the quick assault is the only choice. You see, Thjatsi
has Idhunn."

There were few admissions that Loki could have made that
would have been regarded more terrible, or more treacherous.
Heimdall's hand went to his sword and he would have called
the Valkyries, but Odhinn waved him aside and asked in a
calm and dreadful voice for Loki to explain himself. Then
Loki told all, admitting to his great embarrassment that he
cared greatly for Sygyn and had been too afraid for her safety
to try anything else, and that he had honestly believed that
Idhunn could be gotten back without any real danger to
herself.

And so it was proven that he would have done well to have
trusted in the good will of the Aesir. For Odhinn was indeed
moved by his story, and doubly so in his surprise that the
proud and mischievous Loki could have been forced to such
ends out of love and concern. For himself he would have

forgiven Loki, but he knew that the others would not be so kindly disposed.

"Yes, there is a payment that you have yet to make," Odhinn said at last. "If you could contrive to get Idhunn safely away from the giant and return her to Asgardh, then I would speak on your behalf before the Aesir. In fact, you might even earn their forgiveness."

Then Loki looked up and smiled with delight. "Could I? I have a plan. . . ."

"I thought that you would."

"A simple one, but effective. I will employ Thjatsi's own tricks to his disadvantage. I need only a little help to get started."

It was a small party that gathered at the gate of Asgardh at the first light of dawn. The world-gate was already open into Jotunheim, a window into another universe that hung suspended a few yards out from the edge of the plateau. The crystal bridge Bifrost extended up and through that opening, and Heimdall stood now at the highest point of the arch holding the gate open.

"Are you ready now, Loki?" Odhinn asked.

The great falcon beside him stirred and looked up through the gate. It was cloudy again in Jotunheim, low, thick clouds that might hang for many days unchanged. There was a partial lightening in the distant east where the sun was only just coming up behind that gray cover, but it would remain more night than day.

"I am ready," Loki said in the falcon's shrill voice. "There will be a watch, in the event that I am pursued?"

"We will watch. You will be safe, so long as you can beat whatever is chasing you to the gate."

"Then do not fear if I am two, three or even four days in returning," Loki said. "I may have to wait long for my opportunity, for I am hardly in any . . . 'shape' for a major assault. I imagine that the only way Thjatsi could hold such an accomplished shape-changer is to keep her locked away under guard somewhere. But do not fear. I will have her out."

"Good luck to you, then," Odhinn said. "I will not say be swift, but do be cautious."

Sygyn came and checked a final time the curious device strapped to his back. The long, narrow tank on his back was secure, and the two tubes, one curving around below his head and the other facing forward directly above, were in place. Then the falcon spread its wings and ascended with powerful strokes through the open world-gate. Heimdall stood for a time to watch him go, flying off toward the northwest, before coming down from the bridge and allowing the gate to close.

Loki held to a leisurely pace saving his strength for the return journey. Despite his assurances to Odhinn, he was somewhat less than certain that he could make this plan work. The falcon shape was the only one that he could take on his own, and even then he needed a little help from one of the Aesir. Once into it, he was trapped in that form until he found someone with the magic to free him. It was the best form for his purposes, for he could circle about the fortress of Thrymheim for days without anyone suspecting. But if there was a chase to the end, then he would be in trouble. The falcon was swifter in the short race, but the eagle was more enduring.

He had little trouble finding Thrymheim. The massive fortress stood on a narrow strip of land between a great fjord and the northern sea, bound on three sides by towering cliffs. Loki descended for a time and rested in a sheltered place in a corner of one of the broad towers. Now came the hardest part, finding where Thjatsi kept Idhunn. He knew that the search would probably have to be by inference, since he was restricted to the outside of the fortress and Idhunn was locked somewhere within. The problem was compounded by the presence of the weapon strapped to his back, but he could not take it off and he would certainly never be able to get it back on by himself. He wished that he had thought to have someone cover it with feathers, but that was hardly any help. A hunch-backed falcon was almost as strange a sight.

But it turned out to be no problem at all, for he found Idhunn in the first place he looked and where he had hoped to find her, in the very room where Sygyn had been kept. Two guards stood always at the door, and Thjatsi went there often as if to view some treasure that he often desired to look upon. Loki wondered what they found to talk about, or if Thjatsi was beginning to discover that possessing a lady of the Asynjur and being able to command her powers were very different things. Idhunn was typically very mild of temper and could remain as silent and resolute as stone, except when she was piqued and at liberty to indulge her fury. Either way, Thjatsi would find her difficult to deal with.

Loki circled wide about the keep and flew straight in through a window into the hall where Idhunn's room was located. The guards looked up in surprise as he landed on the floor only yards away, although neither left their post. The falcon folded his wings and walked casually over to stand before the two frost-giants. They were not alarmed, nor were they very bright. They bent to look more closely at the strange device on the bird's back, while the falcon stared up at them. Suddenly he bit hard with his hooked beak upon the lower tube, and the upper one shot a cloud of poisonous gas directly into their faces.

Loki scurried out of the way as the giants crashed to the floor like a pair of felled trees, but he was pleased with the results. He had decided upon the use of poison rather than a sleeping potion because it acted instantly and left no witnesses. He was surprised to see that the fall of the guards had brought no one from within the room to look, for they had been armored and made a good deal of noise. He went up to the door and began tapping at it with his beak. A giantess opened the door a moment later, and she was gassed as she looked down at the falcon. Loki rushed between her legs.

Now began the final battle and the most deadly, for there were four giantesses yet in the room who were armed with long swords and frost-magic. Fortunately Loki's gas-cannon shot forth an extremely powerful spray that was very effective even from several yards. Three he had before they could move to stop him, but the fourth was nearest Idhunn and so he was reluctant to shoot carelessly in that direction. He suddenly felt the sharp bite of her cold, and it was enough to stun him for a moment.

But Idhunn herself was not to be counted out of the battle. The giantess' head was well beyond her reach, so she swung both of her fists together and struck the Jotun in the front of her knee. There was a sound of cracking bone, for even the Asynjur were strong beyond their size, and the giantess opened her mouth to roar in pain and fury. An instant later she was hit by the poisonous spray.

"Get to the floor, fool, and give the poison a moment to clear!" Loki yelled in the falcon's shrill voice, then shook violently. "Yeesh, that was cold!"

"You!" Idhunn hissed. "By the stars above, I should turn you into a half-dozen featherdusters!"

"Later, my dear. If you want to get out of here, then leave my feathers intact and get this stupid thing off my back. Be careful, though. You have seen what it can do."

"Indeed," she agreed, and began to look for the buckles. "A fiendishly clever device. Your invention, no doubt?"

"My suggestion," Loki replied. "Heimdall made it, and Frigg provided the ammunition. I provided the bird. There . . . ah, that feels good!"

He stretched his back and wings and shook his head a second time. "Just put that in the fireplace, if you don't mind. There are enough explosives in that to blast this turret off the side of the castle. It should go off in about ten minutes."

Idhunn looked down at the device in her hands. "First tell me how you plan to get me out."

"I will fly you out, of course. Now make yourself small."

"Small? The smallest animal that I have ever been was a fox."

"Well, you will have to do better than that," Loki declared. "I certainly am not going to try to fly three hundred miles with a fox on my back. I had in mind a mouse."

"A mouse? You want me to convert into something that reduces my significant mass to such a small percentage?"

"Yes," he insisted. "By the way, what happens to the rest of you?"

"Do you really want to know?"

Loki thought about it for a moment. "No!"

Idhunn carried the spray device over to the fire and placed it on top of the burning logs. She then returned to where Loki waited and stood before him for a long moment, her eyes closed as she concentrated. Suddenly her form flowed and seemed to dissolve until there was hardly anything left, then reformed into the shape of a small brown field mouse. She bounded across the floor and scurried up into the special harness strapped to the falcon's back.

"Now get us out of here," she said in a tiny voice. "I do not trust your device to go off on time."

"All right," Loki said as he turned and walked toward the door. "Hold on tight. I will be flying two to three times the speed of an ordinary falcon."

Once out into the hall he spread his wings and flew out the window into the morning sky. He rose quickly and headed off into the southeast at almost his best speed. There was now no doubt of his destination, for he could sense the presence of the world-gate from much farther than this. Idhunn clung to his back by the leather straps and nestled down into the cover of his feathers, not because of the cold wind but for fear of being blown off, although for the first few minutes she stared back toward the fortress of Thrymheim. They had not yet come five miles when the southern turret of the keep was shaken by an explosion and crumbled in ruin.

"Ten or fifteen minutes?" she asked. "More like three or four."

Flying direct, Loki estimated that the journey to the gate would take some two and a half hours. He did not hold his quickest pace, for he would have been spent in the first hundred miles. But the speed that he did hold to was only slightly below that, the highest speed that he could maintain for the required distance. Idhunn clung tightly to his back, hidden beneath the feathers, but she lifted her head often to look back. After some time she pulled herself up as close as she could to his ear.

"I think that we are being followed," she said. "I have sensed a presence behind us, and it is now no more than five miles back. Mouse eyes are very small and weak, but you have a pair of hawk eyes beneath that beetled brow."

"Hold on, then," Loki said, and bent his head around to look behind. He needed only a glance, and immediately picked up his pace. "It is him, bearing hard upon our tailfeathers. This is even better than I had planned."

"Better!" Idhunn squeaked. "You said yourself that he could beat us to the gate."

"Not now," he corrected her. "Our lead is too wide, and we have perhaps only fifty miles to go. Let him follow us

through the gate. Then we can kill two birds with one stone
. . . or at least one oversized vulture.''

So the chase began. Loki knew from the start that he had
won the race, for he could already see the distant hills where
the world-gate opened. He had not forced his pace and was
still good for a last run to safety, while he was certain that
Thjatsi had flown hard and was nearing the end of his strength.
He saw his chance to lead Thjatsi through the world-gate, if
he used himself as bait in the final moments. It was a
dangerous game, and for that reason he decided not to tell
Idhunn.

Minutes passed while the eagle continued to gain on his
prey. Loki could not look behind for fear of dislodging his
passenger, but he could gauge the distance by Idhunn's fran-
tic shifting. After a time she turned around backward to watch
for the eagle, but her eyesight in her present form was so
limited that it was a long time before she could see him. But
she could sense his approach even more clearly, until she
eventually seemed to lose her fear of falling completely and
began turning back and forth nervously, watching for some
sight of either their pursuer or their destination.

''Loki, I can see him!'' she shrieked, beating his head with
a tiny paw. ''I see him! He cannot be more than fifty yards
behind!''

''Alright, then. Hold on!'' Loki called back. ''The gate is
two miles ahead and a quarter of a mile below.''

He nosed over and began to descend, and his speed did
increase somewhat, but the eagle flew slightly faster. Idhunn
clung tightly to her harness, chittering and chirping loudly
and constantly, although if she actually said anything he
could not hear it. The eagle came closer, and as Loki leveled
out for the final run through the gate he seemed to falter.
Idhunn lifted her head to look behind, and screamed profani-
ties when she seemed to find herself eye to eye with Thjatsi.

''Loki!''

''I am spent!'' he gasped. ''I will get us there if I can.''

He weaved about until he settled into a path that would
take him through the world-gate and the open portals of the
walls of Asgardh, for there was not room enough at his speed
to rise after coming through the gate to pass above the wall.
Idhunn screamed a final time as he shot through both in the

space of less than two seconds, and the eagle was not ten feet behind. But as Thjatsi followed, the farther opening of the short tunnel through the wall was suddenly blocked off by a sheet of flame.

Thjatsi had time only to flinch before he hit that curtain of fire. Even then he might have survived, except that the flames proved to be a thick, burning liquid that clung to his feathers. Then he panicked and lost control of his flight, so that he struck the ground. And so great was his speed that he tumbled for some distance. There he lay on the white street of Asgardh, broken and burning.

Loki circled back around and landed before the gate. Heimdall was there waiting for him, and Odhinn also. Idhunn jumped from his back and was her former self almost instantly, laughing and dancing with delight for both her return and her safe arrival.

"I received your warning," Heimdall said as he knelt beside Loki to remove the harness.

"So your device did work," Loki said. "The squirt-bottle worked as well, and even took the front off of Thrymheim Castle. Now we have a tale of giant-slaying so unique that even Thor will be envious."

"Well, you are to be congratulated as well, especially for delaying so that Thjatsi would follow you into Asgardh. If I had missed him with the flame, he would have had you."

Idhunn stopped short in her account of her trials to Odhinn and turned to glare at Loki. "You let him come that close to taking you on purpose, when you could have been well away?"

"Of course. You know well enough why Thjatsi had to be slain."

"Yes, but why did you not tell me?"

"Would you have approved?"

"No, and I should still pluck you for your tricks."

"I would rather that you help me out of these feathers entirely," Loki replied. "I will not expect your complete forgiveness, but I do remind you that our most deadly enemy has been exposed and destroyed. Everything came out just as I planned."

"Perhaps more than you expect will come out in the end," she said as she placed a hand on his head to begin the transformation. But it was Odhinn who finally had to assist Loki into his true form, and Idhunn kept a handful of the falcon's tailfeathers as payment.

When Thjatsi did not return to Thrymheim by the next morning it was assumed that he never would. Then Skadi was forced to leave the castle that had been her father's. Trivoldi, captain of his lord's cavalry, took the command and the rule of Thrymheim upon himself, and no one protested. Skadi was a warrior-maiden and the rightful heir, but she lacked an army and the cultivated favor of soldiers to support her claim. Most other usurpers would have slain her, but Trivoldi permitted her the grace of taking her weapons and going.

Skadi was at a loss for what to do, for none among the giants looked with pity or mercy upon dispossessed rulers but rather with scorn and loathing for their weakness. Therefore she had no hope of gathering an army of her own to retake Thrymheim or even of finding a place where she could dwell in peace, as long as her true name was known. With nothing else left, her thoughts turned at last to exacting some payment from the Aesir. Not weregild for her father, but for her own satisfaction.

So it was that she came silently to the crystal bridge and stood there calling upon her father's murderers to face her in combat. The Aesir were by no means frightened of her, but they did not take her seriously. Then, by some talent of magic inherited from her father, she forced open the world-gate and beat upon the golden portals of Asgardh. This Odhinn could not allow, and at a loss to know what else to do he sent the Valkyries to place her under a forced sleep and take her prisoner.

In that way Skadi became a captive of the Aesir. She was kept first in Himinbjorg, the hall of Heimdall, and the Valkyries attended her. But after some time her mood softened, and she was removed to Frigg's Fensalir where she could spend her days in Idhunn's garden that was enclosed within its walls. Idhunn soon found that Skadi had her father's powers of shape-changing and the tending of living things, and she was helped to develop the powers that her father had jealously refused for her to have.

And so it happened that Njordh of the Vanir saw her one

night as he was walking in the garden, for he had been away in his own world and had never seen her before. And he thought it exceptionally strange and wonderful that a young girl of the Jotnar could be so beautiful, for all that she was twelve feet tall. At last he resolved to talk to her, and joined her where she sat.

"Good evening, fair lady," he said as he came up to her. "I am Njordh of the Vanir. It is strange that I have not seen you before."

"Strange indeed," she replied. "For I am very hard to miss."

"So you are, for such beauty is very hard to hide," Njordh said. "It is good that you have come to dwell with us here in the Garden of Idhunn, for they tell me that you have the powers of a life-tender. Are you to remain with us?"

"It would seem that I must, for I have learned many things that were my father's death to know," she said cautiously, uncertain as to whether he was sincere or merely teasing her.

"But do you not like it here?"

"I suppose that I do," she admitted. "I am much less a prisoner here than I was in my father's fortress, and I do go often into the other worlds with Idhunn. Everything is so beautiful here, but so small. I do not fit into most parts of the palaces of Asgardh. That is why I remain here, in the garden."

"Perhaps you could come with me into my world at times," Njordh suggested. "I have a great citadel by the sea, and several great ships with open decks."

"Perhaps I could, if it is allowed."

They talked long into the night, and Njordh decided then that he would take no other companion but would find some way that he and Skadi could be together. But that seemed unlikely, for they could not even live together at ease in the same house. Skadi was slow to give her love, and reluctant to admit it when it came. Njordh came to visit her often in the garden, and for the next few months he spent more time in Asgardh than he had in the entire preceding century. But at last he had the answer, and with Idhunn's help Skadi changed her shape so that she remained the same in appearance but of a suitable size.

And so everyone was pleased in the end. Njordh had Skadi, and Loki had Sygyn. Odhinn had a better understanding of his enemies, and a major threat had also been removed. And Idhunn had all the revenge she required. But even then the tale was not complete, for years later the union of Njordh and Skadi brought forth the twins Freyr and Freyja. And they proved later to possess very great powers indeed. Freyr was afterward among the highest of the lords of Asgardh, while Freyja inherited both her father's wisdom and powers and her mother's great beauty. She was held to be the most beautiful of all the Asynjur and was called the Vanadis, Queen of the Vanir.

CHAPTER FOUR

Of the Binding of the Wolf Fenrir

The guardians of Valhalla were the wolves Geri and Freki, spirits of power who had assumed animal form. The Aesir esteemed wolves, and did not hold them in low regard because they had to hunt and kill for their food. Rather did they consider the wolf to be the most versatile of hunters, at home in many terrains and working as well alone as in packs. But these were special wolves indeed, larger than a dwarf's pony with thick gray coats, and like the horses of the Valkyries they possessed the power of flight. But they seldom ventured beyond the walls of Asgardh except on special errands for their lord, and when the Aesir sat in council the wolves stood attentively at either side of Odhinn's chair.

There came a time that the wolves had between them a cub, and the only one that Freki ever bore. Now Idhunn did not know what to expect, for she had made the physical forms for the pair from her own design, not modeling them directly upon any existing wolf. She had not considered them a viable species, and even after Freki's pregnancy was discovered she was still not sure of that. There was no denying that a spirit of power inhabited the unborn body, but it remained to be seen if the cub would survive.

Freki carried the pup for eleven months, and so no one was surprised when it was born as fully developed as any normal wolf cub of two or three months. His eyes were open from the start, and he had a respectable set of teeth; and he was nearly as big as an adult wolf of Midhgardh. But he was very playful and mischievous, well-liked by everyone but especially so by Tyr. Fenrir he was named, greatest of all the wolves of the nine realms, although Tyr most often called him simply the Gravargur.

The wolf cub grew quickly, and soon left Valhalla to stay with Tyr. For whatever reason, Tyr and the wolf got along very well together, and that was a very unusual thing. Not so much perhaps for the wolf but for Tyr, who generally preferred no company but his own. So it became obvious that Thor would be without his usual companion for some time yet, although Odhinn did not begrudge it. But it is possible that Thor did, for he had shunned the wolf since the day of his birth, sensing something that he found disquieting, and he did not like it that Tyr or anyone would adopt Fenrir. That seemed stranger still, for everyone knew that Thor was very kindly beneath his rugged and remote exterior.

But soon enough Idhunn's fears proved true, for there was indeed something strange about the wolf. At the end of his first year Fenrir was already larger than either of his parents, and as big as most horses. And yet Idhunn saw that he was still young, and only a fraction of the size that he would eventually attain. Already Fenrir was pleased with his size, and with the strength he possessed which was far beyond his size. For it seemed that he had the same powers as the great horse Svadilfari, both supernatural strength and the gift of flight. Often he and Tyr would go out into the wilds to hunt, and after a swift kill Fenrir would proclaim in his pleasure that when he was fully grown then no prey in the nine worlds would be able to escape him. At this Tyr would smile, for he loved the wolf as a child.

But the others were not so pleased with that thought, for it seemed to them that the wolf grew larger with each passing day. In his tenth year Fenrir finally achieved his full growth, and he was vast beyond all comparison. Twenty feet in height he stood at the shoulder, and nearly sixty feet in length excluding an extra twenty feet of tail. Then everyone feared him and would not approach him alone, except for Idhunn and Tyr, who was more proud and pleased than even the wolf. Fenrir was at first troubled that those who had once been so fond of him now feared and avoided him. Then he thought how very great and powerful he must be indeed, if even the mighty Aesir were afraid of him.

The months passed and Fenrir's strength and skill increased steadily, but still Tyr did not worry. The wolf was his friend, dearer to him than anyone or anything, and he could find no fault in Fenrir. Rather he thought that the fault lay in the Aesir themselves, that they harbored foolish fears and were faithless to lay aside their trust. At last he resolved to never again go to Asgardh except upon the most pressing business, and spend all the rest of the time with Fenrir in the wilderness doing whatever they liked.

There came a time that Tyr had business in Nidhavellir, the realm of the Dvergar. At that time Durinn was still king of the northern mountains, although very old. In his earlier years, centuries before he had completed the unification of the cities of the dwarves in the north begun by his father Modsognir the Great. And in only the last few years had his new city and palace of Gyllirhall beneath the towering peak of Hvitfrakki been declared complete, although expansion was likely to continue for as long as dwarves lived there.

Tyr warned as they approached that Gyllirhall had only one vast gate, and a most unusual guardian sat there, for a dragon was King Durinn's gatekeeper; not a sly fire- or icedrake of caves and tombs, but a true lord of the dragon breed, Hrosdhrull by name. Thus Durinn was the one dwarf-king who enjoyed having a dragon at his gate, for with the greatest of menaces guarding him none of the lesser menaces were likely to win past. And it was an excellent arrangement, for the dragon asked only for his meals.

"But do not let the dragon provoke you," Tyr said. "Only the Dvergar of Durinn's kingdom may pass unchallenged, and any of the Aesir who will endure a minute or two of his threats and insults. We have leave to pass freely, but the dragon is stubborn and proud and still does not like us, even if he has turned from evil."

"Why do you endure it?" Fenrir asked, amazed and an-

gered at the thought of Tyr's having to remain silent through
the dragon's verbal abuse.

"Because this is Durinn's hall, and we do not begrudge
him the right to have such a formidable guardian," Tyr
replied. "And somewhat for the dragon's sake, for he is
valiant and has devoted himself to the destruction of evil
creatures, even his own kind, who prey upon innocent folk."

Fenrir was not able to enter the underground citadel, for he
was too big for many of the narrow halls. He sat down
beneath a tree where Tyr had left his horse, and watched with
growing impatience as Tyr neared the gate. Hrosdhrull did
indeed unleash his expected assault, pouring forth such abuse
as if he brought forth every word with a breath of flame. But
Tyr walked calmly toward the gate and seemed to take no
notice, and the dragon made no move to stop him.

After his anger abated, Fenrir laid down beneath the tree to
watch the coming and going of the short, bearded dwarves.
Indeed on the whole they were not as small as he had
expected, although they were shorter and stockier than either
men or elves. But they had also heavy, powerful builds, so
that they weighed as much as mortal men. But of course even
Jotnar seemed small to him. After a time he noticed that the
dragon was seated on the road not fifty yards away, staring at
him.

"Do not stare, unless you mean a compliment by it," he
said.

"Please forgive me," the dragon answered contritely. "I
have never seen a dog as big as yourself. Surely you have
outgrown your master's lap."

Fenrir rose and tried to look menacing, for all that the
dragon was twice his size. He had never been insulted in his
life, and he lacked the strength of will to ignore it. "Hold
your fiery tongue, lizard! I am Fenrir, Lord of the Wolves.
My strength is many times greater than yours, and I can fly
faster and longer even if I have no wings. I will not take such
abuse from you, so beware."

"Lord of Wolves?" the dragon asked scornfully. "Lord of
dogs, more likely, but still a beggar at his master's hand. But
then two misfits like yourselves belong together, a fool and
his slave."

If Hrosdhrull meant no actual threat with his words, then

he had chosen the wrong one for playing this game. All conscious thoughts seemed to flee from Fenrir's mind, leaving his instinct unrestrained, and his anger turned to a killer's rage in an instant. Without warning he drew back and sprang. The dragon tried to bring his flames to bear, but he was startled and unprepared. Fenrir's powerfull jaws closed about the dragon's long, supple neck, and an instant later Hrosdhrull lay dead of a crushed spine. Standing atop his prey, the wolf raised his head and howled.

Tyr heard that howl even deep within the halls of the dwarvish citadel, followed moments later by the echoing peal of the alarm bells. Immediately he knew what had happened, and without hesitation he turned and hurried back to the gate. There he found Fenrir still standing over his prey, as if guarding his prize from the advances of a score of dwarvish warriors. Tyr called the Dvergar back, for not even Durinn's entire army could have defeated the wolf. Then he approached Fenrir cautiously.

"That was an ill deed," he said. "Greater ones than you have forgiven this dragon for his foul but harmless words."

"He did challenge, and I accepted," Fenrir insisted. "I have endured hate and scorn most of my life, and for no reason that I could see. I will not accept it now from some foul worm."

"No, do not speak," Tyr said. "I understand well enough. There is that in you which must rise to a challenge. I hold myself to blame for this, for I brought you here knowing what might happen."

Tyr mounted his horse and led them quickly from that place, back into the forests of Asgardh. He was fearful that the Dvergar might have come in force, and that Fenrir would attack again. He regretted having to leave without explanation, but he had to get Fenrir away quickly. But early the next morning he went to discuss the incident with Odhinn. The proper apologies would have to be made and perhaps also some payment, even a weregild to King Durinn for the dragon's life.

Fenrir was again left outside to wait, and he took to wandering about the citadel of Asgardh. After a time he came near the hall where the flying horses of the Aesir were lodged, attended by elves. Many of the horses were standing about outside, talking and laughing in their curious manner. For it happened that Tyr's own horse was among them, and had only just finished telling of the killing of the dragon. Svadilfari himself was among them, and seeing Fenrir he trotted quickly over to the wolf.

"So, the great dragonslayer himself!" the horse snorted indignantly. "So you think yourself the greatest flyer, and by far the strongest in the nine realms?"

"You know yourself that I can outfly any horse in Asgardh, as I proved in my younger years," Fenrir replied. "And I will match my strength against yours any day."

"Dog of Tyr, no one is stronger than I!" Svadilfari proclaimed, rising and kicking out with the heavy hooves of his forelegs. To a horse that was only a challenge, but Fenrir saw only a threat as those sharp hooves came within inches of his face. He struck out with a single paw, but the blow was enough to send the giant horse tumbling.

Svadilfari was shaking his head as he pulled himself up, and he knew full well who the master was. Then he saw that the wolf was already charging him, and he had only an instant to turn and leap into the air. But the chase was a short one, for Fenrir was also the faster. He took the horse in the air directly above the citadel of Asgardh and killed him in an instant, and let the body fall. It tumbled broken into the great marble plaza before Valhalla.

The Aesir were angered by this deed and began to call for Fenrir's death. But none of them, not even Thor, were willing to face the wolf in combat. Heimdall would have led the Valkyries into combat at his lord's command, but Odhinn restrained him. He knew that they could not fight the wolf without serious loss, nor was he even certain that they could defeat Fenrir. Instead he had Tyr take the wolf away from the citadel, and then returned to his hall to contemplate what he could do to insure that the wolf would never again kill unjustly.

Then next day Odhinn called a council of the Aesir in Valhalla. Tyr was there, although very much against his will, for Fenrir was banished from Asgardh until the hearing was over. Geri and Freki were also present, not as guardians of the hall but as members of the council. Their testimony, along with Tyr's would decide Fenrir's fate.

Tyr knew that he must do all he could to preserve Fenrir's life and freedom. He knew his friend well, and in both acts Fenrir had indeed been provoked. But he knew also that something was very wrong, that somewhere deep within the wolf's being was a terrible evil, a mindless, murderous rage that Fenrir could not control. Indeed it now seemed to be hidden just beneath the surface, and that Fenrir indulged it as payment for all past indignations.

"My friends, we have a problem and I simply do not know what to do about it," Odhinn began. "Fenrir has killed twice in two days, and he is as likely to kill again if he is crossed. Now if Fenrir had attacked in defense of his honor, and his pride is beyond doubt most precious to him, then I would forgive him. But it seems to me that Fenrir is subject to uncontrollable, unpredictable rages. Convince me that Fenrir can be made harmless and trustworthy, for otherwise I must do what I can to restrain him."

"Then allow me to speak on his behalf," Tyr said immediately, rising. "He is not to blame for what has happened. I am. I brought him up as best I could, but there are certain aspects of his character that I have overlooked, and that was my failing. I have taught him no control to overrule his instinct to kill when his inner desire urges him to do so. Somehow, I fear, killing has become his answer to all problems.

"But I also hold the Aesir partly to blame. Fenrir is very proud of his great size and strength, and it is all that he has to be proud of. And yet it is because of his size that you fear and distrust him, and a long time ago you made him unwelcome. He has never understood why, and he was hurt deeply and bitterly. Now his bitterness is such that he can no longer bear the hate and rejection of others. And you have done this to him."

"I agree completely," Idhunn said. "But whatever the cause, Fenrir is now insane. Nor is it a thing of the mind of the wolf, but of the spirit of power that is the true Fenrir."

"No!" Tyr exclaimed. "I can teach him to control himself. Give me time. Let me take him to my lodge in the wilds of Asgardh, and there we will remain until he learns how to better handle his fears and frustrations. It can be done, even if it takes a hundred years."

"No, Tyr, it is not that simple," Idhunn insisted. "I

perceive that the only remaining control over Fenrir's murderous rage is his love and respect for you. But you have seen
yourself that he is paranoid. What if he should come to
suspect you? I cannot foretell the direction that his growing
madness will take, but I do know that if he remains free then
it will eventually end with his own destruction.''

"Then you say that Fenrir must be restrained?" Odhinn
asked.

Idhunn nodded reluctantly. "I do, for both his own protection and for the safety of others.''

"But you cannot!" Tyr responded hotly. "If you do that,
then there will be no saving him. Caging him will destroy
what sanity he has left.''

"And I fear that you are right," Odhinn agreed. "But the
only choices I see, in light of your own assertion that Fenrir is
insane, is to retrain him if we can, or destroy him. He is safer
dead than in a cage, and that would be kinder also if there is
no hope for his recovery. What would you have me do?''

Tyr turned away and did not answer. He remembered those
long, gentle years of Fenrir's youth, running through the
grass of the windswept plains of Asgardh and riding the
winds of starry nights. Those were the delights of Fenrir, the
times when he was happy and free. Taking that away would
indeed be death to him. And yet perhaps there was some hope
that it could be that way again.

"Cage him, then," he replied weakly. "But afterward give
me leave to try to undo the damage that it will cause.''

"And what do you say?" Odhinn asked of the wolves.
"Have you any insight or special understanding of Fenrir?"

Freki looked about nervously before answering. "Indeed it
is so. We dwell in the forms of wolves and we have only the
minds of wolves to serve us. They are less complex and
function in only the simplest terms, wanting this or fearing
that, without sophistication. We rely upon our metaphysical
consciousness to make up for the lack. Fenrir's judgment is
impaired on both levels. He is beyond hope.''

"What then would you have me do?''

"He has no life, and yet I would not have you take away
what remains. He is mine. . . .'' Freki could not continue,
but closing her eyes she began to weep uncontrollably. And

the Aesir were amazed and deeply moved, for the tears of a wolf were a strange thing to behold.

"So be it," Odhinn declared. "Fenrir will be bound by a leash and removed to some remote place where he can be at peace. He will be well tended, and we will do all we can for him. But he will not be released until I am assured that his recovery is complete."

"That is all very well," Thor remarked. "But aside from the problem of finding a leash to hold him, how do you propose to get it on the wolf?"

"We will convince him to wear it, if we can," Odhinn answered. "And that will take a subtle tongue indeed."

Loki glanced up apprehensively, and looked about the assembly to see who that might be.

Fenrir was told that the council had found him innocent of any wrongdoing. Tyr would not lie to him, so Odhinn himself went to deliver the news. Even then Loki was considering ways that he might get the wolf on a leash, and it seemed to him that there was only one way. And so the preparations were made and two massive chains were brought to serve as leashes.

A few days later it was announced that there was to be a special celebration in Asgardh. All of the Aesir and the Vanir were to be there, and all the spirits of power allied to them. And a special invitation was delivered to Fenrir, for Odhinn had declared him the guest of honor as a token of their desire to be forgiven for having doubted and mistrusted him. The invitation held such glowing praise that the wolf was flattered and happily replied that he would not miss it.

At the celebration Fenrir basked in honor and praise, and sat at the head of the table even before Odhinn. It was a dangerous game indeed, for if something had roused the wolf's rage then it would have blazed forth in unequaled fury. But all went well, and Fenrir was pleased and contented. Afterward he wandered about the gathering for some time, and soon fell into conversation with Thor and Loki. The Thunderer related many of his adventures in Jotunheim in fiery detail, and it was the type of story that appealed to Fenrir.

"Say, why don't you and Tyr and I take up serious giant-hunting," Thor said suddenly. "You know, Tyr and I used to travel together quite a lot, but the three of us would be invincible. I would bet that we could defeat all of Utgardh-Loki's army in one busy morning."

"That is not a bad idea," Loki agreed quickly. "You could certainly make Utgardh-Loki regret it. Why, within a year he would be willing to give half his kingdom to have you on a leash."

"No leash can hold me," Fenrir said confidently.

"I would like to see that, though," Loki said wistfully.

"Would you?" Thor asked. "I have some chains. They were made for Njordh's ships, but turned out to be too big and heavy. I kept them with the thought in mind that I might one day need to tether a dragon."

"Oh? Could we do that?"

"Certainly. We can go over to my place now and give it a try."

Loki turned to Fenrir. "You don't mind, do you?"

"Well . . . no," the wolf replied, somewhat confused.

Thor led them to the green lawn between the north and east wings of his palace Bilskirnir and had them wait while he disappeared inside. Fenrir was completely mystified and very uneasy about this, although he could not say why. He would have been suspicious, but he reminded himself that he was not used to strangers involving him in their games. Thor returned soon, dragging a long chain of tremendous thickness. Each link was an oval section eight inches long, an apparently seamless band an inch and a half in thickness. He attached one end to a heavy post that was set in the ground, while the other was attached to a special collar. By the time that the wolf was securely leashed, a considerable crowd had gathered.

"This chain is called Laeding," Thor said. "It was made by the Dvergar in the greatest of their foundries, and it contains a ton and a half of hard steel. It can hold the largest of Njordh's ships even in a gale, but can it hold you?"

"I think not," Fenrir replied, and leaned back with all his weight against the chain. He braced his powerful legs, and when he pushed the chain snapped after only a moment's hesitation. Everyone stared in amazement except Thor and Loki, who had already known that this chain would not hold. Then, remembering their directions, everyone began to mutter in amazement and appreciation, and many shouted words of praise and encouragement to Fenrir.

"Now that was a deed even the Aesir could appreciate," Loki said. "We just never before understood how great and powerful you really are."

"But I do not understand it," Fenrir said in a low voice. "I knew that I could break that chain easily."

"But they did not know it," Loki explained, and paused a moment in contemplation. "Why do we not bring out the larger chain? It would be a real test of your strength, and the Aesir would be so amazed that they would talk of nothing else for a hundred years."

Now the wolf was hesitant, for while he was proud he was not foolish. He knew that there were limits to even his great strength, and that he would be humiliated if he could not break the leash. But he also liked the admiration that he was receiving, and he saw it as a chance to earn a great and noble reputation. It occurred to him that he must expose himself to the danger of humiliation if he desired fame.

Therefore he agreed to the second test. Thor brought forth another chain, many times stronger and heavier than the first. Indeed it was so heavy that even Thor could not drag it, but called upon the aid of five horses of the Aesir. Each link was half a yard in length and five inches thick. Fenrir bent his neck to the ground so that the collar could be fastened.

"This is Dromi, eight tons of metal," Thor said. "It was to be used by Njordh to lift his ships from the water for repair, but he found another way that is less likely to damage the vessels. Do your best."

Fenrir braced himself as before, and this time leaned against the chain and pushed with all his strength. For nearly a minute he strained against the leash, until it seemed that this one would hold. Then it too snapped with a sound like a breaking harpstring. This time the Aesir were amazed beyond belief, and it was some time before they recovered their composure. Even Loki was shocked as speechless as Hoenir.

But he had also anticipated this. He had known that Dromi could not have held Fenrir for very long, if at all, but hopefully long enough that they might subdue Fenrir and get the final leash about his neck. The wolf was afterward very pleased, for the astonishment of the Aesir could not have been greater and he had surprised even himself. Loki saw that he must move quickly, and he sent Thor to fetch the final leash. This one proved to be only a slender chain of small lengths that even Loki could have broken, the only unusual thing about it being that it appeared to be made of solid silver.

"Now that you have proven your great strength beyond any doubt, there is one thing that you might do to help us," Loki said. "Heimdall has made a chain into which is woven his most powerful spells, so that, as light as it seems, it has the power to resist any effort to break it. We have thought that, if it can resist even your great strength, then it must be very strong indeed."

But this time the wolf was not so quick to agree. He looked at the chain a moment before he glanced up and said, "You believe that I cannot break this chain, so therefore I would not willingly have it placed upon me. Whether I snap this slender length or not, either way it seems that I will get no glory of it. Moreover, if the leash does not break, then I wonder how long it might be before I receive any help from you."

Before Loki could answer, Odhinn stepped forward to stand before him. "You are wise and cautious. But even if we were trying to trap you, then you still have nothing to fear. You will either free yourself, or we will see that there is a limit to your strength and you will no longer frighten us, and we will release you."

Fenrir smiled. "Wisely said, but that is still not absolute proof against treachery. If I should trust you enough to risk imprisonment on your word, then let one of you trust me enough to lay his hand in my mouth as a pledge of good faith."

Each of the Aesir looked to his neighbor, but none were willing to make such a sacrifice. So it seemed that Fenrir was wiser still than them all, and would force them to reveal their treachery. Odhinn was beginning to wonder how he might get out of this when Tyr stepped forward from the crowd.

"I will offer my hand as a pledge," he said.

Then Fenrir was confused, and he wondered if the Aesir did indeed mean him no harm. It was impossible for him to conceive of Tyr misleading him so. "Very well, then."

"Are you sure that you would have it this way?" Odhinn asked Tyr quietly.

"Fenrir trusts me. I do owe him something," Tyr replied.

So it was agreed. Loki placed the collar upon Fenrir's neck, leaving the lock open. Then Tyr placed his hand in the wolf's mouth, and Loki closed the lock.

"This is Gleipnir, the magic chain," he said. "Break it if you can."

Fenrir put his full strength against the leash, and the chain snapped taunt. But it did not break, as any ordinary chain would have broken in that first instant. The wolf pushed even harder, exerting all his might. The post at the end of the chain shifted slightly; it was in fact a metal rod two feet wide and sunk fifty feet into dirt and rock, and was likely starting to bend. A minute passed, then two and three, but the chain held. There was not a sound except for the panting of the wolf and the occasional shifting of the post as it bent even more. In a final effort Fenrir gave the chain several hard jerks, but he gave up at last.

"The strength of the chain is beyond my own," he said from one side of his mouth, not yet releasing Tyr's hand. "Now set me free."

But Odhinn took the key from Loki's hand and stepped forward. "This key I will keep against the day when you might be released. You have proven yourself possessed of a murderous rage, and you will wear that leash until you are cured of it."

Then Loki caused a great ball of flame to explode just before Fenrir's nose, hoping to startle the wolf into releasing his hostage. Startled he was, but that passed immediately into a tremendous rage that was terrible to behold. The wolf thrashed about and fought even harder to free himself, so that the Aesir were forced to flee before the hail of dirt and grass he kicked up. But at last Fenrir fell and lay panting in exhaustion, and Odhinn came forward and was able to place a deep sleep upon him. Thus the wolf was bound at last. But the Aesir were not glad, for Tyr had lost his hand.

While Fenrir still slept they carried him through the world-gate into Midhgardh. They took him into the far north to a lake called Amsvardhnir, and upon the island Lyngvi in its center they leashed the wolf to a new post that was five feet across and sunk two hundred feet into solid rock. A cave was carved out in the rock and made into a den for him, and the

Valkyries afterward guarded him and brought him food and drink. And Idhunn came when she could, doing all she was able to help him recover.

Some time later Tyr came to the island of Fenrir's captivity. He approached cautiously, and found the wolf lying at ease in the sun before the door of his den. Fenrir saw him and rose, the long chain at his neck not even scratched by his exertions. The wolf waited where he was, but Tyr did not hesitate to pass within the radius of the leash.

"Hello, my friend," Tyr called. "I have come to see that you are being treated as well as can be."

Fenrir dipped his head in acknowledgement. "Hello, Tyr. Do not worry for me. I only hope that you can forgive me for what I did to you. I never intended to harm you."

Tyr looked at his mangled arm. "You are sorry? It was the payment I promised for my part in putting you here. I was worried that you would never be able to forgive me."

Fenrir shook his head. "The Aesir were right, and in my saner moments I see that now. I would never willingly harm you, but when that madness took me I did you terrible harm. Even I no longer trust myself, for I sit here and think that on the day when I do break free, then Odhinn will die for what he has done to me. Less often do I think how wrong that is, and I fear that as the years pass I will remember the good thoughts less and less."

"Then you are not angry?"

"Angry?" the wolf asked. "That alien, evil part of me is seething in rage. But I know that it is for the best. Do not blame yourself, for it is easier for me to accept this because you helped to place the leash upon me. Otherwise I would have surely felt bitter rage that you stood by and allowed them to bind me. But it would have been better if they had destroyed me. Fenrir has been dying very slowly for some time now. Soon all that will be left will be a creature of evil hate."

"Perhaps that is true, but I lack the strength of will to do it," Tyr said, turning away. "Is there anything that I can do for you?"

"There is one thing only that you can do to comfort me, and that would be if you would come to see me no more,"

Fenrir answered. "The one you know will soon be gone, and I do not want you to see the evil thing that I will become. Just remember me fondly and with love."

Tyr could find no words, but nodded reluctantly. Fenrir smiled, then leaned forward and placed his great head gently on Tyr's shoulder. Tyr put his arms about the wolf's neck and held him close. Tears came to Fenrir's gray eyes, and as much as he tried to hide his sorrow he wept for a very long time.

"You will remain always in my fondest memories of you as you were when you were young and happy and free," Tyr promised quietly. "Farewell my friend, my greatest and most noble wolf."

CHAPTER FIVE

Of the Making
of Thor's Hammer

Often it is said in the tales of the Aesir that Loki was the most handsome, and the most vain, of all their company. Most of the others wore beards, even Odhinn himself, after the manner of the men of Midhgardh. Thor was most famous for his, and he was known to both his friends and his enemies as Redbeard. But Loki thought so highly of his face that he would not have any part of it hidden, and shaved away his beard.

One day, while Loki was speaking with Idhunn, he commented upon this habit, saying that he preferred to have no beard but disliked shaving. When Idhunn returned to her laboratory she experimented with many of her potions until she invented a special one to suit Loki's need. Then she gave him a bottle of the potion, explaining that it would cause the hair to fall out wherever it was applied and not grow back for many weeks.

It was most likely that all this talk about hair led Loki to think of Sif, the companion of Thor. In beauty she was held to be second only to Freyja, but her long, golden hair was a delight without equal. She received great praise for her hair from all the folk of Asgardh, and even the elves held her

golden mane to be superior in beauty to the glowing silver
hair of their princess Alfrodhull. And Loki was jealous of
such attention. Consciously he wished her no harm, but his
inner thoughts conceived a fitting revenge. To him it seemed
only a wonderfully mischievous prank, and without lasting
harm.

Therefore he stole quietly into Bilskirnir, the mansion of
Thor, and made his way silently to Sif's room. There he
found the table on which she kept her cosmetics, set up
before a large mirror. In a bottle he found the potion she used
to make her hair glow with a golden metallic sheen. He
quickly poured out the contents of the bottle and refilled it
with some of his hair-removing potion. Then he made a hasty
retreat, delighted with his scheme and excited with anticipation of seeing the results.

The next morning Sif rose early. She dressed quickly and
went to her mirror to brush out her beautiful hair. There was
little she had to do, for she wore it loose and it took a shape
of its own with little encouragement. Then she took the bottle
holding the special potion and sprayed it into her hair until it
shown like purest gold. She had only just finished when she
saw to her amazement that the fur trim of her collar was
tearing loose in large clumps. She blamed it on improper
treatment of the hide and quickly changed.

She went downstairs and found Thor seated at the table,
looking pleased and quite content as the elf-servants cleared
away the wreckage of a huge breakfast. Thor attacked meals
in much the same way he attacked giants, although he did not
eat the latter. He rose as she approached and bowed.

"Fair morning to you, my lovely lady," he said.

"Fair morning to you, my bristly bear," Sif answered.
"Did you leave anything?"

"You might find half a loaf in the pantry," Thor replied in
a doubtful voice. As she passed he reached up to give her hair
a jerk, and to his profound amazement a large handful came
loose in his fist. He stared at it in speechless horror for a
moment, then quickly hid it behind his back as Sif turned.

"You know, they told me yesterday . . ." she began, but
paused when she saw that he had something hidden behind
his back and wearing a most comical expression on his face.
She smiled. "You silly boy! What are you hiding?"

"You don't want to see!" Thor insisted, shaking his head vigorously.

"But I do!"

Thor saw no other course but to tell her, and held up the fistful of golden hair. Sif stared at it for a long moment, then screamed in unrestrained fury. That terrible cry echoed throughout Asgardh, and all who heard it leaped up in alarm. In Valhalla the wolves howled, and Heimdall took up his great horn and blew the deep note that signaled peril.

It was not long before a noisy, impatient crowd had gathered before Bilskirnir, but Thor would allow no one to enter save Odhinn. Even then Thor only asked him to follow and led the way upstairs, never once offering a word of explanation. They entered Sif's chamber and Thor hurriedly locked the door. When Odhinn turned around, he saw a sight that was rare indeed.

"Leaping lightningbolts! A bald-headed woman!" he exclaimed, then looked more closely. "Sif, is that really you?"

"Of course it is me!" she snapped.

"I . . . but . . . well now, what happened?"

"I know what happened!" she said, and began to pace in her fury. "I sprayed Idhunn's potion on my hair this morning, as I often do, and it made my hair fall out. It even made the fur fall out of my jacket. Honestly, that stuff could take the needles off a cactus!"

"I assume that it has never done that before?" Odhinn asked.

"No, never. In fact, I have already used half of that very bottle. Something might be wrong with it, but it seems more likely that someone has changed the potion."

"You are probably right," Odhinn agreed. "First I think that we should take this bottle to Idhunn and allow her to see what she can make of it."

They found Idunn alone in her garden, so intent upon her work that she had noticed nothing of the confusion reigning throughout the rest of Asgardh. She rose as they approached.

"Idhunn, do you know of some potion that will cause hair to fall out?" Odhinn asked.

"Odd that you should mention that," she said, mistaking his question as a request for the stuff. "I gave Loki a bottle of some just yesterday."

The answer was obvious, even to Thor. He made threatening wringing motions with his hands and muttered, "I will surely strangle him!"

Now if Loki had considered the consequences of his act, he would have already hidden himself in the darkest hole in the nine worlds. But he was so delighted with himself for what he considered to be a sly and cunning trick that he could not help but watch to see what came of his mischief, and when the deed was done he was among the first to come running to discover what had happened. And so it was that he was caught. Two huge hands suddenly closed upon his neck and lifted him from the ground. The grip was crushing, and he was shaken fiercely like a dirty rag. Then he knew that he had made a mistake.

"Well, if it is not the barber of Asgardh!" Thor's deep voice came from behind him.

"No! Help! Gag!" Loki gasped. "Spare me, my good friend. I certainly meant no harm. It was just a little trick. A game."

"Is that so? Well, now we will play a game with you," Thor said.

At that moment Loki saw Odhinn approaching from one side. He walked slowly, arms crossed, as he looked upon this scene with detached interest. "Odhinn! Oh most glorious Lord of the Aesir, do be so good as to make this beast release me."

"Release you?" Odhinn asked. "Why should I do that?"

"Because the sanctity of Asgardh should not be disturbed by senseless violence," Loki suggested.

"Why, you are right! Thor, kindly take Loki outside this realm if you are going to do senseless violence on him."

"Oh, alas for poor Loki!" he cried as loudly as he could. "Such great things he has done for the noble Aesir, but they forget that and hold him to task for his minor indiscretions."

"And what great things have you done?" Odhinn asked.

"I arranged to have a great wall built about our noble citadel, and it cost us nothing."

"It cost us considerable worry," Odhinn pointed out.

"I exposed and destroyed our greatest enemy."

"After you helped him kidnap Idhunn."

"I keep things in Asgardh from ever getting boring!"

"Yes, I will grant you that," Odhinn agreed. "Thor, put him down."

"Oh, just let me squeeze him a little," Thor begged, and squeezed until Loki's eyes bugged out and he began to turn blue.

"No, my good friend has reminded me of something," Odhinn said. "Every time Loki makes trouble, he has also been made to correct it in payment. Let him now make payment for this deed."

"Yes! Anything!" Loki was quick to promise.

"Then I bid you to go to the Dvergar and find a smith who can forge new hair for Sif out of gold, so that it will become real when placed upon her head and grow."

"But that is impossible. What if I just buy her a nice hat?" Loki suggested, and Thor squeezed again. "All right! I will see what I can do."

"Also, you will have them make some other fine gifts as a token of your repentance."

"Of course."

"And you will pay them fairly for their work."

Thor had to squeeze Loki's neck a very long time before he would agree to that. Then Odhinn said that he might go, although Thor was very reluctant to allow that. It seemed better to him to first break a few of the villain's bones, but Odhinn reminded him that he could either lay aside such vengeance or spend the next year with a bald wife. Loki hurried off as quickly as he could to find his horse.

"I still do not understand this," Thor said after Loki was gone. "No dwarf has the power to spin gold into living hair, and Loki knows that. Only Idhunn knows such tricks."

"And who do you think I was talking to while you ran off in search of Loki's neck?" Odhinn asked. "Idhunn and Heimdall are going to make a little trip into Nedhavellir."

"And what good will that do?"

"They have a saying in Midhgardh about people like Loki and the amazing things they can do if you give them enough rope," Odhinn explained, and smiled. "They also call me the Lord of the Gallows."

Just then Loki came riding by on his horse at a gallop,

pausing only a moment before Odhinn. "My lord, where can I find such clever dwarves as this deed requires?"

"Seek the sons of Ivaldi. That alone will I say," Odhinn answered.

For once Loki did not argue or beg for more, but turned his great charger toward the gate of Asgardh as fast as the children of Svadilfari could run.

Loki had no idea who these sons of Ivaldi might be or where he could find them, but he could be sure of getting information at Gyllirhall. Dvalinn was then king of the dwarf-realm, newly come to the throne following the death of Aldhjof, son of Durinn. Loki did not even have to enter the city, for he received the information he needed from the gatewarden. Hledloff he was by name, less mighty than the dragon Hrossdhrull but greater in the king's favor, and considerably less rude.

The way was not hard to find, for there were few roads in Nidhavellir and the cities of the dwarves were large but few. For a time he followed one of the main roads west before turning north into the most rugged and remote regions of the mountains of Nidhavellir, and after some time he came upon the hall of Ivaldi suddenly as his horse rounded a ridge and descended into a narrow valley. Steindalur it was by name, and the valley was indeed littered with great boulders and slabs of stone. But this was no humble burrow of some petty dwarf. A gate with double portals was inset within a smooth wall of rock, with a row of trees standing to either side. Now Loki was hopeful. Either the sons of Ivaldi owned one of the richest mines in Nidhavellir, or they produced goods that were very valuable indeed.

His horse descended to land before the gate. Loki dismounted and approached the closed portals cautiously. The doors were of some white stone, inlaid with gold with the designs of the hammer and the anvil of a master-smith and the insignia of the mansion. Curiously, the crest of Steindalur Hall was that of a fox holding aloft a sword, while an eagle descended from behind to take his unsuspecting prey.

"Go ahead and knock, Uncle Fox," his horse said impatiently.

"Do not call me that," Loki snapped, and used the door's bronze knocker to thump loudly.

"Yes, grandmother."

The door opened almost immediately, but no more than a crack. A dwarf peeped out, and a rather young one indeed. His beard was barely two inches long, and rather thin by dwarvish standards.

"I am Loki of the Flame," he began when the dwarf said nothing. "I seek the sons of Ivaldi."

The dwarf drew back the door without a word and indicated for him to enter. Loki was led to the main hall of the mansion and left alone while the dwarf went in search of his master. Loki used the moment to look about the hall, and his earlier estimate about the wealth of these Dvergar was confirmed. These sons of Ivaldi were as rich as any dwarf-lord of the greater mansions of the south and west, and they showed exceptionally good taste even for dwarves.

"May I help you?" A dwarf, richly dressed and still well in his prime, entered through the farther door. He stopped and bowed low. "Brokkr, son of Ivaldi, at your service. No, do not bow! I know well enough who you are."

"Then let me be brief and to the point," Loki began. "I need something very special made for me. It will take considerable talent, but I was directed to seek your services."

The dwarf bowed again. "You flatter me, kind sir. But what is this thing you need, and perhaps I can tell you if it can be made."

And so Loki spoke of his need to have hair spun of gold for Sif, made with spells of powerful magic so that it would merge and become her own. Brokkr nodded thoughtfully and assured him that it could be done. Surprised and delighted, Loki then spoke of two additional gifts for the Aesir, a magical weapon for Odhinn himself and some piece of jewelry of unsurpassed beauty for to grace the lady Freyja. Brokkr assured him that all could be ready by the following morning.

The deal was finalized according to the customs and practices of the Dvergar and a contract was signed, with the name of Odhinn invoked as witness. In truth that last part was never wisely done, for while Odhinn endorsed the honoring of contracts he was not obliged to protect any save his own.

Many people, especially men and dwarves, were dismayed when Odhinn did not support such oaths and contracts, and so he earned the undeserved name of Oathbreaker.

Brokkr personally showed Loki to the door, as was fitting for an honored guest, and stood beside the door as Loki's horse leaped into the air and was quickly gone. When he returned to the hall, he found his other guests waiting with his older brother Sindri.

"Excellently played, my friend," Heimdall exclaimed, and actually bowed to him in dwarvish manner. "Of all the heroes and warriors of the nine realms, you alone can claim to have made a fool of Uncle Sly. You are a skillful liar."

"Of course. I am a merchant," Brokkr replied, and they all laughed.

"Then it is settled," Idhunn said. "I will provide the golden hair, and Heimdall will make a magic spear. If we provide a wealth of precious gems and jewels, could you make a necklace of unsurpassed beauty in the time allowed?"

"Certainly," Brokkr replied. "But one thing does bother me. I would not take payment for all these things when I have done nothing more than string together jewels that you have sent me."

"You are honest indeed, but do not be concerned," Heimdall assured him. "Consider it payment for your part of our little joke. Loki must pay in full if he is to be properly humbled by this lesson."

Loki returned at the appointed time, and Brokkr took him down to the workshops of Steindalur to show him the agreed-upon goods. And Loki was amazed, for he had not believed that any dwarf could make such things of skill and quality that they might have come from the hands of the Aesir themselves. But he saw also that he would have to pay dearly for things of such quality. By the time that he had returned to the main hall with Brokkr, he had already conceived a plan. It seemed to him that the dwarves could never make anything of greater quality than he had already seen, and he had a way of insuring that.

"Those are very fine goods," Loki said. "I must admit that I had not thought it possible until I saw it. But with this you have surely outdone yourself. Certainly you could not make anything better than you have already shown me."

"I honestly do not know. It might well be that I could."

"Oh, but that I would like to see!"

The dwarf shrugged. "It would be a challenge. But I cannot devote the time and expense to such a project simply for my own entertainment, and I do not know if I should ever be commissioned to make such fine things again."

"Ah, then perhaps I could hire you!" Loki proclaimed, as though a wonderful idea had suddenly come to him. "Three more gifts you could make for me to present to the Aesir, by which you could win lasting fame and I might win their good graces. And we could have a competition to see which set of gifts are the best."

"Yes, I suppose I could."

"Then we will make this deal," Loki continued. "You will make three more gifts. If they are judged to be of surpassing quality, then I will pay twice what I owe you for all six. But if you fail, then I will pay you nothing."

That offer appealed to both the dwarf's pride and his purse, and yet he could not accept. He began to pace nervously. "My lord Loki, please forget this notion. We dwarves . . . I know that we have a reputation for greed, but we are not gamblers. We fear losing too much. You offer me something that I want very much but dare not take."

"Then you have no faith in your abilities?"

That brought the dwarf up short. Like all of his kind, he was very proud of his skills. While he had made only the necklace for Freyja, Loki had judged it to be the most fair of the three. "Of course not!"

"Then prove it. Accept the wager. I will even offer my head in payment should you win."

"I . . . ah," Brokkr paused, and seemed to collect himself. "I must discuss this with my brother."

"Of course," Loki said, but the dwarf was already halfway to the door. Loki sat back and smiled, thinking that he was leading this dwarf exactly where he wanted, and anticipating his quick return to the good graces of the Aesir and paying nothing in the bargain.

As always, he was placing too much trust in the certainty of his own plots while failing to consider the alternatives.

Brokkr left the room as casually as he could, knowing at the same time that he did not appear very subtle, and almost ran directly into Heimdall as he slipped quickly through the doorway. The Aesir motioned for him to be quiet, and they retreated down the hall and around a corner.

"You heard?" Brokkr asked.

"Do you jest? Has no one told you about my ears?" Heimdall asked. "Stars above, this is beautiful! Now I see what Odhinn meant about rope. You accept the proposition, and I will see that you win. But insist upon these terms. . . ."

When Brokkr returned to the main hall he was very much his old self, calm and quietly confident. "I accept the wager, but it must be according to these terms."

"Name them," Loki said.

"First, the judgment must be made by the council of the Aesir in Valhalla. Second, I must go myself to present the gifts for judgment. And no one, not even you, will be allowed to look upon the second set of gifts until then."

"Done!" Loki agreed, and drew up the contract.

Hemdall, Idhunn and Sindri were waiting when Brokkr returned from seeing Loki away. Heimdall was still delighted with this unexpected turn of events, and even Idhunn was amused. She remembered the times when Loki's plots had worked, and had failed to work, at her own expense.

"Now we will return to Asgardh and devote all our skills and powers to making three new gifts," Heimdall said, then paused for a long moment. The others looked at him questioningly.

"Heimdall, what is it?" Idhunn asked.

"That little thief! He has not left!" Heimdall exclaimed, then looked at the others. "He has turned himself into some type of insect and is flying back here to do some type of mischief."

"He is becoming a very accomplished shape-changer," Idhunn remarked. "You return home and start to work on those gifts. The brave sons of Ivaldi and I will stay here and distract Loki."

"Brave indeed!" Brokkr chuckled. "But more than willing to help. I have a score to settle with that double-dealer."

"Welcome to the group!" Heimdall called back as he departed.

"What must we do?" the dwarf asked.

"Go to your workshop and start to work on some project, as if it was one of the special gifts," Idhunn said. "Loki will no doubt seek you out, either to spy on you or distract you. I will be there to deal with him."

Within minutes the dwarves had retreated to their workshop. Sindri was of the pair the greatest smith, while Brokkr was far more adept at making small things of skill and cunning. Choosing a workroom that had a small forge for light but precise work, Sindri built up the fire to very precise specifications and set about fashioning a great war-hammer. After a few minutes Idhunn warned that Loki was almost there, and then she left. Brokkr and Sindri prepared themselves for their own parts.

A large blue horsefly buzzed noisily through the open door and lighted on the table. Both of the dwarves knew that it was there, of course, although they pretended not to notice but continued their work.

"Now, when I place the iron in the fire, you must blow vigorously on the bellows and continue until I return," Sindri instructed. "If you stop, even for a moment, then it will be ruined."

"I understand," Brokkr said. "I will not stop for anything."

"Very well, then. Start pumping the bellows," Sindri said, tying a roll of heavy parchment that appeared to hold his plans and laying it close at hand. When the coals were glowing with a fierce white heat he thrust a block of iron into it. "Now do not stop until I return."

And so he left, leaving his brother alone at the bellows. Brokkr worked hard at his task, pumping vigorously. Straight away the horsefly flew up and made its way purposefully toward the smith. Brokkr did not even look up from his task, and seemed not to notice. But just as the fly was about to light on the back of his hand and sting him, Brokkr snatched up the rolled parchment and gave it a swift, powerful swat that sent it hurtling into the corner to bounce off the wall.

Sindri returned at that moment and walked over to the forge to look at the block of metal. He frowned. "The metal is not heating evenly. Surely you did not stop?"

"Only for a moment," Brokkr admitted. "A large fly was about to sting me, so I swattted him."

"'I will see what I can do about that. Keep pumping the bellows," Sindri said and left.

A few moments later the fly returned, this time moving stealthily toward the back of the dwarf's neck. The only trouble was that the fly was unable to be very subtle, for it was large and its wings buzzed no matter how slowly it flew. Just as it was about to land on the dwarf's neck, Brokkr spun around and gave it a second swat that sent it sailing out the open door. Sindri returned only a moment later.

"The fly again?" he asked as he inspected the block of iron critically.

"He is most persistent."

"Then I will get something to deal with him for good," Sindri said as he turned to leave. "Keep blowing."

Soon the fly was back again, this time approaching straight across the forge from where the dwarf worked. It advanced openly and moved in on its prey with determination, but Brokkr pretended not to notice. Suddenly the fly darted in, directly for his eye. This time Brokkr was almost too late. Unable to raise his simple weapon in time, he struck the fly on the upswing. It shot up to bounce off the ceiling and came down inside the forge. Fortunately for Loki, he landed atop a coal in one corner where the fire was not so hot. The fly leaped three feet straight up and darted away, and it seemed to Brokkr that he could hear a squeaky little voice cursing furiously.

Sindri returned a moment later, bearing a large basket. "So that fly is still following you?"

"Worse than ever," Brokkr replied.

"Then we will let Stearkvaengir handle this," Sindri said as he set down the basket and opened the lid.

As soon as the basket was open a bird shot out. It was a swift, small and quick, whose special delight was large, slow insects it caught on the wing. Now the fly knew this and saw its peril, and it sought to escape. Three times the pair flew around the room before the fly found the door, and it shot off down the hall with the swift close behind. The dwarves were not bothered again.

*   *   *

Loki came early in the morning with several of the Valkyries, and they bore the dwarves and their goods swiftly to Asgardh. As agreed, the gifts were tightly wrapped in black blankets, and the sons of Ivaldi allowed no one to see them. The Aesir were to meet in council that morning in Valhalla, and the first order of business was the judgment of the gifts. As soon as they arrived, Brokkr and Idhunn went alone with Sif to prepare her golden hair.

First Sif entered, her new hair in place and trimmed and every bit as long and full as it had been. The only difference was that it was even more beautiful to behold, for now it was gold in truth, with a metallic sheen that was irridescent in the sunshine. And the Aesir judged that she was better for it, for while Freyja was fairer still, it was certain that no one in the nine realms had hair that was more beautiful and unique.

Then Brokkr brought forth a great spear and presented it to Odhinn. Gungir it was by name, and in all the worlds there was only one weapon that was more unusual and deadly. The point was of some strange gray metal, so made that it would never dull or break, while the shaft was of polished wood cut from a branch of the great world-tree. Thus it could serve to hold and channel Odhinn's great powers, and launch from its tip searing bolts of tremendous energy.

The last of that first group of gifts was the one thing that Brokkr had made himself, and it was a testimony to just how great his talent as a jeweler and metalworker really was. It was a necklace of outstanding cunning and beauty, with gems of many colors surrounding a single diamond of immense size. Brisingamene it was called, the necklace of the Brisings, that being the family name of the dwarf who made it. But it was also known as the dragon's bed, so great was the wealth of jewels and gold in it. It was Freyja's gift and that was only fitting, for such a thing of beauty truly belonged to the most beautiful of the Asynjur.

Thus the first of the gifts were shown, and the Aesir declared that the second set would have to be very unique to surpass the beauty and workmanship of the things they had already seen. Then Loki smiled and relaxed somewhat, for even though he had not been able to upset their work he still believed that the sons of Ivaldi could not have exceeded their previous work.

But Brokkr was not in the least worried as he brought forth the second set of gifts. The first was a plain-looking golden ring, heavy but completely unadorned. It was a gift to Odhinn; Draupnir he named it, and so proclaimed it to be the greatest of rings. For it had the talent that it duplicated itself nine times every ninth night.

The second gift was to Freyr, Freyja's twin brother, and at first the Aesir looked upon it in amazement. It was a most curious machine, and in form it looked somewhat like a large boar. The similarity was not accidental, for it had great rending tusks projecting forward from its snout, and its eyes shot forth beams of light. It was gold-plated but protected against even the hardest blows by the spells of protection, and there was great power in its four mechanical limbs so that it could outrun even the horses of the Aesir, and it was thereafter called Gullinbursti.

Last was the great hammer that the dwarves had pretended to work on, and it was a gift for Thor. With it went a pair of gloves and a wide belt made of hinged gold plates backed by leather. When Thor wore the belt he was given tremendous strength such as Svadilfari had possessed, and the belt also controlled the hammer through the gloves. Brokkr explained that Thor could strike as hard as he desired at any target without fear of breaking either haft or head, that he could throw the hammer however far he wished and never miss, and it would always return to his hand. Thor called the hammer Mjollnir, but he had so many pet names for it that only he could keep count of them all.

Then the council made its judgment, and there was little doubt of what their judgment would be. Although the greatest beauty was to be seen in the first three works, the greatest skill and cunning was evident in the second. Nor could it have turned out otherwise, for everyone but Loki was in on the scheme. Then Loki made the required payment, and in truth he begrudged the losing more then he begrudged the gold he had to pay. But Brokkr remembered that there was something else that Loki had promised, and now he demanded it.

Loki had not forgotten this either, and he was already trying to slip away even as the dwarf spoke. But then two powerful hands closed upon his neck, and he was lifted even as before. Thor carried him before the council and forced him to bend before the dwarf, his neck exposed.

"Take his head and be welcome," Thor said. "Loki will be a more likeable person without it."

Brokkr drew his short sword slowly, making a great show of it. Of course, this part had been well rehearsed beforehand, and was meant only to give Loki a good scare. And it was most successful at that.

"Now wait a minute!" Loki exclaimed when he saw the sword. "You know that I would not think to break our agreement, but I must remind you that our contract specified that you may have my head and nothing more. You have no claim upon my neck, nor can I allow you to touch it."

"I believe that the agreement was clear enough," Odhinn said. "You promised your head, and that in truth means only one thing."

"No, I will not argue the point," Brokkr said. "I do not want his head, nor anything else to remind me of how he tried to cheat me. There is only one thing that I desire, for my own satisfaction, if Thor will hold him a moment longer."

Then Brokkr took out an awl and a thong, afterward known as Vartari, and sewed shut Loki's mouth. That was considered a fitting punishment, and an excellent way to prevent him from causing any more trouble for himself or others. Of course, no one intended him any real harm, and they soon released him. They hoped that he would learn a lesson from this, but they also knew better than to expect it.

CHAPTER SIX

Of the Theft
of Thor's Hammer

It was a quiet, sunny day in Asgardh. Birds were singing in the trees, and the horses were chatting on the lawn by the fountain. It had been some time since anything had happened to disturb the peace of the Aesir; indeed there had been little trouble of any major type throughout the nine worlds for some time. And so it seemed strange when dark storm clouds descended upon the citadel of the Aesir on such a clear, calm morning, and stranger still that three separate storms should be moving in, each from a different direction.

Now Odhinn saw immediately that something was wrong, and he knew also who it involved. Only two among the Aesir possessed the power of calling forth storms, and he knew that he had not done it. He and Loki set off at once for Bilskirnir, the mansion of Thor. They walked up to the main door and Odhinn knocked tersely. It was some time before anyone answered, and when the door finally opened it was Sif who stood there. She glared at Loki when she saw him.

"You!" she hissed. "What did you do with it?"

"Now wait a minute! I did not do it, at least not this time. You always blame poor Loki!" he raged, sputtering in fury.

Then he stopped short. "By the way, what am I accused of doing?"

"Thor's hammer is gone. He is looking for it now, tearing apart the house faster than twenty elves can pick up after him."

They found Thor in the ruins of his search. He had already decided that Loki must have taken his hammer, and he thought that the quickest way to find it would be to squeeeze the little troublemaker until he confessed. Loki not only denied everything but actually got quite angry, and even Thor had to admit that this behavior was not typical—and therefore might be the truth.

"Why do you not just call it to you?" Odhinn suggested at last.

"That would be very dangerous," Thor replied. "If the hammer is within range, then it will go through wall, tree or even hill to reach me."

"I know that, but do so anyway," Odhinn said. "That hammer is our greatest defense against giants. If it has been taken, then we should learn of that quickly."

Thor put on his gloves and held forth his hands, but even after several minutes there was no response. Then they were sure that the hammer had been stolen, for it was not within Asgardh. The Aesir consulted for a time, and they decided that Loki should take the form of a bird and fly out in search of it, using a stone provided by Heimdall that glowed ever more brightly as it neared the hammer. Loki would not willingly agree to this, for it seemed to him that the Aesir still blamed him for its loss. But they asked him, and very nicely, if he would do this thing for them, and Loki was so flattered that he had to accept.

Loki took his falcon shape and, with the guiding stone hanging by a string about his neck, he flew out into Jotunheim, the most likely place to find the stolen hammer. There were at that time three great lords of the Jotnar who could have arranged the theft; Utgardh-Loki himself, Trivaldi of Thrymheim, Thjatsi's self-appointed successor, and Thrym of Klettastadhur. If Loki had to choose the one most capable of successfully arranging the theft, then it would have been Utgardh-Loki. Trivaldi was not subtle, and Thrym could only be described as stupid even for a giant. But the fact remained that only the hammer had been stolen when the gloves and belt of power had also been at hand, and the possessor of all three would have had Thor's own powers. That was the result of short-sighted stupidity. Loki flew straight to Klettastadhur.

Loki landed on a grassy hilltop some distance from the massive fortress and stood watching it for some time. As he watched, he eventually became aware of a faint rustling in the tall grass behind him. Turning, he saw a cream-colored ferret standing on its hind legs a few yards behind him. It was, of course, a landvaeta, a guardian spirit in animal form. He considered it no threat, even though the ferret, being a local variety of the animal, was almost as big as a wolf.

"Good day!" the ferret chittered. "You wish to speak with my lord, perhaps, you do?"

"Oh? Why would I want to do that?" Loki asked casually.

"He has what you seek, he does," the landvaeta replied. "Do come in."

"Now that would be impossible. If your lord wishes to speak with me, then he must come out."

"Oh, I see," the ferret agreed. "Do wait."

The animal raced off across the grassy slopes, disappearing inside the open gate while a pair of guards who stood to either side did not even seem to notice. Loki was not sure what to make of it, although he did wait. He could not believe that the giant was willing to make a deal for the return of the hammer but he knew also that the Aesir probably would not recover it otherwise, not without a battle. He thought it best to hear what Thrym had to say.

Only a few minutes passed before Thrym himself appeared at the gate, flanked by six armed guards. He was hardly the handsome, sophisticated figure of Thjatsi, but plain and un-kept and rather stocky even though he stood sixteen feet high—ugly, in a word. He was, like those he ruled, a rock-giant, related to the hill-giants like Thjatsi but with certain elements from their cousins the rock-trolls, particularly their great strength and their equally great stupidity. It came from having heads as hard as rocks.

"You've come for something," he said as he strode boldly to the top of the hill and stopped. "Of course, I'm not going to just hand it over. And don't expect that you'll find it if you come sneaking in."

"I hardly expected it," Loki replied. "But I did wonder if you had a price. They say that every Jotun has his price."

"Oh, Loki Quicktongue, they don't call you that for nothing!" The giant laughed. "And what do you think I want? Gold? Precious stones? Yes, bring me a jewel, the most beautiful one you've got. A fair bride to brighten my days."

"You want Idhunn?" Loki exclaimed. Did giants think of nothing else?

"Idhunn? Poo!" Thrym spat in contempt. "Idhunn is one of the old ones; too much to handle. That was Thjatsi's mistake. I want Freyja."

Loki was so stunned that he tried to sit down, forgetting that he was in falcon shape. Birds cannot sit down that way, and so he rolled over on his back with a startled squawk.

"Now you remember the deal," Thrym said. "I am not willing to bargain with you. Just send Freyja on alone when she's ready. There's no time limit, but I'll just hold onto that hammer until she comes. Only then will my burglar return it."

"Your burglar?" Loki asked.

"Take a bow, Sinir," Thrym said, and the ferret did.

Loki knew that his report would not be received favorably, and in that he was right. He thought it best that only the greatest of the Aesir should be present when he spoke in Bilskirnir. Odhinn was there, and Freyr and Freyja, as well as Idhunn and Heimdall. Sigrune and Brynhild came also as captains of the Valkyries. He made his report quickly, fearing what would come at the end, hurriedly relating the giant's terms for the ransom. Then it was as he had expected. Thor positioned his hands as if holding the stolen hammer while distant thunder began to rumble. Freyr also reached for his weapon, outraged for his sister's sake, while Freyja herself panted in such fury that her wonderful necklace was shattered.

"I will blast them all! I will roast them slowly and feed them to dragons. I will . . ." Freyja's curses faded away when she could think of nothing worse.

"And I will help you," Thor said grimly.

"You will do nothing of the sort without my approval," Odhinn said firmly. "Our first and only task now is to recover the hammer. Heimdall, can the hammer be duplicated?"

"Only too easily," Heimdall replied. "I have no doubt that there are master-smiths of Jotunheim capable of eventually understanding the spells of power within the thing. Then they can build such weapons in large numbers and prove to be a serious threat to us."

"Then we must get the hammer back," Odhinn concluded.

"And that will not be easy," Loki insisted. "Thrym has the place locked up as tight as a dwarf's vault. Nor is he as stupid as we might have thought. He thinks in a simple manner, but he does find simple answers. What he wants, as those before him, is one of the Asynjur to enhance his own powers. If Freyja did go to him, I believe, then he would hold both her and the hammer as ransom against our interference."

"If Thor could get inside Klettastadhur and get his hands on the hammer, then the problem would be solved," Heimdall commented.

"And if rock was water, then Thor could swim inside," Loki snapped. "For otherwise he will not easily get inside."

"No, he would not," Heimdall agreed. "But Freyja could. Indeed, she is expected. A carefully guided shape-changing might help."

The bride who made ready to depart for the wedding was indeed a reluctant one. Thor had fought giants and dragons quite regularly and even enjoyed it, but the prospect of shape-changing into Freyja's form filled him with such terror as he had never before known. Earlier he had been so desperate to find his lost hammer that he would have willingly agreed to anything. But he had thought about it much since, and he had decided not to be gracious about it.

Loki found himself elected to go along in the guise of an attendant, and he submitted to the shape-changing first to prove that it was not morally fatal. He emerged as Fulla, who was in truth a student and companion of Frigg. But the Jotnar did not know that, and Fulla seemed to be a better choice for Loki's assumed role because of her own great beauty, an important point in distracting lusty giants. Still the completeness of the transformation was no reassurance to Thor; it seemed to frighten him more to see that it could be done.

Idhunn finally had to force him into her workroom, and she

made the transformation as quickly as she could. At least Thor was not to be weaponless. His belt of strength was hidden within a jeweled sheath made of gold cloth and his magic gloves were trimmed with white silk. There was no hope of trying to hide the fact that the gloves were heavy leather with metal plates. Instead the bridal dress was to be like in fashion to the special armor that the Valkyries wore at ceremony.

And so it was that a very small group set off for Jotunheim the next morning. Thor went forth in the likeness of Freyja, dressed, in the manner of the Asynjur when they went abroad, in pants and tunic and low, soft boots. Loki rode behind in the likeness of Fulla, while Brynhild of the Valkyries went ahead. She alone pretended to be no one but herself, a special guardian to insure her lady's safety in the wilds, although she also wore the white tunic, pants and cape of her companions rather than her usual armor. She still bore her mighty sword and rode her horse Glaerfaxi, as they all rode the wind-borne descendants of Svadilfari. But for appearances sake they stayed on the ground, and that made it a journey of several days. Thor passed the time muttering curses, contemplating a well-earned revenge for his indignities.

The three slowed when they crossed the top of the last hill and descended toward massive Klettastadhur. It was obvious that they had been expected, for it seemed that most of the population of the fortress had turned out to greet them. Perhaps it was an honor guard, for the soldiers were standing in line beside the road with as much honor and precision as rock-giants could ever achieve, which was to say that they were all standing. Brynhild made a face when she smelled them even two hundred yards downwind.

"My, what a big family you are marrying into!" Loki exclaimed quietly.

"Shut up, Fox, or I'll wring your neck!" Thor threatened in a low voice, never once breaking his well-rehearsed smile.

"Which one is the bashful groom?" Brynhild asked.

"The tall one with the lusty grin," Loki replied.

"Do you mean the stocky one standing beside the large weasel?"

"Yes, but that is Sinir, the ferret," Loki explained. "He is the burglar, and I wonder if it was also his idea to take the hammer in the first place. He has more intelligence than any score of rock-giants.''

"I will wring his neck, too!" Thor said, still smiling.

Moments later the travelers drew their horses to a stop before the crowd at the gate of Klettastadhur. A great cry of greeting went up from the group, like the delighted squeal of an equal number of pigs at a long-awaited meal. Catfaced trolls scurried out to attend the horses, but Thrym only stood and gazed covetously at his three guests with such a lecherous grin that even Loki was momentarily speechless. At last he bowed to the Valkyrie who stood nearest to him.

"My lovely Freyja . . .'' he began courteously enough.

"Hey, stupid. That's Brynhild of the Valkyries," Loki interrupted. That was, of course, the proper way to speak as friends among rock-giants.

"Excuse me," Thrym said, and turned to the next. "My lovely Freyja. . . .''

"Dunceling! I'm Fulla.''

"My mistake. My lovely Freyja . . .'' the giant began a final time, then paused and looked up to see if he had found the right one. "Most radiant one, you are exactly as I pictured you. You are as beautiful as a winter's morning after an all-night drunk and as skinny as a weasel.''

"Oh, you flatterer," Thor said just a little coldly, not liking the comparisons at all. Fuming and impatient, he reached out in a habitual gesture to stroke his beard. There was, of course, no beard, but what his hand did find as it moved down his chest surprised him, and he looked down. He glanced up self-consciously and actually blushed. Thrym naturally assumed the gesture to be a rather suggestive one, and his broad grin became even broader and more lecherous.

"By Ymir, she is a bashful one!" he exclaimed.

Loki cleared his throat to keep from laughing. "Oh, Freyja is the gem of Asgardh. Naturally, we have treasured her and guarded her well. She is shy . . . even . . . inexperienced.''

"Oh really!" The giant cried in delight. "Do you think that I might . . . ah, steal a little kiss?''

Before anyone could answer, he bent to take the kiss, puckering like a beached salmon gasping for breath. But he paused halfway through the motion, taken aback by the murderous glare his bride-to-be afforded him. He quickly straightened and looked startled and confused.

"You must excuse dear Freyja," Loki said quickly. "She has not slept in days, so eager she has been since the arrival of your kind and generous summons. Besides which, we have this silly superstition that it is bad luck to kiss your bride before the wedding."

"Oh, I see," the giant said contritely. "Might I show you to your chambers? We have prepared a fine suite of cells for you."

He led the way inside the fortress, while the trolls shuffled along behind with the luggage balanced on their shaggy heads. Half the population of Klettastadhur followed also, staring in frank curiosity at their new mistress until Thrym finally chased them away with such a string of oaths and obscenities that even Thor blushed.

"Your room," he said, kicking open one of the heavy wooden doors that lined the countless branching corridors. The trolls scurried through without pausing, pushing past the others. They threw the baggage on the floor and hurried off, never saying a word. Rock-giants found trolls very useful. Especially about the kitchen, where they could both fill the pots and stir them. Naturally, they tended to be very quiet servants.

"Then we'll see you at dinner this evening," Thrym said hesitantly after the trolls were gone. "Ah . . . are you sure about that kiss? Not even on the cheek?"

"Freyja might just be persuaded . . ." Loki began, then saw that same murderous glare turned in his direction. "No, forget it."

"Then we shall just have to wait," the Jotun said reluctantly as he turned to leave, then paused at the door. "Oh, dinner will be ready in about three hours. We will be having a feast in your honor. You will probably wish to clean up." He shrugged, as if he could not understand the reason why.

"Thank you," Thor replied. "I do feel most unclean."

It was indeed quite a feast that Thrym had prepared for his guests. Nearly everyone in Klettastadhur was gathered in the great hall of the fortress, and it was different from the usual drinking and gluttony that went on every night in that the drinking and gluttony followed a pre-established plan of attack, and both the food and the drink were of decidedly better quality. For once the trolls at dinner were the ones doing the serving, rather than being served. There were just enough brawls to keep the party lively.

The guests of honor sat at the main table with the Lord of Klettastadhur. All eyes were on the blushing bride, and so it was not long before they began to notice her rather healthy appetite. Soon even Thrym was staring in wide-eyed amazement, for Thor, forgetting both his role and the restrictions of his present form, had skillfully put away a whole roast haunch and three salmon. The Jotnar might eat as much or more, but not the dainty Vanadis. When Thor finally pushed away his plate, the entire hall rose and applauded in honest appreciation.

"That was quite a feat!" Thrym said approvingly. "I have never believed that such a little lady could eat so much."

"The Lady Freyja has not eaten since your offer of marriage reached her ears," Loki hastily improvised an excuse.

"Oh, I see," Thrym said, duly flattered. "Can I offer you more drink?"

"Do you have an excellent wine in stock?" Loki asked before Thor could demand another beer.

"Wine? Lots of wine. Good wine." He looked up, searching for a troll to send after the wine. The first one he saw was on the far side of the hall, about to go out the door, nearly a hundred yards away. Thrym picked up his empty cup and threw it at the unfortunate servant. The metal cup flew straight and true, and bounced harmlessly off the troll's thick skull. The entire hall cheered and applauded his skill.

"Bring the best wine you can find!" Thrym bellowed, and the troll scurried off.

"Oh, Thrym! The troll never lived who could tell a good wine from a bad one," Loki exclaimed. "Why do you not go and choose a good one for us."

"Yes, of course," the giant agreed, and hurried off.

"Nuts, Thor! Talk about your gut instincts!" Loki hissed in a low voice. "Show more restraint. These rock-giants would be suspicious if they knew better."

"So what was I supposed to do?" Thor demanded. "I was hungry!"

"You are just nervous."

"And who would not be? If this does not work, I'll be married to that brute."

"Infinitely preferable to being mated to a horse."

"Oh, really?"

Loki thought about it for a moment, then frowned and nodded. "You are right. This is worse."

Thrym returned presently with a large skin of wine. Loki frowned upon seeing this; he was used to the better wines produced by the elves and had come to appreciate the fact that good wines only came in bottles. But, by the standards of the rock-giants, it was a good wine, having been mixed with honey after fermentation, so that it was both sweet and potent. Of course, Thor thought it was wonderful.

"Now there are certain arrangements to be made concerning this marriage," Loki began after the wine was served.

"Oh?" Thrym looked confused. "Such as?"

"Such as the type of life you have in mind for Freyja. You cannot take one of the Asynjur and put him . . . her in some dark corner by the fire with a spinning wheel. That," Loki said ominously, "is the quickest way to get yourself in real trouble. Surely you know that you cannot hold the Vanadis against her will."

"Yes, I see," the giant said thoughtfully. "But have no fear. I was looking upon this as more of a business investment. Freyja and I can do great things, if she is willing."

"Ah, so we thought. Now you realize that you can have us as your enemies, or as your friends. We were looking upon this as an alliance."

"An alliance?" Thrym brightened at the prospect.

"Yes. You know that we have never been at ease with Utgardh-Loki. Now if someone was to replace him, someone who was in alliance with the Aesir and privy to their councils, why then he could rule his own kingdom in absolute security! Do you know what I mean?"

"I do indeed!"

"And if he had the support of the Aesir beforehand," Loki continued, "then it would be a simple matter indeed for him to replace Utgardh-Loki."

"Yes!" Thrym was all but panting with excitement. "And what do I have to do to secure this alliance?"

"Begin even as you have. Marry Freyja as quickly as you can."

"Yes! Yes! The wedding is tomorrow morning," the Jotun declared. "But Freyja . . . ?"

"She was sent by the Aesir to secure the alliance I have described," Loki explained. "Not to get the hammer."

"Oh," Thrym said, thoroughly pleased. "And will you be staying also?"

"Most of the time. I am to act as a messenger between yourself and the Aesir."

"Good!" Thrym declared, even more pleased. "Your tongue is almost as potent a weapon as any power of the Aesir. It's almost like having my own copy of that mealy-mouthed Loki."

The day of the wedding broke cloudy and dark, a fitting tribute to the auspicious occasion. The tables had been removed from the hall and replaced by row upon row of long wooden benches that now filled the room, and every space was quickly taken by hundreds if not thousands of rock-giants, frost-giants and even fire-Jotnars. Trolls in trollish formal wear scurried up and down the aisles, seating the guests and serving refreshments. There were even a pair of small dragons, a firedrake to warm the food and an icedrake to keep the beer cold. Thrym had spared no extravagance.

After a time the guests grew silent and the music began. The dragons sat up on their haunches and sang. It was not half bad, for the musicians were hill-giants with a fair appreciation for music, and the dragons were in excellent voice. But they were more entertaining than tuneful; the soprano scorched the rafters with every high note.

Then the bride arrived, riding her horse slowly down the center aisle. Her handmaidens rode ahead and to either side, their weapons drawn. Their role was not just ceremonial; they served, according to Jotunish custom, to insure that there were no last-minute hesitations on the part of the groom. All three were dressed in brilliant white, but in pants, tunic and cape rather than the flowing robes more typical to the occasion. Unknown to the giants, they anticipated something of a brawl to close the ceremonies and robes were too cumbersome for that.

"This had better work," Thor said in a very low voice.

"I have done my best, and that was what I was sent for," Loki replied. "You just go through with what we planned. That little talk we had last night should make him somewhat less hesitant about producing the hammer."

Brynhild looked around in surprise. "So that was what that was about! Forgive me for thinking that you were just wasting time."

"You are excused," Loki said graciously. "If Thrym believes that we are here to strike that unholy alliance, and not to get back the hammer, then he will not worry about showing it."

They were now proceeding up the front of the aisle, where the more important guests, and those sober enough to pay attention, were seated. There were a fair number of comments flying about like bats on a dark night, and not even the wailing of the dragons could drown it all out.

"They're an oddly mismatched pair," someone commented. "It'll never work. He's three times her size. The first time he tries to. . . ."

The giant's wife, who had somewhat better manners, silenced him with a quick punch in the jaw. "Watch your language, Smoort. You just mark my words. She'll lay him out flat the moment they're married."

"Well, I heard that they had to get married!" someone else said loudly. The entire hall rippled with laughter, and even the draconic duet hesitated in mid-note.

The bride's party arrived at the raised stage at the front of the hall and dismounted. Thrym approached from one side and held out his hand to his bride-to-be. They were indeed a mismatched pair, for the false Freyja looked even more like a child at his side. The pair turned to face the crowd, and everyone applauded and cheered and shouted obscene encouragements. Thor took it all in surprisingly good grace, his fixed smile never faltering.

They turned back to stand before the tall bookstand that supported a single vast, leatherbound volume. There was a stepladder against the back of the stand, nearly as tall as Thor, and he was beginning to wonder if a dwarf had been called to invoke the ritual of joining. Just then Sinir scurried in from one side and mounted the ladder to perch on his haunches on the top step.

"A ferret?" Thor asked incredulously.

"Why not?" Loki asked, trying hard to hide his amusement. "Considering the circumstances, it seems only fitting to have a weasel read the rite."

"Besides, he's the only one in Klettastadhur who can read," Thrym added. "And he has written a truly inspired passage for the rite."

"Oh, thank you!" Sinir chirped.

"Not at all," the giant said. "Do proceed."

The ferret lifted himself up and leaned over the book, his forelegs braced against the open pages, and began to read. "Good people, giants and giantesses, dragons and trolls of all types. We have gathered here to witness the rites of joining of this Jotun and this fine lady of Asgardh. Let us first consider the true meaning of this blessed act, for what is marriage if not an advancement, a union of two people each with the thought that their lives will be richer for having each other. A Jotun seeks a wife and through her finds the happiness and contentment that he had missed before, to gain those things which have true meaning, which he has long wanted but always lacked. And what would a fine lady such as this seek in marriage except the fulfillment of her own desires. Standing here before you are two such people, sharing but a single thought of what they stand to gain."

The guests exploded with applause for that moving oration, while Sinir bowed to his appreciative audience. Even Loki was stirred, although it was with a greater respect for the wily ferret and his subtle sarcasm. A shame that it was wasted on such dim-witted Jotnar, although that was to Sinir's benefit. There would be one less ferret in Jotunheim if Thrym knew what he was about.

At length Sinir motioned for silence and continued. "Do you, Lord Thrym of Klettastadhur, agree to take the Lady Freyja for your wife, to love and cherish her for the short time that you have left?"

"Will I!"

"And do you, Freyja of the Vanir, agree to take Lord Thrym for your husband, to love and cherish him for as long as he might live?"

"I guess so."

"Lastly do I ask if there are any here who know some reason why this union should not be allowed?" Thrym glanced over his shoulder at the assembled guests with a look that would have frozen the fires of Muspell. "Then I do proclaim you husband and wife. You may. . . ."

"Wait just a moment!" Thor exclaimed before anything could be said or done. "Before this ceremony can be declared true and binding, I insist that we swear our vows upon Thor's hammer, as is our custom in Asgardh."

"But . . . why?" Thrym demanded. "That sounds like something silly. And this is not Asgardh."

"It is not silly," Thor insisted. "If you swear your oath upon that hammer, then Thor will be bound to protect and avenge me if you ever break that oath. It is my only protection."

"Oh, very well," Thrym reluctantly agreed. "Sinir, do you remember where I have it hidden?"

"Oh, yes!" Sinir said as he leaped down. "I will ferret it out!"

He was back barely a minute later, Mjollnir slung by its thong about his neck. He laboriously hauled it up the ladder and let it fall with a loud thump atop the open book.

"Now what do I do?" he asked.

"Why, nothing at all," Thor said casually, and reached out with one hand. The hammer suddenly stirred to life and leaped into his gloved hand. Thor leaped back with a cry of joy and, bracing his legs, swung the hammer widely over his head. It was quite a startling sight for the dainty Freyja to suddenly seize the hammer and be possessed of a sudden battle fury. Everyone in the hall stared in astonishment, while Thrym only stood with his mouth hanging open.

"It's the real one!" Thor declared triumphantly, then focused on the unfortunate giant. "And you can be the first to experience Thor's wrath!"

With that he gave Thrym a quick poke on the stomach, and when the giant doubled over Thor landed a firm crack on his head. Thrym straightened and stood motionless for a long moment, until it seemed to everyone that his thick skull had proven itself the harder. Then the giant slowly toppled over backward like a huge, ugly tree.

For a moment longer the guests simply sat and stared, then rose and applauded long and fiercely. They still had not realized that this was not Freyja, and they were understandably impressed by her ability to dispatch her husband even before the wedding was over. Then they drew their weapons and charged by the hundreds, for they still had a dead lord to avenge. Then Thor's hammer was given a furious workout, and tested to the limits of its abilities. After only five minutes the survivors fled.

"Yes, that is indeed the real Mjollnir," Thor said, stepping carefully across the carpet of Jotun carcasses. "Let us get our baggage and get out of here."

"If you can get those two away from here," Brynhild said, and pointed with her sword.

"Two?" Thor asked and looked, only to find that it was more like five. Loki and Sinir had already descended upon the refreshments, and their three horses were not far behind.

"Loki!"

"Oh, hold on a moment," Loki called back. "If you're not going to cut the cake, then I am."

"Let's join them," Brynhild said, pulling at Thor's arm. "After all, it is your wedding day."

"All right, but we have to hurry," Thor insisted. "I want to get home and change, and I don't mean my clothes. Sif is going to be jealous; I'm prettier than she is."

CHAPTER SEVEN

Of Thor's Journey to Utgardh

The safe return of Thor's hammer did not prove to be the end of that matter. Utgardh-Loki was outraged that the simple-minded rock-giant Thrym had been plotting against him, but he was also encouraged to learn that the walls of Asgardh were not impenetrable. It seemed to him that if Thrym could get one thieving ferret past Heimdall's gate, then he should be able to get a fair number of spies and saboteurs inside. The small expedition of Jotnar entered Asgardh undetected and left several hours later by the same means. They did no damage of any consequence, but the thing that filled the Aesir with real fear was simply that spies had again invaded their sanctuary. And what frightened them most was that they had obviously come and gone under the protective cover of a very powerful illusion.

When Thor heard of what had happened, he resolved to go after the spies. It was certain that within their group was the one who had created the illusion, and his loss might be a serious one to Utgardh-Loki. Thor chose only two to accompany him. Loki, of course, had little choice. He was always called for when giants were involved and he was now Thor's most frequent companion. Thor's second choice was Sinir, the landvaeta in the form of a giant ferret, who had joined with the Aesir after Thrym's defeat and whose special magic made him invaluable. He alone could trace the giants, at least with the speed required, and not even an illusion could mislead him.

The trail led over the wall, down the sheer side of the great plateau and out into the wilderness into the world of Asgardh. The giants had not entered by the main world-gate, or they would not have gotten past Heimdall however secure their illusion. Instead they had come and gone by one of many lesser gates which usually joined only two worlds. After several hours they came to such a gate, and found to their surprise that it led into the elf-world. From that the trail led almost due west; Utgardh lay in that direction, once they transferred into Jotunheim.

By night they were well into the wilds of Alfheim, within perhaps twenty miles of the river Glaervatna. King Alflysa's great hall lay almost directly ahead, and it seemed incredible that the giants would attempt a secret crossing of the river by one of the elves' own bridges. Sinir suddenly looked up and, after a moment's consideration, rushed off the path to one side. The others followed, and found him standing with one foreleg braced against a tree, staring into the darkness.

"What is it? Trouble?" Thor asked.

"No, not trouble. Not the giants," the ferret explained. "I feel a strange presence. A witch . . . an elf-maiden of unusual powers. And her brother, he has some unusual talents also. Like the belt gives you, but directed into swiftness rather than great strength."

"Unique powers?"

"Oh, yes!" Sinir replied emphatically. "Great power. Half of the Asynjur do not possess such powers."

Now Thor hardly knew what to do. He believed that such powers belonged in Asgardh, where they could be used for good or at least protected from evil. But he did not desire to abandon his chase. After a moment he decided that, since they must soon stop for the night anyway, they might at least check this out and be on their way in the morning. But Loki was quick to urge caution. Witches and warlocks who possessed such powers, and especially elves, did not care to be found. Thor quickly agreed that they should proceed with great subtlety; Loki's advice was not to be ignored, even if it was not always reliable.

Half an hour later the small group of travelers, with the addition of one large ox, rode up before the simple house that stood alone in the woods. Wood-elves lived apart from all others, and it was easy to assume that they were a lesser folk than the high elves because they did not build great mansions or live in fine cities. But they were skilled beyond compare in simple things, such as the working of wood or metal by hand, and yet their magic was subtle and complex, and they understood the dark forests of their twilit world even better than the animals who dwelt there. A wood-elf in his own element was as secure as a dragon in his den, a fact shown by the ease and confidence with which this small group came out to greet their unexpected guests.

Because the Alfar were an immortal folk, it was often impossible to tell the parents from their grown children. But there was an unmistakable feel of power about the slender girl with the wood-brown hair, and her obvious similarities with the tall elf who stood beside her marked the pair as twins. It was indeed the other elf, shorter and not quite so thin, who stepped forward as the lord of this hall.

"Good evening to you, travelers," he said, bowing shortly and quickly. "You are, I hazard to guess, lords of the Aesir? Thor, the Thunderer, and Loki Laufeyarson?"

"Are we that obvious?" Loki laughed, as if amazed at the elf's perceptiveness. But it was, in fact, no great trick. Loki could and often did pass as an elf, but Thor could be mistaken for no one but himself.

"Be welcome, then," the elf said, and bowed again. "I am Gylfi, a woodworker. My mate is Veiga, and our children are Thjalfi and Roskva. Our home is a simple one, but you are welcome to spend the night."

"We thank you," Loki said as he slid down from his saddle. "It is indeed a comfort to find such hospitality in the wilderness. In some parts you cannot even beg a warm fire out of a dragon. But let us return the favor by adding something to your dinner, which is simply a matter of practicality. Thor can eat you out of a week's worth of food in one setting, so we make special provisions."

Thor drew his famous hammer and stepped over to the ox

that had been following obediently behind their party. It
looked up, as if in weary anticipation of what was to come,
before Thor fetched it a smart crack on the head that laid the
beast out. Soon it was dressed, trussed, spitted and set to
cook over the fire, and dinner was not long in coming. Of
course, it was not a true ox, but illusions could have turned a
rabbit into a dinner for seven. Since Sinir tended the spit and
Loki served the meat, no one noticed that it appeared to
shrink considerably as it cooked.

"Now let me warn you about one thing," Loki said as he
began serving out dinner. "Do not damage the bones in any
way, but save them whole. This is a magic ox, and it can be
restored to life in the morning if the hide and bones are
intact."

Now everyone heard that and took note except for Thjalfi,
who had heard nothing. He sat at the far end of the table,
momentarily isolated by illusion, so that he was not even
aware that Loki had spoken. And later on, when no one was
watching, he gave a small leg-bone to the dog to take outside
and gnaw.

The guests spent the night in the best comfort that the
wood-elves could provide. Elves were always very serious
about the courtesy they showed their guests, whether friends
or strangers, and wood-elves were no exception in spite of
their reputation for inhospitality. It was true that the Lady
Veiga did not especially like having a wolf-sized ferret in her
house, and the horses stayed up half the night telling bad
jokes and laughing. But she bore it with good grace.

When morning came everyone had a hasty breakfast and
gathered outside to see the travelers off. It was at that time in
the autumn months and moving toward winter; there was a
chill in the air, and silvery mist drifted among the trees of the
forest. The horses stood saddled and laden outside the wood-
elves' home, blowing thin clouds of steam in the morning air.

Thor appeared at last, carrying the bones of their dinner
wrapped in its own hide like a bag. Then Redbeard did a
curious thing, taking the bones and arranging them carefully
before throwing the hide over the crudely rebuilt skeleton.
Then he brought out his hammer and held it over the ox's
remains. The beast suddenly leaped up alive and well, to the
amazement of the elves. But when Thor tried to lead it over

to the horses they saw that the ox was lame; a lower bone was missing from its hind leg.

"So! It was only a simple thing that we asked, and yet you still did not deal carefully with the bones!" Thor declared, and held the hammer above the head of the ox. It collapsed back into a hide filled with bones.

Then he turned to the elves and glared at them beneath a lowered brow while his hand gripped the handle of his hammer until his knuckles whitened. And the elves, to his surprise and consternation, threw themselves down and begged for forgiveness. Gylfi offered anything that was his to give in exchange for the damage that had been done. And that of course, was what Loki had been waiting for.

Then Thjalfi stepped forth. "My lords, the fault was mine, for I did not hear the warning. I will make what payment I can, or accept any punishment. But I have only myself to give. My strength is great and my speed is beyond that of any elf; that is my magic."

"Oh?" Loki sat down on a rough wooden bench and seemed to consider that. "You know, Redbeard, he might be right. His talents are great, and his sister's magic is even greater. They could do you great service. And not, mind you, as thralls."

"Yes, I would agree to that," Thor said as he put away his hammer. "Thjalfi would be very useful to me, but I believe that Roskva would be worth even more when a sorceress' talents are required."

The two young elves leaped up, laughing and clapping and congratulating each other until Thor was given to wonder if he had been the one to fall into their trap. Loki was even more surprised, for in his plans he had never considered the possibility that they might actually want to go.

They were off again as soon as the two young elves were ready. Thor took Thjalfi up on his own horse, and Roskva rode behind Loki. Sinir brought them quickly back to the giant's trail and ranged on ahead, covering more ground than a ferret's short legs suggested possible. Soon they were drawing near the great river Glaervatna and more inhabited regions. Glaervatnadalur, the city of the elves, was barely five miles ahead. Already they could catch an occasional glimpse of King Alflysa's marble palace atop the cliffs overlooking

the river. Thor cursed in his beard when he saw that the
giant's trail led directly over the bridge, although the elves on
guard swore that none had passed that way the day before.

Late that evening they came to the second of the world-
gates the giants had used. This one led directly into Jotunheim;
the giants were now in their own home world. They would
either continue to press on quickly or consider themselves
safely home and slow down somewhat. Even Loki was unable
to guess, so it was only logical to assume the former and keep
up the chase. He thought it best that they should overtake
their prey as soon as possible. Just now they were in the
wilderness northeast of Klettastadhur and far from help. But
he did not fancy the thought of this chase leading into the
heart of Utgardh-Loki's kingdom, although he was afraid it
might well come to that.

Several days passed as they tracked their prey across the
barren plains of Jotunheim, and Sinir reported that they were
gaining slowly but steadily. But by that time they were
coming very near to Utgardh. Then it was that the weather
turned bad, for a terrible storm descended in violence from
the north, bringing lightning and wind and icy rain. Soon the
fury of the storm was such that the travelers were forced to
abandon the trail and seek what shelter they could find. They
were struggling up a steep slope beneath the lashing fury of
the rain when they saw the dark form of some immense hall
standing atop a nearby hill. The horses needed no encouragement when they saw it, but turned and headed directly toward
the hall.

It was so dark that they could not see the structure properly
except to tell that it appeared to be a fairly typical farmhouse,
but of unusual size. There were no lights to be seen, nor any
other indication that it was inhabited. Loki's horse arrived
first and immediately found the door, a simple piece of
canvas hung over an open frame. The horses pushed through
without hesitation and stood for a moment in absolute darkness until Loki brought forth a glowstone.

As bright as the crystal was, its soft light did no more than
push back the shadows into the corners, revealing the place to
be a barren shell. There was no sign that anyone had ever
lived there, for even the floor was covered by a thick carpet
of grass.

"Well, what is this place?" Thor asked as he slid down from his saddle. "A barn? This was never anyone's home."

"Yes, perhaps a barn," Loki agreed uncertainly. "Perhaps someone began to build a homestead here."

"But the grass?" Thjalfi asked in confusion.

"Oh, that's not odd," Thor said indifferently as he looked around. "The grass in this world is as insidious as mildew; it needs no light, just a fair amount of dampness. It even grows inside caves."

There were enough sticks and twigs littering the floor to build a respectable fire, but they decided against it. Thor had had to tie the canvas door tightly shut to keep the cold wind and rain from blowing in, and there seemed to be no other ventilation for the smoke. At last they resigned themselves to cold rations and the pale light of Loki's glowstone.

At dawn they were suddenly awakened by a terrible noise. There was a sudden crash like thunder just outside the door, and the ground shook beneath them. Then Thor took his hammer firmly in hand and opened the door to investigate. What he saw took even him by surprise, and for the first time his courage failed him if for just an instant. For there stood the tallest giant that he had ever seen, thirty feet and more in height. The giant was swinging an ax of immense size, breaking up a whole tree for firewood. There was already an immense fire burning off to one side, heating a teakettle that held twenty gallons or more of water.

"Ho, ho, ho!" the giant exclaimed as he saw Thor peeping out from behind the canvas door. "So I had visitors in the night and never knew. Do not fear! You are welcome to share my tent any time."

Thor looked up and saw that what they had assumed in the previous nights' darkness to be a great hall or barn was indeed the giant's travel tent. He stepped forward and faced the giant squarely.

"We thank you for your hospitality," he answered. "We did not mean to trespass, but in the darkness and the storm we took your tent to be some abandoned farmhouse or barn."

"A barn? Ho, ho, that is rich! But you are such little folk. No, my Lord Thor, take no offense." He held up a hand in entreaty. "Yes, I know who you are, and that your bashful friend behind the tent flap is Loki the Fox. None other would be so bold as to come so far into Jotunheim. But you have nothing to fear from me, at least. I am Skrymir. Will you not join me for breakfast? Then we must be on our way. My path takes me within sight of the gates of Utgardh, and you may accompany me, if you like.''

Now the others hardly knew what to make of this offer, but they at last decided to accept. Sinir reported that their trail now led directly to Utgardh, and that the lead was widening again. So he said that they must either abandon the chase or go on to Utgardh. They decided to go on, at least for now. Skyrmir was delighted, and he packed their supplies into his own bag so that their horses might travel as lightly as possible, the only way that they might keep up with his long-legged stride.

Skrymir traveled long and hard throughout the day, and he covered a very great distance before he stopped. As night fell he found them shelter beneath a stand of immense oaks. He threw down his bag and ax and explained that they should take what they wanted from the provisions, and immediately laid himself out like a fallen tree and began to snore. And he was a lusty snorer indeed.

Thor immediately set about untying the knot that secured the giant's bag, but the thing eluded him completely. After several minutes he was forced to admit defeat, and Loki took his turn. But the knot remained firm, even after they had all taken a try. Then Thor began to grow rather cross, and also very hungry. It seemed to him that Skrymir was trying to play him for a fool, and taking Mjollnir in hand he walked over and fetched the giant a sharp knock on the head. The blow was more than enough to lay out an ox, but Skrymir only yawned and lifted himself up.

"Hello, Thor," he said, and yawned again. "Is dinner ready?"

"No, indeed!" Thor said sharply. "We were not yet hungry. But if you will join us, then we will eat now."

Skrymir untied the bag with no difficulty at all, and they dined that night on smoked salmon and small round loaves of bread that Thor thought must be harder still than the giant's skull. Then Skrymir laid himself down and went back to sleep, and it seemed that he snored even louder than before. The others withdrew from him as far as they could, and yet the noise was still deafening and none of them, except Sinir, could get any sleep.

At last Thor could stand it no more. Taking his hammer in hand a second time, he walked over to Skrymir and shook him violently. But no amount of shaking would wake the giant, and Thor was finally forced to take more extreme measures. This time he brought the hammer down even harder than before, and there was a sound like metal striking rock. And he might as well have been striking rock, except that a boulder of equal size would have broken. Skrymir woke with a start and looked about in confusion.

"An acorn must have hit me on the head," he remarked. "Oh, hello Thor! Is something wrong?"

"No, nothing is wrong," Thor said as he walked away in disgust. "But we do wish that you would not snore so loudly."

"What? Don't be silly! I never snore," Skrymir declared as he laid back down. And only a moment later he was snoring as loudly as before.

The noise did not abate once during the night, and Thor sat and fumed in indignation. Actually he was not certain which annoyed him more, the snoring or his apparent inability to slay this giant. At last he saw that morning was close at hand, and he decided then that he could take no more. With hammer in hand he approached the giant a final time. He swung as hard as he could and landed a blow on the giant's head that would have shaken a mountain. Skrymir's eyes popped open and he sat up quickly.

"Oh, hello. Nice of you to awaken me," he said congenially, "for indeed we must be off, if you are to reach Utgardh by nightfall."

As soon as breakfast was over they were off again, and as the day before they traveled hard and fast. They were now climbing well up into the mountains that had been rising like a vast barrier before them for the last two days. Late that morning they came upon a road that cut across their path. Skrymir stopped and opened his bag to return their provisions.

"Here we must part," he said. "Follow this road to the north, and it will take you directly to the gate of Utgardh by some time this evening. My path lies on ahead."

*   *   *

They rode on until very late in the afternoon, climbing ever higher into the mountains until the path became steep, twisting and treacherous. Coming around a sharp bend in the road, they suddenly found before them a narrow valley like a deep sword-cut in the mountains, and on the other side of that valley they saw what was surely the greatest of all castles in the nine worlds perched atop sheer cliffs. For a long moment they simply stared at the immense fortress and tried to remember why they had even wanted into it in the first place. They would have done well to remember that they had never meant to enter Utgardh, but it was too late for that. The horses stepped out onto the bridge that spanned the narrow valley.

The bridge led them directly to Utgardh's immense gate, but its portals were closed and locked fast, and there was not a sign of life inside the hall or out. The travelers slid down from their saddles, and Thor walked purposefully up to the vast wooden door and knocked with his hammer.

A long moment passed before they heard the door being unlocked from the inside, and the portal opened just enough for a single giant to look out. He was indeed a very ordinary giant, not particularly tall or massively built but slim and almost gentle in his features, and with an intelligent and pleasant face. Even more unusual, he was neat and clean and very well-dressed.

"Welcome to Utgardh," he said and bowed politely. "I know your names, but may I inquire of your business?"

"We thought that we owed Utgardh-Loki a visit, being in the neighborhood," Thor replied with mocking dignity. "Returning the compliment, don't you know."

"I see. But would you happen to know the password?"

"Would you like a dent in your head?"

The giant swallowed nervously and pushed the door open for them to enter. "Close enough. I am Skuli, King Loki's seneschal and warder of his castle. If you will come with me, then we will see if King Loki will receive you."

Skuli led the travelers into Utgardh-Loki's great hall, where the king and his warriors were seated in attendance. Two long benches ran the length of the hall to either side, and on these benches sat some two hundred of the largest Jotnar that Thor and Loki had ever seen. And yet the biggest of them was

Utgardh-Loki himself, seated upon a massive throne at the far end of the hall. He was tall and rugged in appearance, dressed in leather and fur and an iron breastplate, the largest and most powerful of the Jotnar save only Skrymir. All talking ceased when the giants saw who entered, and they stared long and hard at the visitors as they were led up the long aisle between the benches.

Utgardh-Loki smiled scornfully as he glared down at his guests. "Welcome and well-met indeed; or can I be mistaken, that this little boy can possibly be the mighty Thor? But it must be, for that horse's tail on his chin marks him as no mere child, and he is surely no stone-burrowing Dverger in spite of it."

"It is I, beard and all," Thor replied. "And if you do not recognize my beard, then I would be delighted to show you my hammer. A great many giants have met it, and it left a lasting impression upon them."

Utgardh-Loki laughed heartily. "No, withhold your hammer! You may indeed be greater than you appear. But what great deeds and accomplishments would you and your fellows be ready to attempt to prove yourselves? For I must tell you now that I will allow no one here as my guest unless he can do at least one small thing of craft or cunning surpassing the abilities of anyone else."

Then he proposed the first contest, that one of their company should be able to put away a bowl of meat faster than his own champion. That seemed a strange contest, and Thor might have seemed the likely choice. But while he could indeed eat more than anyone in Asgardh, Loki ate faster. Then the benches were drawn back against the walls and a table was brought in and set up in the center of the room, and two huge plates piled high with roasted meats were set upon it. Then Utgardh-Loki called forth a strange fellow named Logi, who was in form like a giant but smaller than the shortest dwarf, barely two feet in height. Loki was surprised when he was seated at the table across from this curious competitor, thinking that Logi could surely eat no more than a single piece of meat from the heap piled in his bowl.

The race began and Loki addressed himself to the contents of his bowl, and he did not look up until it was empty. But when he did glance up with bulging eyes, he was surprised.

Logi had grown to unusual proportions, not yet the size of a true Jotun but larger than himself. Even more surprising was the fact that he had eaten not only his meat, but also the bones, the bowl and a large portion of the table itself.

The giants laughed heartily as much at their victory as at Loki's amazement; no one had to point out that he had lost. Utgardh-Loki called for the servants to clear away the wreckage, but before they could intervene Logi consumed it all without a trace and abruptly disappeared. Loki meekly rejoined his companions.

"Something is wrong here," Roskva said quietly. "We are being tricked."

"I suspected as much," Loki agreed, and belched. "But I do not know just what is going on. Do you?"

The girl did not have time to answer, for at that moment Utgardh-Loki came up to them.

"Well done, Sly. You are very quick indeed, but well below the standard that has been set for us." He looked perplexed as if he regretted their loss. Then he suddenly brightened. "But why can we not try again? Is anyone here fit for a race?"

"I will race your champion," Thjalfi said. And it seemed a safe bet, for it was his talent that he was the fastest runner on two or four legs.

Utgardh-Loki laid out a course from before his throne, out the castle gate and across the bridge, a path that was in fact perfectly straight with the only turn coming when the contestants doubled back at the end of the bridge. Then he selected his own runner, a wiry lad by the name of Hugi. The pair looked evenly matched, for Hugi was young and no more than a hand taller than the elf. Hopefully the Jotnar did not know of Thjalfi's special talent for speed.

But when they ran the first heat, Hugi proved the swifter and won by a good ten strides. Utgardh-Loki smiled tolerantly as he greeted the runners. "Well, Thjalfi, you will surely have to try harder than that. You are fast, but I must warn you that Hugi is faster than the swiftest bird. But we will try again."

The second race was run, and this time Hugi finished more than a third of the course ahead. Utgardh-Loki frowned in embarrassment, as if he could not understand what was wrong.

He insisted upon one more race, but not before Thjalfi was well rested. But this time Hugi finished the course before Thjalfi had even reached the half-way point.

"Enough of this," Utgardh-Loki said at last. "It seems to me that we could stage races all year, and Thjalfi would never win. Perhaps there is some other game that we might try."

"More tricks?" Thor quietly asked Roskva.

"Of course. But I cannot say how the trick was done."

"Is Hugi really something else?"

Roskva shook her head helplessly. "By my magic I cannot say that he is anything else. I sense no living presence."

"Oh? What do you make of it, Loki?" Thor asked, then saw that Loki was seated at the end of the bench, one hand over his mouth and the other on his stomach, and his face was green. "Sly? What is wrong with you?"

"I think I ate too much."

"Well, Thor, your companions have failed you," Utgardh-Loki proclaimed loudly as he walked over to the group. Thjalfi followed closely behind, as blue in the face as Loki was green. "But it may well be that you have been saving your best for last, for you have not yet yourself tested your skills. Are you now willing to try your own talents in some game?"

"Yes, I am ready," Thor said. "Then you will see what I can do."

"Yes, we will indeed," the giant said, with a note of sarcasm. "I have often heard it said that your greatest renown lies in your tremendous strength. All I ask of you then is that you lift the cat lying over there by the hearth. The only condition is that you lift it completely from the floor."

Thor looked at the cat, which was sprawled out and fast asleep on the stones before the fireplace. It was, of course, of Jotunish proportions, and so was as large as a lion. Even so, it could not weigh more than a few hundred pounds, and therefore, no great task for him to lift. At least not under normal circumstances, but he also knew that there was most likely some trick. He agreed to try, for indeed he could not refuse. Instead he hoped that he would be able to uncover the trick once he had his hands on the cat.

The giants gathered about in a circle as Thor marched up to the cat and placed his hands firmly about its middle. The cat did not bestir itself except to twitch its tail in annoyance. Then he began to pull and found, as he had expected, that the cat did not weigh a couple of hundred pounds but at least several tons. He was able to lift it, but it bent like soft rubber. Even when he lifted it well over his head, the beast was still bent double, so that its front and back ends were still on the floor. At last he threw it down and stood panting, red in the face from his exertions.

"I can do no more," he said. "I can lift the cat, even though it must be the heaviest house cat ever. But I cannot lift it high enough to get it completely off the floor."

"Oh, but that is too bad!" Utgardh-Loki declared. "I do not know how to judge the game. Clearly you can lift it but, as you say, you are too short to lift it high enough to clear the floor. Let us say that it was a tie, and that you failed only by default."

"My, but that is generous of you," Redbeard said with blatant sarcasm.

"Oh, not at all!" Utgardh-Loki laughed as he picked up the cat with one hand and tucked it under one arm, then turned to walk slowly back to his throne. "You know, I have always thought how fine it would be to have Thor, mightiest of warriors, to sit as a guest at my table. And here you are, but you and your companions cannot pass even one of my tests. Am I to lay aside my rule for you? I gladly would, and yet it makes me wonder if I am dishonoring Thor by allowing some poor imposter take his name and place."

"Then give me a true test. One without tricks. Then I will show you plainly who is Thor."

"Do you imply that I have been less than honest?" the giant asked incredulously.

"Imply? I imply nothing, but state facts."

"Then, if you believe that you have been misled, I must redeem my honor by allowing you one more chance. Will you attempt another game?"

"First show me the game."

"Only this," Utgardh-Loki said, then turned to take one of the tall drinking horns that a servant was holding. He drained the horn in a single swallow and wiped his mouth on his sleeve. "It is a custom in this hall that a warrior drains his horn in a single quaff. Some require two, but no one is so poor that he cannot drain it in three. Will you try?''

Thor took the horn and sniffed at the ale to see if there was anything in it that would render it unfit to drink, but it was pure and very good. He put the horn to his mouth and drank long and deeply, and at first he thought that he would not need a second try. But when his breath failed he knew that the horn was not empty, and yet it surprised him to see that the level of the ale had hardly dropped at all.

Utgardh-Loki raised an inquisitive brow. ''You did not finish it off in one try? But no matter. Because you are so much smaller than us, the horn is larger in comparison. Try again.''

Thor said nothing and took a second drink, knowing that he would have to drink considerably more than he had the first time if he was to empty the horn. He drank well past the point when his breath gave out and until he could force down no more, and yet he saw that the level inside the horn did not seem to have gone down any at all. He raised the horn a final time and drank again as long as he could, and still the horn remained nearly full. He could drink no more, but gave the horn back to the servant and returned to where his companions waited beside the bench.

''Now do not be ashamed,'' Utgardh-Loki said. ''You did the best you could. Perhaps it is true that Thor is not so mighty as rumor says. But with rumor that is often so.''

''Then devise for us a fair test,'' Thor said angrily. ''For if you have heard any rumor then you know that I am a giant-slayer beyond compare. Would you put that to the test?''

''No, indeed!'' the Jotun laughed. ''You are welcome and safe in my hall, but I do ask that one of you show me some small trick that you can do better than anyone else. Do any of you have a special talent?''

''Yes, I do,'' Roskva said suddenly. ''I have great magic, and it gives me the ability to judge true from false. And in that I have defeated you at your own game. Do you declare me the winner? As proof, I ask you who is the true lord of this hall, or how many are really gathered there, or where in fact this hall actually stands.''

For a moment Utgardh-Loki looked dismayed as he listened to her words, and then he laughed uncertainly. ''Yes, I must concede to you the victory, for you have proven your-self in the greatest game of all. You have earned the hospital-ity of my hall for the night, and you will feast with me at my table. And tomorrow I will send you on your way with fresh provisions and my true blessings. I will find rooms for you; Skuli will come and attend to you presently.''

Utgardh-Loki turned and stalked from the room, and it was only a moment before Skuli came up silently behind them. ''My Lord Loki has sent me to show you to your rooms. Would you like to come and refresh yourselves before dinner?''

''Dinner?'' Loki asked, swallowing fearfully.

''Why, yes. And, in your honor, we will have roast ox and fish, venison and pork, with sweet wines and hearty ales. What more could you want?''

''Out!'' Loki yelped, and ran for the door with his hand over his mouth.

Thor and his companions were shown every courtesy, and they sat at the king's table that evening and were held as guests of honor. And indeed they had a very pleasant time and enjoyed themselves immensely. For their hosts were hill-Jotnar, far more wise and restrained in manner than other giants, agreeable and quite easy to get along with in spite of their previous jeering and mockery during the games.

They spent the night in huge beds of unsurpassed comfort. But in the morning, with the first light of dawn, Thor and his companions rose and made ready to depart. Skuli met them at the entrance hall, where their horses stood packed and ready to go. The warder of the castle led them outside and across the bridge, but there he paused and begged them to spare him a few minutes of their time.

''You were not kindly received yesterday, and for that I must explain,'' he said. ''But first let me ask you how you think your business at Utgardh turned out, and if you have met anyone mightier than yourself?''

''I cannot say that I am greatly shamed by how things turned out,'' Thor answered. ''I know that we were tricked, and so I do not feel that we were dishonored by losing the games. But I do regret that Utgardh-Loki was able to fool me. Nor would I have anyone dismiss me as one of little might.''

"Oh, rest assured that no one here underestimates your worth," Skuli insisted. "But let me tell you the truth, now that your visit is past and you are out of my castle. And, if I have my way and prevail in the end, then you will never again come within my walls. Indeed you would never have come here at all, had I known how mighty you are, and what powers your companions possess. It was a dangerous game, and I cannot say that I won. Now let me remind you of how this strange adventure began, with the unexpected visit of my agents to your own great citadel."

"Yes, of course," Thor recalled. "We were pursuing them. . . ."

"To prevent their safe return to Utgardh," Skuli finished for him. "Your intention was to destroy them before they could reach it, but you never meant to go there yourself. You see, I was in that group, and I am perhaps the greatest illusionist of all the Jotnar. I knew that you were following us soon after you entered this world, and when it became obvious that you would not give up the chase I knew that I had to distract you.

"And so I stayed behind the others and, leaving a false trail for your ferret to follow, I led you far away. Then I arranged my trap and laid in wait for you, and because I knew better than to try to fight you I sought to mislead you. Do you remember that first time I came to you?"

"You were Skrymir?" Loki asked incredulously.

"I was, in a sense, but in truth there was no Skrymir except in your own eyes. Nor was there any tent to shelter you, but that hardly mattered since there was no storm. Skrymir put the idea into your heads that you wanted to go to Utgardh by offering to show you the way, and then he kept you distracted with his little tricks. First you were annoyed that you could not open the provision bag. The bag was real enough. But you could not open the knot because I had complicated it with an illusion."

"Yes, and I gave you a knock on the head that would have killed a dragon," Thor said.

Skuli shook his head. "There was a huge boulder of solid granite on the ground where Skrymir's head seemed to be. Your first blow chipped it and the second cracked it, but the third was so great that it was reduced to rubble. Now I had thought to annoy you even more by filling your ears with such noise that would keep you awake all night.''

"But why would you lead us to Utgardh, if that was the one place where you did not want us to go?'' Loki asked, confused. It seemed to him that the giant had contradicted himself.

"But I did not say that,'' Skuli answered. "What I wanted was to distract you from your task. And after spending the night listening to Skrymir snore, you had quite forgotten why you were even here. Then, when you arrived at my hall, you were distracted even more by the games I had you play, and especially by the annoyance of being unable to win those games.

"The first game put Loki out of the competition for the rest of the evening. I was fearful that he would not be easily fooled, for I have heard much of his reputation for shrewdness. Of course, he gorged himself enough to make anyone sick, but I put special herbs in his meat that upset his stomach even more. After that he could think of nothing but his discomfort. But the reason that he did not win was because his opponent was fire, hidden by the illusion of Logi. I had poured liquid fire over the other bowl, and of course the fire consumed it all, meat, bones, bowl and even table. You saw how Logi grew as he ate, and abruptly disappeared when he had consumed it all.''

"Yes, I should have recognized that by his name,'' Loki said. "Logi is one of the words for fire in the language of Midhgardh, even as my name means the same in the ancient language of the Aesir.''

"Then Thjatsi ran his race against Hugi, which means thought. Hugi was indeed nothing more than my thought, an illusion created by my mind; as so, no matter how fast Thjatsi ran, my thought could always run faster.

"Now Thor was nearly my undoing, his strength is so great. The 'cat' that he tried to lift was indeed a huge dragon, weighing more than fifteen tons. No giant could have lifted him and I had not believed that Thor could, but I was wrong. Of course, the dragon was so long that his head and tail remained on the floor, and so Thor lost on a technicality.''

"But Utgardh-Loki, he lifted the cat!'' Sinir pointed out.

"That was only an illusion, meant to make Thor believe that his strength was small in comparison. Now the drinking horn was the only part that was not an illusion. It was connected by a magical gate, not unlike the world-gates, to a twenty-gallon keg. A special valve filled the horn from the keg as fast as Thor was drinking, and the only reason that the level went down at all was because the level inside the keg went down as much. And I grant you that it was an amazing feat in itself, not just that Thor could drink so much but that he held it without getting drunk."

Skuli shrugged. "I had always wondered what would happen if I had to stand against Thor, and I saw this as a chance to test my powers against his under controlled conditions. But I must admit that he gave me cause to fear. But you do not understand even yet, although Roskva has guessed it. Do you think that, under any circumstances, I would invite Thor into my castle, endanger my henchmen and guests, especially after what he did at Klettastadhur?"

"But you speak as though . . . ." Loki paused, and suddenly looked up in amazement. "You! You are the real Utgardh-Loki!"

"Oh, now you do understand!" the giant said, and executed a deep formal bow. "One thing I did to protect myself was to pretend to be the servant while an illusion took my place. Then, if Thor had answered my baiting with his hammer, it would have been to no more effect than his blows to Skrymir's stone head. Also, you must agree that I am hardly the imposing figure of my imitation. But I warn you now: Do not underestimate me. My powers are great, and my cunning greater. My reputation is as well-earned as your own."

Thor stroked his beard thoughtfully. "Yes, perhaps it is well for us both that this test of our abilities was not a serious one."

"Yes, but now we must part," Utgardh-Loki said. "And perhaps it would be better if we did not meet again. For if you ever again seek me out, then I will defend my castle and my people with such cunning as you have already seen, or in other ways that you do not expect, so that you will never get the better of me."

Thor frowned when he heard this, and he reached for his

hammer. "But what will protect you now that you do not have your illusions?"

"Have you not learned my ways better than that?" Utgardh-Loki asked, and abruptly disappeared. Then, as Thor watched, the immense castle also vanished, and the very mountains about them dissolved and reformed into a vast and level plain. And so the travelers understood what Roskva had guessed the night before, that they had never been in Utgardh nor anywhere near it. Thor and his companions had no choice but to admit defeat and turn for home.

PART TWO

CHAPTER ONE

The Otter
and the Dwarf

In the earliest moment of the star-realm there was a great explosion as all existence came into being in a single instant, and all things of substance and energy and time itself were blasted outward from that primordial core. Of the wreckage of that beginning the stars were formed, and in the furnace of their fiery hearts simple forms of matter were made into those more complex. And as the stars themselves grew old and poured forth their substance into the void, as if in imitation of that most ancient explosion, then greater and far more complex things came into being and were set adrift into the star-realm.

But in all the star-realm there was no thing so strange and terrible, so innocent in appearance and yet so dangerous, as the gold. It was a rare substance indeed: In all the long ages of his wandering, Odhinn had come upon its like only once, a small lump no larger than a pebble. The faint aura of power it radiated had attracted him to it, and he had kept it for a time. For he found that the gold responded to his will, merging with the mind and will of its possessor, taking identity and awareness for itself and returning an even portion of power. Tremendous strength of will was

needed to awaken the gold to life, but the power it gave back
was awesome.

And then, within a very short time of his finding the gold,
Odhinn had destroyed it. In the ages since, after he had taken
physical form, he could no longer remember why he had
done so. He remembered only that he had come to distrust the
thing, and eventually to fear it, in a very short time, and the
only reason seemed to be a very vague and uncertain memory
of a growing apprehension that the thing had been coming to
life, gaining a will and identity of its own as it fed upon the
will of its possessor.

In the mountain lands it began as a trickle of water through
a crack in the rock, joining with other courses as it slipped
and bubbled along its stony path down from the heights. Soon
it was a lively brook that leaped and played past rapids and
over falls. Spring thaws and summer storms thrust their burdens upon it, yet even in the driest times the river ran swift
and deep. Northward it rushed from the mountains that gave
it life, down among the lowlands where it cut a looping,
twisting path through rolling hills, and finally eastward through
grassy plains laid by its own burden of silt over the long
years, carried down from distant mountains and abandoned as
the great river paused to merge with the sea.

The river was the life on the northern lowlands. For the
men of Midhgardh it was as constant as the rising of the sun.
It had been as they had always seen it throughout the short
history of their kind, ever flowing yet never changing, like
the long and uneventful passage of years. Their lives were
short and they cared nothing for the long tale of years behind
them, nor did they even conceive of a time before themselves. Farmers tilled the rich soil of its borderlands, and
lordlings built their halls upon its shores and sailed dragon-
prowed ships down its unerring path to the sea. And they
called it the Rhine.

The waters of the Rhine held many secrets, as all rivers
hide their share. But one secret laid buried in its icy depths
that was greater and more deadly than any other, for in its
stony bed lay a piece of the true gold. It was not a thing
originally of that world, but had come out of the star-realm
long ago. In the ancient-most days, during the forming of the

world that was to become Midhgardh, the gold had been drawn in and swallowed in its molten mass. For many long ages it had lain buried in the very substance of that world, until the slow but persistent hand of time had cut it free of the stone that held it and the waters of the Rhine washed it down from the heights.

The waters of the Rhine hid also a pitiful creature called Andvari, a dwarf who had fled his kin and his world for the obscurity of the wilderness of Midhgardh. Andvari had been born small, misshapened and ugly, but of even greater harm to him was the shame and resentment that he had taken upon himself. He was the son of a wealthy and successful gold-smith, as his fathers had been before him throughout the history of the dwarf-kingdom, and Andvari himself was an exceedingly fine smith. But he nursed his hatred until it dominated him and made him enemies of all those about him, even his closest kin.

After a time Andvari had fled his home in the mansions of Gyllirhall and disappeared into the wilderness of the middle world. But his was no blind flight into unknown lands but one well-planned, for he was always one to plan for his own needs. It seemed to him that in the world of mortal men, where travelers from worlds beyond the gates were seldom seen, his malformities might pass unnoticed by men who would consider him no different from other dwarves. He also knew that since he was an exceptional smith even among the artisans of Nidhavellir, then he would be thought one of unsurpassed skills in the wilds of backward Midhgardh.

It was not by accident that he came to the Rhine and settled there. He selected a site well back into the lower mountains behind a high fall where the water ran swiftly through a narrow gorge. There he found extensive caves that he could convert easily into a mansion according to the manner of his kind. And he had all the length of the Rhine below to carry his goods to the lordlings that dwelled along its shores and to merchants who sailed their round-bellied knorrs along its way.

But one other thing attracted him to the great river. For Andvari was a shape-changer, and had the ability to take the form of a large pike. It was a secret that he guarded jealously throughout all of his younger years, for in his piscine form he

was strong and swift and he knew no greater joy than when
he swam in that shape. His talent was the one thing about him
that was special and unique, and for that reason he wanted to
protect his secret from the envy and criticism of others. He
could swim to his fullest contentment in the wild waters of
the Rhine and escape all the miseries and failings of his
land-bound self.

So it was that Andvari found the gold in the depths of the
Rhine and soon discovered its power to lead him to sunken
treasures hidden within its icy depths. As he considered it,
still gloating over his find, it must be a talisman of good luck
and a very powerful one at that, perhaps even a gift of the
gods. He wondered if Freyja had taken pity upon him for the
cruelties he had suffered, or if the thing had been a token
from Aegin the Seafarer or even Njordh himself, the great
god of the seas. But it was just as likely from Odhinn,
Andvari thought cynically; perhaps the gold made him a
useful tool in the Allfather's plans.

Whatever its source, Andvari meant to wring as much
profit from the gold as he could. And so he took the gold and
carefully cut a tiny hole through it. He ran through the hole a
strand of the best wire that the dwarves knew, light yet strong
and resistant to rust. In that way he could always carry the
Rhinegold about his neck as he swam, and the wire was so
light that it always caught on the rough surface of his forward
fins.

After that the depths of the Rhine were always open to
him, for the gold's brilliant glow could pierce the darkest
waters. And he was able to find and loot all the wrecks that
the river had swallowed over the years. The Rhinegold brought
such wealth that Andvari enjoyed most of the privileges of the
dwarf-lords of his own world, and he gained the happiness
and satisfaction that he had always sought but never known.

Beyond the falls of River Hall, the Rhine entered a swift
and narrow course as it twisted its way down through the last
few miles of rugged highlands where it was born and grew to
youthful vigor. Here lay a twenty-mile stretch of the river that
was known as Andvari's Force, the bane of the river-bound
merchants who had already rowed and pulled many hundreds
of miles up the length of the Rhine to trade with the skilled

but reclusive dwarf. They were obliged to off-load at the start of that course, and pack their goods in and out of River Hall overland by sturdy ponies.

So it happened through the years that a small holding of men grew up at the place where the ships were forced to put ashore. Hreidmar, son of Arnor, was the lord of that hold, a good and honest man and a valiant warrior. Three times he had repelled packs of river pirates come to loot River Hall, and Andvari paid him and his people well in both gold and friendship for that service, while they also made good money supplying ponies to the merchants. But the years passed and Hreidmar grew old and feeble, while Andvari, being of the mortal but longer-lived Dvergar, looked as old and withered as he had even in the days of Arnor's youth, yet still hale and strong.

Three sons did Hreidmar have. Fafnir was the oldest and his father's heir. He was exceptionally tall and strong and very handsome, as brave and skilled a warrior as his father and a hunter beyond compare; only an elf could have moved more silently through the woods. And it seemed that he was worthy and well-able to take over his father's holding, even though he possessed less patience and wisdom than Hreidmar or Arnor before him. Reginn was younger by little more than a year, and of less stature and considerably less skill in arms and battle. As a boy he had spent much time at River Hall, where Andvari had taught him as an apprentice and had shown him many of the skills and tricks the dwarvish smiths employed in their art, and Reginn became a very capable smith in his own right,

The youngest of the three was Ottar, although that was not his real name. He had a special power much like the one that Andvari possessed, and could change at will into the form of a giant otter. For this reason he was very special to Andvari; the Dvergar had first recognized his talent and had helped him to develop it. The two often swam together in the river, and it almost seemed that Andvari was as much Ottar's father as Hreidmar was.

It was a cool, clear morning in early autumn. The nightly dews were only just beginning to turn to frost and the leaves of the trees were still more green than brown. It had been a good and gentle year along the Rhine, the third such since the

Dark Winter four years earlier when the great river had
frozen from Andvari's Force almost down to the sea. Ottar
hurried down the long, sloping path toward the river, thread-
ing his way among the boulders and stunted, bushy trees. He
was perhaps seventy yards down from the last of the great
rapids that choked Andvari's Force, about twice as far down
from the place where he usually entered the water. That he
could hear the roar of the tumbling rapids as loud as ever
meant that the river must be running about as deep and swift
as it ever did.

He came to the edge of the river and stepped out onto a
large, flat stone that protruded out like a pier into the water.
A few tendrils of white mist curled up from the waves, and
patches of lazy fog had gathered in sheltered places. That
meant that the water was cold, nearly as cold as the morning
air, although that was of little concern to Ottar. In his animal
form he seldom felt any discomfort from the cold, even at
those times when he had to break the ice to swim.

He paused only a moment before he gathered himself up
and leaped as far out as he could. As he arched out over the
water his form shifted and flowed, and it was an immense
brown otter that slipped into the water. Andvari had taught
him many useful tricks, but the one that he appreciated the
most was the one that allowed him to transfer in all his
clothes and have them back warm and dry when he returned
to human form. That took the dread out of leaving the water
on cold days.

The river closed about him as he dove into its depths. The
river was swift, treacherously swift and turbulent. No human
could have survived long in that swirling flood, but for an
otter it was a place of play and delight. He swam out into the
center of the course and dived, forcing his way down into the
depths while the current lifted and carried him along. He
thought that there must be nothing so close to flying free on
the wing as when he dived into the river's swiftest channel
and allowed it to catapult him through the rapids, half swimming and half riding that powerful blast of water.

As he neared the end of the course the channel began to
carry him down into the depths. Darkness closed in about him
quickly, for the morning sun was still behind the mountains to
the east and there was no direct light to penetrate the depths.

In the full daylight this course would be as clear as crystal
and as cool and bubbling as the costly white wines from the
lowlands. But he had no fear of swimming this course even in
complete darkness, for he had an otter's feel for the currents
and eddies, and his stiff whiskers could feel the shift and pull
of water around hidden rocks. There was no part of the world
he knew as well as the Rhine's rocky bed.

The channel dissipated and he swam off into the calmer
waters near the bank. Suddenly he saw a faint but piercing
glow approaching from behind, and he turned and launched
himself toward that light. He came at it swiftly from behind,
and soon saw that an immense pike swam lazily at the core of
that golden radiance. The fish saw him only a moment later
and darted toward the bank. But the chase was close, for
Ottar was only ten feet behind when the chase came to a
surprising end. The pike broke the surface near the bank and
threw itself well into the air with a mighty leap. As it sailed
in a graceful arch above the water its form changed, and it
was Andvari the dwarf who landed atop a large, flat stone
like a tiny island just out from the bank. He spun about to
glare at the otter, its head lifted up above the waves to stare
back at him.

"Ottar, is that you?" he asked uncertainly.

"Of course it is me," Ottar replied. He had the advantage
of being able to speak in his animal form, if in a shrill,
chittery voice. "Did you think that one of your mythical sea
otters was after you?"

"Oh, one can never know," Andvari insisted, settling
himself on the stone. "I have seen enough sea otters—real
sea otters, mind you—at such times as I have left the Rhine.
One even chased me, just as you are fond of doing. And
twice I have indeed seen them nearly this far up the river, so I
do not take chances."

"So you say," Ottar said as he began to back slowly away.
"But I suspect that you are more afraid of restless ghosts
chasing you for stealing their funeral gold."

"Ha! I have no fear of ghosts!" Andvari declared. "And
dead men have no need for gold. I do."

Ottar, who had paused to look back, lifted his head even
higher above the waves. "All right, then. But you still watch
out. Some day you will be so busy hunting gold in the

riverbed that one of your mythical sea otters really will eat you."

"Mythical?" the dwarf demanded in mock anger. "Listen to this! First the child gives me advice, and then he questions my word. Some day you will meet a sea otter, an otter-maiden, and you will fall in love and raise a litter in a hole in the bank."

Ottar stared back at the dwarf. "Surely you jest! If we had the habits of our animal forms, then you would have swum up river to spawn a long time ago."

Andvari then proceeded to hurl a string of choice insults at the boy, and he meant some of the lesser names he used. But Ottar did not hear, for he had dived beneath the waves and disappeared.

Now by strangest chance, Odhinn, Thor and Loki were traveling through Midhgardh that same morning, and had indeed camped for the night not very far away. The Lord of Asgardh was becoming concerned by reports that many evil creatures, especially dragons, had been making their way into Midhgardh in the past few years, and he had come with the others to look for himself. They had camped that night beneath the trees only a short distance from the lower rapids of Andvari's Force, and were still packing their gear when Loki hurried down the bank for water. A few minutes later they were startled by the sight of him hurrying back, obviously excited about something. He was running in a half-crouch, so that he was loping along like some bow-legged troll, alternately waving his arms and signaling for them to be quiet.

"You wanted to know of anything strange?" he demanded in a hoarse voice best described as a shouted whisper as he slipped to a stop before them. "Well, I have just seen something strange! There is a ferret in the river. A giant ferret, as big as Sinir if not larger. And in the river!"

Thor crossed his arms and snorted. "Is that strange? You know that Sinir spends the summer in the fountain. The horses always complain, because they like to drink there."

"Ferrets everywhere," Sleipnir, Odhinn's flying mount, added. "And who wants to drink their bathwater?"

"No! No!" Loki was jumping in exasperation. "This is a

big ferret, a great deal larger than they get here. And it's on its back, in the water. Sleeping!''

"Sleeping on its back in the water? Why did you not say so?'' Sleipnir said, and snorted much the way Redbeard had. "Now that is odd.''

"Oh, shut up!'' Loki snapped, then turned to Odhinn. "Will you not come and see? I do not come here often, but I know that it does not belong in this world.''

"Yes, I do want to see,'' Odhinn agreed.

They followed him down to the edge of the bank, where they paused in hiding behind a hedge of tall, thick bushes, and peered through an opening at the river on just the other side. There indeed they saw an animal, lying blissfully asleep on its back in the center of a small, tree-shaded cove. There were no currents here to carry it away, except perhaps for the faintest trace of a circular movement that kept it in the very center of the cove. It knew that it was safe there from both predators on the shore and from being carried away into the rapids.

Thor crossed his arms and snorted again. "It is obvious that you really do not come to Midhgardh often. That is an otter, not a ferret.''

"Oh,'' Loki said meekly, as if that explained everything.

"Now wait,'' Odhinn said. "That beast is several times larger than any ordinary otter of this world, and I do not believe that it is a sea otter either. There is indeed something strange here.''

"Do you think that it might have come in through one of the lesser world-gates?'' Thor asked. "From Jotunheim, if the size is any indication.''

"That is likely,'' Odhinn agreed. "I wish that we could take it back to Asgardh with us for Idhunn to identify.''

"That is easily done,'' Loki said, and bent to retrieve a large, round stone. Before Odhinn could stop him, he threw it at the otter. The stone flew straight and true, and hit the otter almost squarely on top of the head. There was a faint hollow, wooden sound and the animal bobbed somewhat in the water but remained on its back, nor did it move thereafter. There was no doubt that it was dead.

"Loki, that was an ill deed,'' Odhinn said sternly. "If you had waited, I would have told you that I thought the otter to be a landvaeta, or perhaps something similar. There was something about its actions that suggest to me that it was intelligent.''

"You worry too much," Loki said scornfully, not wishing to discuss it. "At least now we can take the hide back to Idhunn, for her to do what she can with it."

"And how do you plan to get it?" Thor asked. "The thing is twenty feet from shore."

Loki turned to look at the horses, which had followed them down to the bank to watch. He singled out his own. "You! Go fetch that otter."

"Ha! Do I look like a dog? You go fetch it."

"I meant for you to fly."

"And I meant for you to swim."

"Hold it!" Thor said, chuckling softly. "Give me a moment, and I will get it for you."

He went to his horse and took from the saddle a length of slender rope. With this in hand he walked a third of the way around the circular cove, until he came to a place where the bank was unobscured by brush and rocks. But there he paused, for they saw three large salmon lying in a row on the thick grass near the edge of the bank.

"It seems more and more that my fears are true," Odhinn said. "That was an intelligent being you slayed. Only ill will come of it."

"That means nothing," Loki insisted. "And what if it does? By its size it was of Jotunheim, and that means that it was an enemy, a spy. But I do not see what difference it makes, now that it's dead."

"Then retrieve the hide for Idhunn's study, and let us be on our way."

Odhinn turned and walked away, and now Thor came up to the edge of the bank. He made a noose in the end of the rope, and with this he snared the otter and drew it in to shore. But after that he would have nothing more to do with it and followed after Odhinn, leaving Loki to take the hide. He found Odhinn standing on the rocks a little way up the river, staring in the direction of the great falls that they could hear in the distance.

"Was it a spy?" he asked bluntly, for he was never subtle. "And if so, then who could it be spying upon out here?"

"Who indeed?" Odhinn asked. "Behind that falls lies River Hall, the only great dwarf-mansion in Midhgardh. Andvari, the smith, is lord of that hall, and he is a small and stunted creature and wealthy beyond compare. And that is also strange. Perhaps strange attracts strange, so that one who has no business in this world has come to spy upon another."

"Oh," Thor muttered, looking upriver. "And will we speak with him?"

"Andvari? We would get nothing from him," Odhinn said, almost scornfully. "Brynhild reports that he seldom leaves his hall. He spends his days at his forge and his nights counting his gold, and he takes no heed of the world outside his door."

"Hey! Come along, you dodderers!" Loki called from the road. "I have it, so we can go now."

"We can go now?" Thor muttered into his beard and they started toward the road. "When did this become his party?"

CHAPTER TWO

Unwelcome Guests

H reidmar's holding was a small one, nestled into the northern portion of a long but shallow cut within the towering cliffs of stone that bordered it on three sides. There was but a great hall atop a low hill, a carpenter's shed large enough to house a sea-going knorr, twice a score of lesser dwellings and half as many barns. There was a long stretch of sand-blanketed beach, enough for a fleet of ships to draw up, and a short pier that had been erected in calmer, more sheltered waters. The native woods still enclosed the holding and so completely hid it that a ship on the river might pass it at night without anyone aboard ever knowing it was there. But there was no danger of that, for lights were placed out on the pier every night to welcome and guide ships.

Odhinn and his companions rode out of the forest along the portage road to River Hall even as the morning sun was climbing over the mountains. At first it seemed that no one saw them, but as they drew nearer to the holding people began to stop and stare, and others came out of their houses to look. For there was no denying who these travelers were, not when they looked upon Thor, his hammer in his belt, or Sleipnir with his eight legs trotting in unison.

Hreidmar himself hurried out to greet them as they rode up to the great hall. He was an older man in appearance, but not so much that he would have been called elderly in spite of his snow-white hair and beard. At one time he must have been a man of powerful build, for he still stood tall and straight. Only the slightest hesitation as he started down the broad steps indicated that he had grown too old for sword and armor. Here indeed was one who deserved to be called a lord among men, who could command respect with a kind word and a smile and yet be firm and just in his decisions.

He welcomed them most graciously and invited them to dinner, and to rest for the night if they would. Odhinn knew that he could not delay long, for he planned to be five hundred miles away by nightfall. But he did indeed wish to speak with Hreidmar, and a brief stop for lunch would provide a good excuse. Hreidmar's landing was the final stop for all traffic coming up the river, and for all the news and gossip for the length of the river and beyond; if odd creatures were abroad in Midhgardh, then some tale of it might well be found here.

Hreidmar's hall was not like that of many other lordlings. Elsewhere a lord's men would be seated on benches about a large table, drinking and laughing and singing loudly. Here the folk, both men and women, were free to sit at ease in the evening hours, to talk softly or to listen to music or stories. It seemed more like a home, peaceful and comforting, even to those who were visiting for their first time. It was hard for some to believe that these were the best warriors along the Rhine, but Hreidmar and his people were of a nobler stock than most.

A handful of servants entered with them and hurried to the task of preparing dinner. The three visitors took chairs that were farthest from the fire, not caring for the heat, allowing Hreidmar the nearer chair since he apparently did enjoy the gentle warmth. Odhinn saw that the older warrior was not so old as he seemed, but forced into an earlier retirement than he would have wished by a growing pain in his joints. A young girl brought them cups of mead while they waited.

"I must say that I am honored by your visit," Hreidmar began immediately. "But I also know that you did not come all this way just to confer with an old warrior who has outlived his time.''

"Now you should know better than that," Odhinn scolded him lightly. "It might perhaps seem fitting that heroes of the old tales should die in honorable battle, but you and I both know that it is strenuous work and a good warrior deserves a few quiet years of rest. And I also deem that you are a wise man; the world never has enough of those. But I did indeed come to confer with you."

"Did you indeed?" Hreidmar was rather surprised to hear that. "What might I know that you would need to hear?"

"Just any rumor you might have heard of strange creatures where they do not belong," Odhinn explained. "Rumor has it that such things have been coming into this realm, more than ever before."

"Yes, I have indeed heard such rumors," Hreidmar agreed, surprised with himself. "Yes, they do say that there are bands of dark elves raiding the smaller holding to the east and north, and trolls waylaying traders in the far north. Such things have not been seen along the Rhine, at least not yet, and I am thankful of that."

"It is the Valkyries who deserve that thanks. They have been hunting down such invaders every night, and steadily cutting away at their numbers. No, my concern here is for spies, and other strange creatures who would do small mischief and disappear into the night. Landvaetir for the most part, not too unlike animals you may have known all your life, but many times larger than usual. They are often seen in the form of large hunting birds, or animal forms such as badgers, ferrets, stoats or . . . otters."

Hreidmar was obviously startled at the mention of that last, but calmed himself quickly and hid his surprise. "No, we have seen no such animals except those that belong here."

But Odhinn knew that to be untrue; the giant otter was known to the lord of this holding. And yet he could not understand why Hreidmar would wish to hide that, unless the landvaeta had dwelled in Andvari's Force for so long that it was considered a protector and bringer of luck. Men often did not know that landvaetir served only those who knew how to summon them, as did the giants.

"But what would such creatures be spying upon, so far up the river?" he asked suddenly.

"Why, the richest prize of all the Rhine," Odhinn explained. "Giants and dragons both hold dear thoughts of raiding one of the great dwarf-mansions, but those of Nidhavellir are too well protected. But River Hall has no such armies to protect it; only a small force at best."

They talked of that and other matters for some time, although Odhinn did not press for an answer concerning the otter, until they were called to dinner. Several trestle tables were set up in the main hall, piled high with food and drink while servants brought still more. A great many people were taking their places at the table, mostly the unattached warriors and craftsmen of the hold. The three visitors were given places of honor at the main table, though Odhinn insisted that Hreidmar should not surrender his usual place.

Everyone was quickly seated and the last of the food was brought to the table. It was a common enough dinner, but it was good and plentiful and the travelers had no cause to complain. There was fish from the river, and meat, and bread that was still hot from the oven. But there was little else, for the people of Midhgardh did not as a rule enjoy a great variety. But Odhinn had been in Midhgardh often enough to know that they did indeed eat better than most.

Dinner was over and the tables were being cleared away when the door of the hall opened and two young men stepped in. Odhinn did not have to ask, for he could see clearly that the taller of the pair was Fafnir, so much did he appear to be a younger version of his father. They quickly hung their cloaks over pegs beside the door and walked over to where their father sat with his guests beside the fire.

"Ah, so there you are," Hreidmar said, looking up. "We have some very important visitors today."

"So I have been told," Fafnir said, and bowed politely. "Good day to you all, lords of Asgardh. Had we known, we would have hurried home sooner."

"Have you seen nothing of your brother?" Hreidmar interrupted.

"Ottar?" Fafnir asked. "No, not since dawn. He went with us down to the river, as we were leaving for River Hall. But we did not see him on the way back just now."

"What could he be doing down at the river all morning?" Thor asked. "Is he fishing?"

"Fishing, but mostly swimming," Hreidmar explained. "Ottar has the gift of shape-changing. He can, at will, take the form of an unusually large otter, and his one great delight is to swim and play in the river while he wears his animal form."

"Why, is that not odd?" Thor remarked. "Loki killed an otter in the river this very morning, not fifteen miles upstream."

Then he paused, seeing the stricken looks of both Odhinn and Loki, and he knew what they had already guessed. Fafnir had risen from his seat and stood with his hand almost on the hilt of his sword, as if only remembering who it was he would have drawn weapon against stayed his hand. Hreidmar looked up at him, the younger man removed his hand and seated himself. But for several long moments Hreidmar only sat in silence, his expression vacant and remote, as if no emotion could push past the barrier of shock for what he had heard. The three travelers waited apprehensively, and for once Loki looked very small and frightened.

"These evil creatures you spoke of," Hreidmar said without looking up. "Is there perhaps some mistake?"

"I fear not," Odhinn replied slowly. "I had asked you of such things only because we had seen the otter so near. Your son is dead."

Hreidmar nodded slowly, staring into the fire. Still there was no indication of what he thought or felt. The hall cleared in an unnatural silence while he continued to sit in wordless grief and stare into the flames. Gradually his blank expression gave way to one of loss and sadness, and it seemed as though he grew years older in those passing minutes. The last person left the hall and the door closed with a hollow boom, overly loud in the stillness of the empty room. At that sound Hreidmar stirred and rose with considerable effort. He walked slowly over to open the door and looked out across the holding, down to the dark waters of the river. Odhinn, who alone dared to follow, stood in patient silence behind him.

"My friend, I know of no words or deeds that would truly make up for what has been taken from you," he said after some time. "Neither I nor my companions ever meant you any harm. But even we are not immune to misfortune, whether we bring it upon ourselves or others. Is there any favor that I might grant you or any payment I might make? For if it is within my power, I will grant it freely as a token of our good will.''

Hreidmar shook his head sadly. ''No, I ask no weregild for my son, for I do not hold you or anyone to blame. Nor do I say that because of who you are, for it would be the same for anyone.''

He paused, and sighed in helplessness before turning to walk slowly back to the fire. ''I knew, you understand. I knew from the first day that Ottar went alone into the river that he would be easy prey for any hunter's arrow. And with merchants coming and going most of the year, the danger was a hundredfold. Who would not have tried at so tempting a target, an otter many times as large as he should be, unafraid and perhaps careless in his joy. I know that I would not have stayed my hand, if I knew not the secret. Judging by that, I knew that I could not blame the one who slew him in ignorance, meaning no harm.''

Hreidmar lowered himself slowly into his chair, and returned to staring into the fire. ''I had thought, this past year, that Ottar's love of the river would win out, that he would go away to some wild and uninhabited region, and be safer there than he ever could be here. In my heart I did not want for him to go, but I knew that it would have been better for him if he had. Now it is too late.''

''No, not too late,'' Odhinn said suddenly. ''This much at least I can do for you. I can call forth the Valkyrie Brynhild, who rides through the mortal realms on her nightly patrols. I shall bid her to seek out the spirit of your son and bear him to Asgardh, even as my Valkyries have brought me so many valiant warriors. And there Idhunn will restore him to eternal life. Thus for the few years that he has been robbed of in this world, I can give him back an eternity of life and happiness.''

''You . . . you will do this?'' Hreidmar asked hesitantly.

''I will do it gladly. Only I cannot return him to you here. One who has in truth been dead would always be easy prey for the death-maidens of Nifheim, and they would steal away his soul from his living body to take in tribute to their queen, Hel. But I will have him taken into the elf-world, to the great river Glaervatna where King Alflysa dwells in his white palace, and Ottar will be forever under the protection of the elves. Nor can the death-maidens reach him there, for death itself cannot come into the undying realm. Would that help to pay the debt I owe you?''

"My Lord Odhinn, that is more than I could have hoped for.''

"Then so it shall be,'' Odhinn declared. "For I do not forget that I owe Ottar an even greater debt for what was done to him. Come with me, for Ottar is in danger every moment that we delay.''

Then Odhinn took up his spear and hurried the others outside, and standing upon a low hill near the hall, he bade Thor to blow the notes of summons upon the horn that he wore at his belt. For it was indeed a magic horn, such as all of the Valkyries carried, and its notes carried soundless upon the winds throughout Midhgardh and even into the other realms. Several minutes passed as the Aesir watched and waited, until a dark, violent storm raced through the mountains to the east and descended swiftly toward the holding. Many of the mortal folk drew back fearfully, but Odhinn waited patiently. At last he lifted his spear, and a small figure astride a flying horse dropped out of that churning mass of clouds to drop toward them, a Valkyrie in silver armor and a long cloak of sky-blue.

Brynhild brought her horse to a halt not twenty yards away, still prancing impatiently in mid-air. Then Odhinn called out to her his instructions for her to find the spirit of the boy Ottar, and have him returned to life. Brynhild lifted high her own spear, and lightning shot down from the clouds to strike its tip and set it aflame with golden light. Then she turned and raced away on her errand, disappearing quickly again into the clouds.

"My friend, I have done the best for you that I can,'' Odhinn said as he turned back to Hreidmar. "Brynhild is the wisest and most capable of my Valkyries, even if she is not their captain. She will find Ottar if anyone can, even if she must ride into the realm of the dead.''

Brynhild did not have to search long for the place of Ottar's untimely death, for all death drew her like a scent. But she found to her dismay that she was only minutes late, for the boy's spirit had only just been drawn into the realm of death. She turned without hesitation and sent Glaerfaxi hurtling through the upper ways back to Asgardh. The great horse took the world-gate at a run and landed on the pavement before the portals of Asgardh. Then she took her own horn from where it hung at her saddle and blew the horn-call of the Valkyries, summoning her sisters from wherever they might be.

Sigrune, the captain of the Valkyries, was the first to come. She threw open the golden portal, weapons in hand, then leaped back as Radgird hurtled through the open world-gate to bring her horse down nearby.

"Brynhild, what is your need?" Sigrune called. "Why have you summoned the Valkyries?"

"I ride at Odhinn's command," Brynhild replied, and quickly explained her errand.

"That is a dangerous path," Sigrune commented thoughtfully.

"That I know well. I can deal with this death-maiden, for our powers have grown since days when we were of their kind. But, even so, I would not ride into that realm alone."

Sigrune nodded. "That is wise. But I can order no member of our company to take that path. Any who accompanies you must go by her free will."

"I will ride with you!" Radgird proclaimed from her saddle, lifting her spear.

"And so shall I," Sigrune added. "But the task remains yours, Brynhild. Command us as you will; we ride when you are ready."

Brynhild was off again within minutes, this time with a following of seven Valkyries. None who came to her call would remain behind, for the death-realm held no terror for them so long as they rode in force. Not even the Allfather would have lightly taken that path which the Valkyries rode without hesitation, for this was the place of their origin. The beings of Nifheim were neither good nor evil, but in a curious and often dangerous manner aloof from such concerns; the Valkyries were set apart from their sisters in that they had pledged themselves to serving good.

Nifheim lay before them like an entire world encased within a cavern of vast size. The land below was of bare rock,

smooth and flowing yet uncut by wind or water, while bizarre
things grew there that were as much rock as plant. And above
hovered a low ceiling of dark, unmoving clouds, like the
black smoke and ash of a volcano. The world-gate stood open
just above ground level, and from it a strange white road
snaked away through the low, flowing hills. No one, not even
the Valkyries, knew who had made the roads and why, for
the only travelers, the death-maidens, rode flying steeds.
Most likely they traced familiar runs for the death-maidens,
for all roads had their beginning and end with the great road
that ran to the gate of Hel's fortress.

Brynhild followed it now, for the road from the gate was
one of the major ones and the one she sought lay ahead. She
fastened down her helmet and urged her mount to all the
speed she dared. The others trailed out somewhat behind,
giving their horses room to fly. Sigrune rode just behind her,
ready to give her power in any sudden need. But Brynhild
took the vanguard, her spear held out as if its point cut a
path through the air before them.

Time passed as swiftly as the desolate land that passed
steadily beneath them. Brynhild made contact with the one
she sought, the spirit of the boy Ottar. But at that same
instant the death-rider sensed her. There was an instant of
open contact between them, and Brynhild felt the other's
astonishment and fear as she discovered who trailed her. Then
the contact broke, and from that moment the chase began.
The death-maiden's horse shot ahead with speed almost equal
to that of the children of Svadilfari.

Almost, but not quite. Brynhild could see them now, a
girlish figure in black robes atop a shaggy beast that looked as
much dragon as horse. Nor did that strange mount have any
endurance. Brynhild pulled slowly to the left and circled
around to intercept her prey. She held forth her spear and a
bolt of raw power shot from its tip to cross the path of her
quarry. So near did that bolt come that both horse and rider
drew back in alarm. With that the death-rider was forced to
admit defeat and instructed her horse to circle down and land
on the crest of a low hill.

Glaerfaxi descended to land facing the death-maiden, while
the others moved to encircle her. Now Brynhild saw, nearly
concealed in the folds of the girl's robe, a curious figure.

Most of the time it was a large otter, but at times its outline flickered to become that of a mortal boy.

"Hail, noble Valkyries!" the death-maiden proclaimed, although it was more a challenge than a greeting. "Fair hunting to you. It has been too long a time since we have seen you, sister."

"A long time indeed," Brynhild replied. "And it will surely be a long time before you will see us again. But for now we have business."

"So I had thought," the death-maiden replied defiantly. "Has it come to this? First you are traitors, and now thieves."

"You have what does not belong to you," Brynhild countered. "We seek to take him back, not to keep him for ourselves."

"And are you not content?" the other hissed in pure anger. "You have the advantage over us. You take the best and leave us what you do not want."

"We leave you far more than we take," Sigrune said. "We were once the same, and in most respects we still are. We ride at night, the same as you, and we are entitled to our share of the take."

"And now it seems that you are not content with the best, but come into our realm to steal from us."

"This is an exception," Brynhild insisted. "It has never happened before, nor is it likely to happen again. Now give me the mortal child."

"He is not mine to give. Beg your favors of Queen Hel."

Brynhild did not reply in words, but lowered her spear at the rebellious death-maiden. The point began to glow menacingly. The death-maiden's eyes widened in fear. She had too much respect for the Valkyrie's power, and she knew only too well that she was vulnerable while the boy was not.

"Take him, then," she hissed in rage as she tumbled the boy out of her saddle like a bag of garbage. "But ride quickly when you go, proud ones. Queen Hel is not tolerant of thieves."

"You might find that your mistress is much less concerned than you are," Brynhild said, then gestured with her spear. "Now go."

The death-maiden looked as if she wished to argue more, but her horse had greater discretion. He turned and leaped into the sky, and shot away as though the Valkyries still pursued him. Within moments they disappeared into the cavernous gloom of Nifheim.

Brynhild did not look up to watch her go. She turned to slip her spear into its saddle-strap, then pulled off her helmet and set it aside. Ottar, now wholly in his animal form, sat up on his haunches to watch her inquisitively. When he saw that the leader of these strange and rather daunting riders in heavy armor was in truth a young girl he smiled. Brynhild smiled in return and held out her hand.

"Come with me, Ottar," she said. "I will take you from this place, to a world where you will live in happiness and peace forever. Hurry now! There are evil things in this land. We must be away."

"But . . . will your horse be afraid of me?" Ottar asked hesitantly. "Most horses do not care for shape-changers."

"Surely not!" Glaerfaxi replied for himself. "As you can see, I am not an animal but a loyal servant of the Aesir. I know that you are neither dangerous nor evil, and I will carry you willingly."

Reassured that even the horses of these curious strangers were his friends, Ottar rushed forward and leaped up into Brynhild's arms. She pulled him around and set him before her in the saddle. Then she set on her helmet and put her arms protectively about the boy, even though he was in no danger or discomfort from the wind. Glaerfaxi leaped into the air and retraced their path to the gate at the same hurried pace. Soon the others caught up and set themselves protectively about Brynhild and her charge as if to shield them from sudden attack. The Valkyries rode with their spears drawn and ready.

"Will it be long?" Ottar asked after a minute.

"No, not long," the Valkyrie promised, and laughed when she saw his look of disappointment.

CHAPTER THREE

The Ottergild

"The deed is done," Odhinn announced to the mortals as they waited in Hriedmar's hall. "My debt to Ottar is paid. But the fact remains that he is lost to you just as surely as if he was dead, and that is a second debt that must be paid. What weregild would you ask for your loss?"

"Weregild?" Hreidmar asked with disbelief. "My Lord Odhinn, I consider myself better paid for my loss than I could have ever hoped. What more could I desire?"

"Not even yellow gold in payment for the trouble we have caused you?" the Allfather asked, and looked at the old man appraisingly. "Hreidmar, you are indeed an honest man. Your grief will not be eased by the tickling of your greed. But I want all matters settled between us, so that no one can say that you would not accept weregild from me because of who I am. Will you not accept some payment, for my sake?"

"My lord, what can I say? You have done so much for Ottar and myself already that I would be ill at ease taking additional payment from you."

"Then let us place the blame where it belongs," Odhinn declared. "Loki slew your son, even if it was an accident. I tried to stop him, even though I did not yet know the truth. But he was so certain of himself that he would not listen. True, I am his liegelord, and so responsible for all acts that he commits in my service. But what would you do with a liegeman who commits such irresponsible acts? This is not the first time.''

''Oh?'' Hreidmar asked, almost with fascination.

''Perhaps you have heard of the trouble he caused during the walling of Asgardh? Or perhaps you know also that he once helped the giant Thjatsi to steal Idhunn.''

''Yes, I had heard. But I had thought those only stories.''

''No, those things did indeed happen. And each time that Loki has had a hand in some evil deed, I have always seen that he is made to pay. That way he is very humble for some time to come. It seems to me that I should allow him to pay the weregild, and a goodly one at that. And you will be doing me a favor by accepting it.''

Loki, seated well to one side, cringed and turned pale.

Hreidmar turned away and worried upon that in his mind for some time. ''Only for that reason would I consider accepting this weregild. A small one, and I want it to be known that you insisted upon it. But you name the price.''

Odhinn considered that for a moment. ''Loki slew Ottar and took the hide; now let him pay for what he took. He will return to Asgardh and fetch enough gold to completely fill the hide, then cover it over so that not one hair can be seen.''

''What?'' Loki demanded in alarm and indignation. ''That is no small weregild! If I must be compelled to pay, at least let it be a fair price.''

''That is the price, and you will return with it before nightfall,'' Odhinn said sternly. ''You were acting in my service, and so your guilt becomes my own. Now you will do what is required of you and clear me of the guilt that you have brought upon me.''

''I simply will not do it. I cannot do it,'' Loki declared, crossing his arms and leaning sullenly against the table. ''It is not fair. That is many times what I would normally have to pay as weregild in this world, especially since I killed the boy accidentally. Let me pay a fair price and we will be gone.''

''You will pay what you can afford, and I know very well that the ottergild is but a fraction of the wealth you have hoarded," Odhinn insisted. "Then, if you pay enough to make you regret it, it may be a very long time before you act so irresponsibly again."

Some persuasion was needed before Loki reluctantly agreed to the task. He saddled his horse and the pair took to the sky at a brisk pace. His companions did not notice that he directed his horse south along the river rather than east toward the world-gate. Then, to the horse's mystification, they set down again on the portage road just above Andvari's Force. Loki leaped from his saddle and stood for a moment staring off at the swiftly flowing river. Then, to his horse's surprise, he began to walk down toward the water.

"Hey, Uncle Fox!" the horse called urgently. "Come back! We still have a task to perform."

"Then you do it!" Loki snapped peevishly. "We have plenty of time, nearly half a day to do an hour's work, and I for one am not ready to do it."

"Loki, you are a fool!" the horse called, but Loki was gone. He sighed heavily, as only a horse can. "But then, everyone knows that."

Loki paused in the clearing on the north side of the cove, the very place where he had first seen the otter. There was no hint of the tragedy that had occurred there only that morning. He did not greatly repent that deed; he never had and, as far as he was concerned, everything had already been set to right. He had told his horse the simple truth. He could not yet bring himself to part with so much of his hoarded gold, even if it was only a small portion of the whole. Worse yet, he could not bring himself to face the scorn of all Asgardh, the Aesir and the Vanir, the Valkyries at the gate and even the smart-mouthed horses.

He sat down in the grass with his back against a large stone, then took a gold coin out of his pocket to stare at it, brooding. The horse was right, as much as he hated to admit it. He had no choice. But, being Loki, he wondered if there might be an easier way. How much would the required amount of gold weigh? He wondered if he might be able to sneak into Asgardh quietly, collect it and be away before anyone knew. Not with the Valkyries watching the world-gate.

"Fox, are you finished brooding?" His horse had followed him down to the cove and stood watching him from a short distance away. "You would do better to get this over. I will help you. We can be in and out of Asgardh in a matter of minutes."

Loki looked up and frowned. "So you believe you know what I am thinking?"

"You are not hard to figure out. I have had you like a monkey on my back for a very long time now," the horse said, and regarded him closely. "Perhaps I could go myself. Sygyn would get the gold for me."

"You are a pest."

"I'm the closest thing to a conscience you have. Now you either come along or I will go myself. Right now!"

"Oh, very well. Hold your horses." Loki struggled up, then paused and frowned. "I can't believe what I just said."

With the horse's help, he resolved to get this over. He tossed the coin into the air and meant to catch it, but he was distracted of thought and missed. His open hand knocked it out over the cove and it hit the water with a loud plunk. Loki hurried to the edge. He saw it immediately, for the water was shallow and very clear near the bank, lying on the bottom and glittering faintly in the sunlight.

Loki bent and was about to reach out to retrieve the gold. Just then it flashed unnaturally, not very brightly but enough to startle him. Then, as he sat in bemusement, the shadowy form of an unusually large fish flashed in to the bank, snapped up the coin in its mouth and disappeared with a thrust of his tail. Both Loki and the horse stared for a moment in complete mystification. Then Loki recalled that the coin was his, and he leaped up and swore in anger.

"That was most peculiar," the horse commented as Loki cursed and stomped.

"Peculiar?" Loki paused in his tantrum to stare. "Peculiar, did you say? I've been robbed by a toad-eating fish!"

"What does a fish want with gold anyway?"

"Nothing, horsewit! He just saw it flash and struck at it."

"No, not that gold," the horse said impatiently. "You were looking at the coin, but I saw the fish as it swam in and I tell you that it had a piece of gold on a chain or wire about its neck that glowed like a golden lamp. There is something very odd about this, something . . . unnatural. Might I even say magical?"

Loki thought about that and nodded. "You might. But how do we find out about it without throwing coins into the river for just a glimpse of this very large and greedy fish?"

He thought about that a moment, and remembered the spells that Idhunn had taught him for giving the gift of speech to common animals. He glanced about and saw a kingfisher perched on a branch on the opposite side of the cove. Who would know the river better? He called forth the most subtle powers at his command and cast the spell. The kingfisher turned to look at him, cocking its tufted head inquisitively, then flew across the cove to settle on his wrist.

"Speak to me, friend," Loki said soothingly. "Tell me what you know of this strange fish that hunts the waters of the Rhine for gold, and wears gold about its neck."

He waited, while the bird seemed to collect its thoughts. Then, when he had almost decided that this one did not know the answer, the kingfisher lifted its head and spoke in a high, sing-song pitch very much like a bird-call.

> "Andvari the dwarf is the one you seek;
> He dwells in dark tunnels beneath the falls.
> This secret he guards, that at will
> He takes on the form of a fish.
> In that shape he hunts the river's bed
> For the gold that he cherishes dear!"

"A shape-changer! Does this river crawl with the like?" Loki muttered to himself, then looked at the bird. "My friend, great help you have been to me. Tell me now how I might capture this dwarf."

> "Bright gold is the thing
> That captures his eye;
> Give him what he seeks
> And he shall come forth.
> In the morning's and dusk's soft light
> He prowls the river's deep path.
> When he steals the gold
> be quick with your net;
> Andvari will then be yours!"

"Ah, an excellent plan! You are a very smart bird!" Loki cried with delight, and held out his arm for the bird to fly away. "Thank you, little friend. Go with my gratitude."

The kingfisher flew off across the cove and lighted upon the very branch he had left. Loki took no more notice of it. He rushed over to where the horse stood, watching silently, and pulled open the saddlepack to look inside. The horse bent his neck around to stare at him.

"What are you doing now?" he asked.

"I am going to make a net," Loki replied as he pulled out a ball of thick string. He carried it back over to the bank and sat down in the grass, and began to measure out lengths of string that he cut with his knife.

"Do you know how?"

"I can put something together that will work."

The horse came a couple of steps closer. "The last question, I suppose, is why? Although I can guess well enough."

"If you can guess, then do not ask," Loki said. "That is, according to Odhinn, one very wealthy fish. He will lend me the gold I need, if I can just find some way to talk to him."

You might just walk up to the door of River Hall and knock, the horse thought. But he kept that to himself. If Loki intended to do this ill-advised deed, then let him do it the hard way. That was what came from listening to birds.

"This is more trouble than it is worth," he said instead.

"It saves me a great deal of embarrassment," Loki corrected him without looking up from his work.

"The trouble that I was referring to comes later."

"Great stars, what a nag!" Loki declared. He looked up, startled, and chuckled softly at his own pun. The horse, insulted, walked away.

Loki hurried, but over two hours had passed before he had something that at last vaguely resembled a net. He used a long stick to lay it out carefully on the floor of the cove, mostly hidden from view in the sand and gravel almost ten feet out from the bank. The ends of the net circled well around to either side, where they were attached to stout ropes. Last of all he laid out the bait, two more gold coins, and he set them among the rocks in such a way that Andvari could see them clearly but could not simply snap them up on the

run. Then, with his trap carefully laid, he sat down on the
bank with the ropes in his hand and watched.

And so the afternoon passed, and the sun sank down
behind the lower mountains of the west. Evening was approaching, and Loki's time was quickly running out. If Andvari
did not come soon, then he would have to abandon this game
and collect his own gold in Asgardh. He had known that from
the start and had at the time considered it a fair deal, but now
he liked it no better than before. The horse came and stared
over his shoulder, caught up in the suspense against his better
judgment.

"Here he comes," the horse said very softly, and began to
move back from the bank so that he would not be seen.

Loki looked up and saw a faint golden light darting into the
cove from the open river. Then he saw the two gold coins
glitter in response, as if calling out to that hunter of the
river's dark ways. But the golden light did not move in to
take that bait. It shifted back and forth through the center of
the cove as if the dwarf feared some trap. Loki wondered if
the same magic that found the gold for him also served to
protect him.

The light suddenly turned and darted in, so swift that Loki
almost leaped back in surprise. He first saw the fish as it
came into the shallows, a dark shape almost as big as himself,
struggling to get its head down into the rocks to snap up the
coins. He took firm hold of the ends of the net and pulled
back as hard as he could, hoping that the slender strands and
makeshift rigging would hold. Why had he not asked the
kingfisher just how big Andvari was in his aquatic form?

It was as if something had exploded in the water just below
the bank. Spray shot out as if from a fountain, and the water
rolled and churned furiously. Loki realized in an instant that
he had made a serious miscalculation. He had known enough
to expect a big fish, big by acceptable pike standards. What
he found in his net was larger than even Sinir, the ferret, and
weighed perhaps two-thirds as much as himself. The hunter
nearly became the prey in that first instant, but he was just
barely able to keep his net in his hands and himself ashore.

Even then he would not have succeeded, but his horse
came to his rescue. He approached from Loki's right and took
firm hold of that end of the net in his teeth, leaving Loki free

to take the other end of the net in both hands. After that it was a very simple matter for them to haul the struggling pike up onto the bank. They pulled him well away from the water, too far for him to work his way back, and left him lying in the grass still tangled in the net.

Loki sat down on his favorite rock and waited as the pike struggled to free himself, twisting and thrashing like any real fish thrown up on the bank. Of course, Andvari would do his best to conceal his true identity and free himself if he could without changing back. But it could not go on for long. A shape-changer he was, but the pike could not breathe air any better than the dwarf could breathe water.

After a minute the pike suddenly ceased to struggle and lay gasping for the very air that was strangling him, then shifted back to his true form. Loki was on him immediately, a knife held to his throat. Andvari was long of hair but sparse of beard, still fairly young but not particularly handsome. He was dressed in dry clothes as rich as those of the dwarf-lords of Nidhavellir. And at that moment his eyes were as round and glazed as they had been on the fish. Loki put his knife away and pulled Andvari to his feet, for the Dvergar continued to gasp loudly until his breath returned. Loki did not travel often in Nidhavellir, for dwarves seldom partied. But he knew enough to see that this one was smaller and heavier of frame than most, and slightly hunched of back. He was more comely as a fish.

"Ah, so you are the renowned Lord Andvari of River Hall," Loki said. "A very wise and prosperous dwarf, by all accounts. It is well that I saved you."

"Oh? And perhaps you expect some reward for 'rescuing' me?" the Dvergar asked, overcoming his fear. He eyed his "rescuer" closely. "Odd, but you do not look like an ordinary robber. In fact, you look like a tree-hopping wood-elf."

"Do I indeed?"

"Yes, you do. I am surprised, even disillusioned. But I suppose that even an elf can be down on his luck." The dwarf shrugged helplessly. "Very well. Take what you will. You will find that I am carrying little of any great value."

"Oh, no! Hardly that, my good dwarf!" Loki cried as if in distress. "I am not here to rob you. In fact, I have a terrible problem, and I need your help."

"Do you now?"

"Oh, yes! You see, I have had a part in a nasty accident. A boy was killed, slain by mistake, taken for an animal. An honest mistake. But now there is a weregild to be paid to a foolish old man, because an even older fool insists upon it."

"Most regrettable."

"Terribly regrettable," Loki agreed. "For you see, it is such a long way home, and I am supposed to be back with the payment this very nightfall, and I am under bonds that cannot be broken. I was hoping that such a wealthy lord as yourself would be able to extend to me a loan."

"A permanent loan?"

"Excellent terms!"

"And how much do you require? I am, after all, a dwarf of limited means, living alone here in the wilderness. Perhaps I do not have enough to cover it."

"Oh, but that would be tragic!" Loki shook his head with regret. "But do not worry. I need only enough to fill the skin of an animal about the size of a wolf, and then cover it over completely."

"That is an odd way of paying a weregild," Andvari remarked, but his mind was on other thoughts. That might require the contents of two full chests, and perhaps a little more. He had a storeroom full of such chests, enough to stuff the hide of a small dragon.

"You can make the payment?" Loki asked.

"I . . . I suppose that I could," Andvari answered, although he had no intention of doing so if he could help it. He was quite willing to pay for his life, but escaping was the best bargain of all. The only problem was that this smooth-mannered robber was between himself and the river, while the horse stood peering over his shoulder in a most disconcerting fashion. Had he not seen that horse help in pulling him from the river?

"Then shall we not be on our way?" Loki suggested. "As I have said, my time is short. Do not think to delay me."

"Patience, my lord. It is not that simple," the dwarf said in desperation, shifting nervously. "The only entrance to my hall is under water. I built it that way, so that I alone could come and go through its gate. Surely you cannot blame me, living alone in the wilderness of a strange land.

I will go and fetch the gold you require. You have my word on that.''

"Is that a fact?''

"So it is, my lord!'' Andvari insisted, shaking now with fright. "Do you think that I would deceive you?''

"I have good reason to believe it.''

"Oh, no, my lord!'' Andvari feigned indignation now, thinly covering his fear. "Surely you cannot mean that.''

"In fact, I do,'' Loki said, and drew his sword. "For I know very well that merchants come from afar to trade for the products of your forge. And I know that behind us is the road that leads to your hall. I do not believe that road descends to the river's bed around the next bend. Do we go now to retrieve the payment? Decide quickly, for I am impatient.''

Andvari drew back in terror, but was brought up short by the horse. He swallowed nervously as his eyes began to resemble a fish's once again. "I believe that I will accept your bargain. If I keep my head, I may some day be able to recover my losses. We do say that a dead dwarf is the poorest dwarf of all.''

"Come along, then. Time is short,'' Loki said, and took the Dvergar by the arm to haul him over to the side of the horse. He pulled himself into the saddle, then reached down and lifted Andvari up with ease to set the dwarf in the saddle ahead of him.

"Away, my friend!'' Loki called. "Follow the road to its end, for there we will find the gate to River Hall, even as I have said.''

With that the horse turned, ran a few steps and leaped into the air. The sun was now below the western heights, and the length of the valley lay in deep shadows. The road was not hard to see. But still the horse stayed low and kept his speed well down, weaving in and out through the trees or along the faces of rocky cliffs when the way grew steep and narrow. But it was still too high and fast for Andvari, who did not care for horses even when they stayed on the ground. Shape-changers had a natural distrust of horses and the feeling was mutual, and his caution had been reinforced by a few hard lessons.

CHAPTER FOUR

In River Hall

By the time they reached River Hall, only a couple of minutes later, Andvari had figured a few things out for himself. Flying horses were understandably rare; as far as he knew, only the Aesir and their servants used such creatures. From that point he had little trouble figuring out just who his unwanted companion had to be. He found that he was not quite so surprised as he might have been had this been a story that he had heard from someone else.

The river valley ended suddenly in a wall of stone, divided up the center by a towering column of water. The whole of the river fell in a single narrow stream of almost a thousand feet, thundering as it crashed upon the rocks below. On the east side of the fall stood a small opening in the bare rock of the cliff face. It was round and rough in appearance, as if it was the exit of some natural cave and not the gate of a dwarfish mansion, most of which had heavy outer doors bearing the insignia of clan and trade. Perhaps it might have been overlooked, except that the portage trail ran directly up to it.

"Why, that looks as though it might be a door!" Loki said with obvious sarcasm. "Do you suppose that it is?"

"It does look like one," the horse agreed. "And yet I cannot easily believe it. The dwarf said that there is none, and I know that he is honest."

Andvari rolled his eyes and suppressed the urge to scream at them to shut up. The one thing that he hated worse than being called a liar was being caught in a lie.

The horse came to a stop on the road at the entrance of the tunnel. It did indeed look like a natural cave, cut by an underground stream, except that it was dry and the road continued as a narrow path inside. Loki lifted the dwarf from the saddle and dropped him to the ground, then jumped down beside him. He took Andvari by the collar, for the dwarf looked like a nervous rabbit about to bolt down his hole. He turned and peered within.

"Say, there does seem to be a light inside," he exclaimed. "Now who do you suppose would keep a light inside a cave?"

"Bat?" the horse suggested.

"Yes, bats!" Loki laughed. "You stay here. I will not be long."

"I had no intention of going in there."

"Shall we be done with this, my friend?" Loki drew his sword with a flourish and pointed it inside the cave. "After you."

Andvari reluctantly led the way down the dark passage while Loki followed at a cautious pace, the tip of his sword held to his captive's back. He had no wish to walk quickly into some hidden trap, while the dwarf's knees were too weak to carry him any swifter. The passage was dark, now that evening was falling outside, but suspiciously dry and free of debris. They soon came to a bend in the passage, and rounded an unusually sharp corner to find themselves facing a door of heavy timbers set in an iron frame. A lantern hung from a bracket beside it.

"Well, my short friend, will they answer if we knock?" Loki asked.

"Someone will come," Andvari replied vaguely.

"No doubt," Loki said suspiciously. "Then I will be around the corner. Just remember this."

He pointed toward the center of the door. The wood exploded into flames, and the metal band across the center snapped and curled back. Then, with a wave of his hand, the flames retreated and were gone.

"I do not become a fish or anything else, except angry," he said. "I could be through that door in an instant. Or that could be you, if you are not quick enough in shutting it behind you. Now why do you not knock?"

Andvari nodded, swallowing nervously, then turned and began pounding upon an unburned portion of the door. The hammering filled the passage and no doubt echoed through the length of River Hall. Loki thought that sufficient to raise anyone within and stepped back behind the corner.

There was quite a long wait before anyone came. Andvari stood at the door and shifted nervously, occasionally glancing back at the corner where Loki was watching him. Every time Loki would wave his sword menacingly, reminding him to turn around and look unconcerned. After a time they heard the heavy metal locking bar drawn back, and the door opened enough for a young dwarf, his servant Kuli, to peer out. Poor Kuli, hopelessly slow of wit, only stood and blinked.

Loki did not wait for the dwarves to make some move of their own. He stepped out and pulled the door from Kuli's hold, throwing it open. Then he used his sword to herd the pair inside and against the wall. Kuli looked mildly surprised, as if he had not yet figured out what was happening.

"That makes two," Loki said, smiling with satisfaction. "How many more rabbits are in this oversized warren?"

"Oh, there are only eight . . . dwarves, I mean, including ourselves. Yes, eight." Kuli replied. Andvari's sigh of exasperation confirmed that; he would have lied. Kuli rolled his eyes upward as he reflected. "Let me see. There is Lord Andvari. And myself, Kuli by name. . . ."

"Introductions will have to wait," Loki snapped impatiently. "For now, I want you to find everyone and bring them to whatever room your master keeps his treasure in. Can you do that?"

"Oh, yes sir!" Kuli agreed eagerly, and hurried off down the half-lit corridor. Loki sent him on his way with subtle encouragement, setting the point of his sword to the seat of the dwarf's pants. Kuli yelped and ran on to complete his task. Loki turned back to Andvari and indicated the way with his sword.

"If you would continue to lead the way," he said. "But remember this. I can avoid any trap or repel any ambush that might be set for me. But will you survive my anger?"

Andvari swallowed apprehensively and edged sideways along the wall until he was well past the sword. Then he turned and hurried on ahead, looking back often to be certain that he was staying ahead of the point on that weapon. The tunnel paralleled the outside wall of the cliff for some distance, for the major portions of River Hall were actually on the other side of the fall as well as higher up. Even so they were soon approaching the inhabited sections.

As Andvari hurried along, he began to wonder why this was happening. If the Rhinegold was his gift from the gods, then why would they punish him so? Perhaps it was a warning. If so, then he would learn his lesson well and accept his punishment with good grace. Anything was better than having to forfeit his gift; at least it had not come to that. He quietly slipped the gold and its light chain from around his collar and let it fall down inside his shirt as he hurried along in the lead. As long as he still possessed that, then he could win back everything he might lose.

He rounded the final corner and saw that half of his people had already gathered. They looked up, questioning and fearful, and so he lifted his head proudly and walked up to the door of that special storeroom, bringing out the key as he approached. He quickly unlocked the door and pulled it open, and stood patiently to one side. But Loki, mindful of the traps and tricks of vengeful dwarfs, indicated for them all to enter first.

What he saw when he stepped inside the room surprised him. Of course, there were no piles of gold or jewels lying in piles; dwarves were too cautious and tidy for that. But the chamber was almost completely full of chests, scores upon scores. They lined the walls from floor to ceiling, and stood in neatly stacked rows that left only narrow spaces for corridors between. There was only a small open space near the door, where the dwarves crowded to one side to leave the rest for Loki.

"My, but you have been busy!" Loki remarked.

Andvari shrugged. "The river hides the wealth of many

men, for those who are able to find it. And I have always made a fair profit in my years of trading.''

"You are a grave-robber," Loki said, eyeing him in disgust.

Andvari shrugged a second time. "I do not fear the ghosts of dead men. They are safely gone, and their gold is to be lost forever. To me, that is a terrible waste. You are the thief.''

Loki might not have even heard, which was as well for Andvari, but simply continued to stare about the room. He stirred suddenly and reached for a leather case that he carried at his side. He opened it and peered inside, but paused a moment to look over at the small group of dwarves before him. There were eight in all, so all were present. His attention centered on an old woman, so bent that she did not even stand above his waist.

"You! Do you sew?"

She took an uncertain step backward and would not look up. "Yes, my lord, I do. I make most of the clothes we have.''

"Then sew up this hide, as if you were making it to put back on the animal. Leave only one small opening so that we can fill it with gold.''

He pulled the hide from the pouch and laid it out on the floor. Andvari stood closely to one side, watching to see what manner of animal it was whose hide his treasure would have to fill. It was larger than he wished but not so large as he had feared, the fur rich and soft, deep brown in color. But then he saw what manner of pelt it was and he stopped, motionless, fearful of looking closer to see if his suspicions were correct. He bent slowly and reached down with a shaking hand to feel the edge of the pelt.

"I will need a stout needle and my other tools, and a slender leather thong with which to sew it,'' the old woman said.

"Fetch it, then. And be quick!''

The old woman hurried away. Loki followed her to the door, to see which way she went as she disappeared down the half-lit passage. When he turned back, he saw Andvari and the other dwarves gathered about the pelt as if it was the body of a fallen companion. Intrigued by such odd behavior, he approached slowly to stand behind Andvari, still bent over the fur.

"Where . . . from whence did you get this pelt?" Andvari demanded without looking up, his voice low and harsh with accusation and grief.

"From an otter of the river, who I took to be a landvaeta and a spy of the Jotnar," Loki replied truthfully, out of fascination. "But he turned out not to be an otter at all, and so I found myself required to pay a weregild to his father."

"Then you are a murderer as well as a thief!" Andvari replied sharply, then seemed almost to forget that Loki stood over him as he stroked the thick fur gently. "Ottar, you were almost like a son to me. We shared a gift, and you indulged a foolish dwarf in his loneliness. Where are you now?"

He rose slowly and stood remote and passive, his back to Loki. "I must share equally in the blame for his death, for I taught him how to command his gift and I encouraged him to use it, knowing well the danger. But it seems that I alone must pay the weregild."

"The guilt in this is a matter of no concern to me," Loki said impersonally. "But if it is of any comfort to you, then know that Odhinn took pity on the boy. The Valkyries took him to Asgardh, where he is being restored to immortal life."

"And can I believe you?" the dwarf asked harshly.

"In spite of what legend might say of me, I am not so low that I would tell you such things to torment you in your grief. He is alive and well; ask that of his father tomorrow. Hreidmar will tell you a tale that will cause you to wonder, and he may pity you enough to return your gold."

The old woman returned, half running, with her tools. She sat down on the floor without a word and took the fur in her lap. She carefully matched the cut edges of the pelt together, and began to sew them securely with slender leather thong. It did not take her long to finish, such was her skill. She knotted the cord and cut it, then passed the pelt into Loki's waiting hands. He checked each of the seams quickly to insure that they would not fail under the weight of the gold, then forced the thing into Kuli's unwilling hands.

"Stuff it full with gold," Loki commanded. "Coins, rings and other small things for the inside."

Kuli looked to his master, who turned his head and nodded tersely. With the help of several of the others, Kuli found a chest that was filled to the lid with coins and brought it out into the open. He held the hide open while two of the journeymen smiths began pouring handfuls of coins into it. The hide was soon stuffed tight with gold and the opening was sewn shut. The dwarves carefully turned it over and set it upright, where it stood, sagging and lumpy, half-supported by its legs but bent in the middle. Andvari glanced over his shoulder at it but turned quickly away, unable to look upon that cruel representation of what Ottar had been. He found little comfort in the thought that the boy still lived in another world.

Then a second chest was brought out, this one filled with stacks of small gold bars, which the dwarves began to stack carefully about the otter's form. When they were almost done, Kuli was sent off in search of a heavy sack to carry the gold in. He returned a few minutes later with both the sack and a large rectangular plate of beaten gold. It was not so thin that it bent easily, but it could not contain more gold than three or four of the small bars. Loki recognized it as a sly attempt on Kuli's part to save a portion of his master's treasure by laying it over the top. But it was in accordance with the terms of the weregild, so he permitted it. Indeed, it made things easier.

"Admirably done!" Loki declared as he inspected the rectangular block of gold that completely hid the otterskin. "Indeed it looks so beautiful I hate to have it dismantled. But time is pressing, so sack up all that gold as quickly as you can."

Andvari did turn then, looking mildly surprised. Loki laughed at his questioning look.

"My good dwarf, do you think that I would have gone through this gold-stacking ritual if I meant to take an ounce more than I need?" he asked. "I did make you a promise."

"I just never met a thief so selective as yourself," the Dvergar replied with obvious sarcasm. "I only hope that the next time you will bring a list."

"Next time I will bring a wagon," Loki answered. "This is all my horse can carry, and he will complain about his precious back as it is."

The loose bars were quickly loaded into the sack, which was tied securely shut. Then it remained only for them to get the sack and the gold-filled hide outside, and that took all the dwarves of River Hall, as strong as they were from their work at the forge. The horse was still standing patiently at the entrance of the tunnel, and he eyed the sack and the hide suspiciously as the panting dwarves carried them out and laid them on the ground. Loki paused a moment to look up at the sky. The sun was down and it was now almost completely dark.

"Up on the horse with those," he ordered. "Place the sack behind the saddle and the hide ahead, and tie them securely. If I lose any of that gold on the journey, then I will be back."

That was threatening enough. The dwarves heaved the sack up first and tied it to the saddle with ropes, then pulled the gold-filled hide up over the horse's shoulders. The poor horse grunted loudly and rolled his eyes.

"Oh, my precious back!" he complained.

"Ha! What did I tell you?" Loki demanded.

The hide was soon tied in place as well. Loki came forward to check the straps, then turned and advanced upon the assembled dwarves menacingly. "Go on! Away with the lot of you! Your master will undoubtedly keep you hard at work at your anvils for many long days and nights to make up in profits what he has lost. Away!"

The dwarves turned and hurried down the darkened passage, while Loki stood at the entrance to see that they were indeed gone. Andvari, standing quietly to one side, watched apprehensively, his hand cupped over something hidden beneath his shirt. Then Loki turned abruptly to look at him in such a way that he knew he was in trouble, a cold and measuring stare that insisted that Loki still had some very hard matters to discuss. Andvari snatched his hand away from his shirt and hid it behind his back, hoping that his captor was both unobservant and short of memory. He gathered up his courage and stood proudly erect as he faced Loki.

"You have what you came for," he said. "Go now and leave me in peace."

"I will go presently," Loki replied. "But there is one other thing that I require of you. I will have that gold that you wear on a chain about your neck. There is something special about it."

"Only to me, my lord," Andvari swallowed nervously. "It is but the first gold that I found in the waters of the Rhine."

"But hardly the last." Loki was growing impatient. "There is a strong power in the heart of that gold, something beyond you. Give it to me before it destroys you, and be glad that I have saved you from your own ignorance."

"Please, my lord," Andvari begged softly. "The gold is precious to me. It was my gift."

"Your gift?" Loki asked, surprised. "Who would give you such a thing?"

"I thought . . . I had assumed it to be a gift from the Aesir," Andvari said in a low voice, suddenly ashamed for his simple trust and assumptions.

Loki laughed aloud. "Hardly so! If the great lords of the Aesir had such things, they would hardly give them away as gifts. Do you not suppose that I would know, if they did?"

Everything was suddenly clear to Andvari. The Aesir gave no gifts of power to lowly dwarves such as himself. They had not even known that the Rhinegold existed, until Loki had discovered it by chance. But that also meant that the gold was his alone. Now he had no intention of surrendering it.

"Give me the gold," Loki repeated.

"No!" Andvari shrieked. "The gold is mine alone. It came to me!"

"Fool! Give it to me while you can, and be glad that you still have your life," Loki ordered, and stepped forward menacingly.

Andvari cowed back, and almost instinctively he placed his hand over the gold. "No! By the power of the gold, you shall not have it!"

Loki came to a sudden stop, as if some unseen force held him back. Andvari stared in amazement, and slowly it came to him what had happened. He had called upon the power of the Rhinegold, and it had answered him in ways that he had never expected. In an instant he saw his advantage, that he now had powers over even the immortal ones. The world could be his. And to begin, he would have his stolen treasure returned.

But in his triumph his control over the gold slipped and failed altogether, and even before he knew it Loki sprang at him. In a sudden, swift movement he seized the gold and snatched it away, still wrapped in a torn scrap of the dwarf's shirt. Andvari fell back against the bare rock of the cliff face and sank slowly to the ground with a terrible cry.

Loki paid the dwarf no mind. He unwrapped the gold from the piece of cloth and held it up by the remains of its broken chain to admire it. Surely he had never seen any gold as pure and radiant, for it gleamed with undiminished beauty even in the growing darkness. Nor could he deny that it possessed a very great and subtle power; it had certainly brought him to a sudden halt. Now it was his, the power to make him the equal of any of the high lords and ladies of the Aesir. He would continue in his role of servant and jester, until he learned how to command it. And on that day not even Odhinn would order him about any more.

"And what bright promise does the gold make to you, thief?"

Loki glanced down in surprise at the dwarf, having forgotten him in the wonder and delight of the Rhinegold.

Andvari laughed bitterly. "Do not stare so! I know what you were thinking. Remember that I held the gold for many years, and I have listened to its whisperings."

Loki looked annoyed, and raised his sword in a half-threatening gesture. "Begone! Crawl back into your hole; you have bought your freedom."

"Free! Am I truly free?" Andvari asked, and laughed harshly. "There is no freedom from the gold once it has been in your hands. Hear me well, thief, and remember my words when your bright toy brings you grief. For I have held the gold and lost it, and now I see the power that it holds over the mind and will of its bearer. It calls you always, promising bright visions and comforting thoughts, until you lose your own will in its radiant beauty. It calls me even now, as I know it will for as long as I live. And if I cannot have it, then I will see that neither you nor anyone else will ever find joy and contentment in the gold.

"Thus do I curse the gold! While it has brought me wealth and happiness, let it now bring only death and betrayal to its bearer. Its bright gleam will bring no contentment or joy, only dark visions to trouble the thoughts and dreams. Fear and care will haunt the one who commands it, while it will awaken envy and greed in those about him. And in the end it will turn upon the one who covets it, bringing deception and death. You have taken my treasure; now take my curse. Let it destroy every hand that holds it until it returns to me!''

Andvari hissed and spit in a murderous rage, and as he cursed the gold it began to glow in response. For so great was his rage and grief, and so strong was his will, that the gold was for the first time awakened into full life. It reached out eagerly, hungry for the purpose and will that would keep it alive, and it seized upon the dwarf's dire curse and made those thoughts its own. It glowed brighter and brighter, filling the night with its golden radiance while Loki cautiously held it at arm's length, fearful of what the dwarf had brought to life. And when the curse was complete it blazed forth blindingly before the light faded swiftly away.

''A fascinating display,'' Loki commented, overcoming his fear. ''It is a thing of great power, I will grant you that. But I fear no curses, for I place no trust in any save my own.''

So saying, he caught up the gold and slipped it into his pocket. Then he leaped into his saddle and rode away swiftly to complete his task. Andvari crouched in the shadows by the tunnel and smiled with grim satisfaction. He did not doubt the power of his curse. Some day, he knew, the Rhinegold would return to him, and until that time he was content in knowing that it would destroy every hand that kept it from him.

Deep in the core of the world other forces were moved and stirred into life. Jordh awoke, troubled by powers that flared and shifted with her sphere of awareness. Great powers, but somehow twisted, and feeling their pulsing glow a fear awakened within her such as she had never before known. She stirred to full awareness and considered for a moment her counter-moves against such forces. Then she gathered herself together and began to move toward the source of that power.

CHAPTER FIVE

Payment in Full

Supper had come and gone and night had fallen upon Hreidmar's Hall, and still Loki had not returned. At least the sense of unrelenting grief that had descended upon this holding had been dispelled by Brynhild's report that Ottar was safe and well, so that the evening meal had become a farewell feast in his honor. The only difficult matter yet to be resolved was that of Loki's continued absence now that the time for his return had come and passed. Thor was of the opinion that he was not coming back. But Odhinn, who thought that he knew Loki better, suspected that he had simply gone off brooding somewhere for the afternoon and had not allowed himself enough time, and that he would be along any minute. In that much he was right.

The door flew open as if caught by a violent blast of wind and Loki poked his head inside. He quickly glanced about the room, while everyone stood and stared at him in silent amazement. He spied Odhinn near the fire and cried out in delight and relief.

"Ha, there you are!" he declared, as if Odhinn had been the tardy one. Then he quickly stepped in and waved his arms about in seemingly pointless gestures. "Now wait just a minute! I have it, I really do!"

"What, the silies?" Thor asked.

"No! No! No! I have the weregild, of course."

"Have you indeed?" Odhinn asked. "And why have you not brought it in?"

The answer to that was soon obvious enough, for the two strong sons of Hreidmar were needed to carry in the gold-filled otterskin while Thor followed with the sack of gold over his shoulder as if it was a feather pillow. The servants quickly cleared away the last of the tables, and the gold was set down near the fire. Odhinn turned to Hreidmar, who stood watching it all in confused silence. The grief of losing his youngest son was still too fresh for the old man, and being thrust into the affairs of the gods only made matters worse. The payment of the weregild, and especially the presence of the otterskin, would not be easy for him to endure.

"My friend, why do you not clear this hall of everyone who does not need to be here," Odhinn suggested quietly. "This is a private matter, and no doubt a hard trial for Loki."

Then, in accordance with the terms of the weregild, Loki began stacking the small bars of gold about the otterskin, covering it over so that no part could be seen within. Hreidmar stood staring with the others, but after a time he became aware of some troubling of his mind. And, as he watched Loki work, he suddenly realized what it was. The Lord of Flames wore it openly about his neck. The old man recognized it instantly for what it was. He had seen the Rhinegold only on rare occasions; he was one of the few whom Andvari had allowed to see it, and one of the fewer still who knew of its powers.

He immediately understood how Loki had come to possess it, and saw the treachery that Loki was capable of. First he had committed murder, perhaps unintentionally, but he had paid for it with theft and perhaps additional murders. Mischievous he was called; but Hreidmar saw him now as a creature of inherent evil, that so many of his deeds turned out so ill. Hreidmar was satisfied that he could at least recover the dwarfs treasure, and the Rhinegold as well, if he could contrive it. He was not the docile, agreeable old man that his guests may have taken him to be.

"Now let the payment be judged," Odhinn said when the treasure was ready. "In accordance with the terms of the weregild for his misdeeds, Loki is to have produced enough gold to fill the otterskin and then cover it over completely from sight. If he has failed to satisfy those terms, then additional payments must be made. Lord Hreidmar, are there any additions that you would require at this time."

"Only one promise," he found himself saying, as if by another will.

Odhinn nodded gravely. "Name it."

Hreidmar shifted nervously, as if fighting some inner conflict for having to do something that he found distasteful. "My lord, I have a duty to protect my holding, my people and my two remaining sons. I want no more troubles or ill deeds to descend upon us, now or ever. Therefore I must ask a promise, that neither Loki, nor any servant of his, nor any member or servant of the mighty Aesir should seek to recover any part of the gold, even the smallest bit, that has been surrendered in payment."

"That is wisely considered," Odhinn agreed, and the oath was sworn upon his spear Gungir, that it should break if that promise was ever broken.

When all was ready, Hreidmar bent low to the floor and inspected the box of gold from every side, and many of those who watched thought that he moved with more ease and vigor than he had these five years past, when they would have expected him to be more worn and tired than ever. After a moment he rose slowly and looked over at Odhinn.

"My Lord Odhinn, do you charge me with holding Loki to the full terms of the weregild?" he asked with slight hesitation.

Odhinn nodded slowly. "Indeed, I must."

"Then I must admit that the terms have not been properly met," he said, glancing nervously at Loki. "One of the bars is flawed, and it leaves a gap through which I can clearly see the whiskers of the otter's muzzle."

He stepped aside to allow Odhinn to peer through the gap. As Hreidmar had said, one of the bars was improperly formed, as if the smith who had poured it had not had enough gold to completely fill the mold. One-quarter of an end was missing, looking as if it had been sliced cleanly off, leaving a small window through which the otter's snout was plainly visible.

The others looked as well, and it was agreed that Loki had failed to meet the terms of the weregild.

"Have you no more gold with which to fill the opening?" Odhinn asked Loki, who had been turning pale in anticipation. "If not, then I must declare that you have failed and specify a second weregild you must pay in addition to the first."

"No, only a few gold coins," Loki answered dismally, wondering if all his trouble would prove to be for nothing.

Odhinn considered that and nodded. "Yes, that would surely be within the terms of the weregild."

Loki reached into his pocket and brought out a small handful of gold coins. They were wide enough to fill the gap, and stacked together they might just make a pile high enough. He bent and began stacking the coins one by one in the opening. He had seven coins in all, and when he inserted the last one he saw that a gap remained at the top large enough for one more. He bent and looked through the small slit, and knew that he had lost.

Odhinn stepped forward and peered through, then brought Hreidmar over to look also. The old man frowned, as if he regretted what he saw. He shook his head sadly. "So near. And yet, in honesty, I must confess that he has failed. I can still see the whiskers of the otter's snout."

"Then I must declare that Loki has failed," Odhinn said. "It remains for you to name the terms of the second payment, whatever you wish, even his life."

"But there remains one way that he might complete the first payment, if you will allow," Hreidmar said, slowly and cautiously as if in doubt, although Loki was not alone in catching the underlying note of slyness that suggested something dangerous—for him. "Can he not give something of gold large enough to fill the remaining hole if it was of another shape, but will not fit as it is?"

Odhinn considered that briefly. "So long as you are willing, then I would say that it would meet the terms of the weregild in theory, if not in fact. But he has no more to give."

"Oh, but I am sure he does, and if he surrenders it then I will allow that the weregild has been paid in full." And with that he turned to Loki, suddenly triumphant and self-satisfied.

"Give me the gold that you wear on the chain about your neck."

Loki was not surprised, for he knew that Hreidmar had seen the gold and marked its presence. But he still drew back in alarm. "Surely you are mistaken, my friend. What gold could you mean? You can see that I have none."

"The gold hidden beneath your shirt, if you have not already slipped it into some other secret place," the old man said so smoothly and dangerously that everyone stared at him, for he seemed indeed another person. "Give it to me, then all will be forgiven and you will be free to go. For otherwise I must demand your life in payment."

Loki made another attempt to retreat, while his hand clutched at something beneath his shirt. "No! I tell you, I have nothing. You cannot have it."

But Odhinn was not misled, for Loki was a terrible liar when he was at a serious disadvantage and upset. "Loki, show us this gold. What could be so special about it that it could be worth your life?"

Even then Odhinn doubted that Loki would comply, and so he took up his spear and called upon its great powers to reinforce his command. As if his hand moved against his very will, Loki drew out the gold and held it forth, dangling from its chain. Hreidmar seemed almost to hiss with pleasure, and his eyes gleamed like those of a hungry predator. Everyone watched, frozen in amazement, as much at the old man's curious behavior as Loki's. So much was Hreidmar's desire that the power within the Rhinegold sensed it and responded. It flashed with golden light and moved slowly toward him until it hung straight out on its wire leash, still suspended from Loki's hand.

"Do you not see!" Hreidmar cried in delight. "The gold recognizes its new master. It comes to me. Release it!"

"No!"

Odhinn recognized it at once. Often of late he had thought of finding new powers, and in ancient, half-forgotten memories he recalled the gold. Therefore he knew it immediately; indeed he wondered how he had not felt its powers before. It sang to him in a voice that he had not heard in a very long time, like the winds of space.

"No!" he declared again, and stepped forward. He held

forth his spear until its head was almost touching the gold. Sparks flared, jumping between the two, and the light of the gold failed and it fell to hang limply from its slender chain. "No, I cannot allow it. Such a thing was not meant for mortal hands. Nor for the likes of a thief and trickster like Loki. Give it to me at once."

He held out his hand for the gold. Loki and Hreidmar both glared at him in shock and open rage, and seemed likely to leap at him and fight for its possession. Then a strange, commanding voice called out from the very air about them, halting everyone where they stood.

"No! Surrender the gold to Hreidmar; it is best served in his hands."

Everyone jumped and looked around for the source of that strange, feminine voice. Fafnir and Reginn put their hands to the hilts of their swords, as if to challenge that unseen intruder. But there was no one.

Then a spark of misty blue flame suddenly appeared before the fireplace, turning in upon itself and spinning rapidly as it grew swiftly in size. Thor and Reginn, standing to either side of it, quickly retreated. The sphere of blue flame grew to greater size, a swirling, revolving mass of glowing plasm that hovered before the fireplace. Thin blue clouds trailed from it and flowed out across the floor, searing the boards, before vanishing. The mortals continued to draw back, and even Thor gave it room. Only Hreidmar seemed to welcome the intrusion; he knew not who this fanciful spirit might be, but it did support his claim to the Rhinegold.

Odhinn stepped forward to face the thing, his spear held before him almost as a threat. He watched it intently for a moment, then bowed his head slightly in recognition. "Hail, Jordh. It is long since last we met. This is no concern of yours, so what has awakened you from your long sleep?"

"Hail, Odhinn," the voice echoed loudly from all parts of the hall, as if the air itself spoke. "Speak plainly with me, for I cannot be deceived. I do not sleep. My being fills this world, and I observe all things that pass within the realm called Midhgardh. Seldom am I disturbed by what I see to the point of taking a direct hand, but I do not sleep."

"That would seem obvious, judging by how you were able

to force your way in here at what must seem to you a very
opportune moment. But why are you here, old friend?"

"I am here to see that you do as you have promised,"
Jordh said. "Hreidmar has a right to the gold; you must
surrender it to him, and then you will leave this place and
insure that no one who claims you as lord shall ever trouble
him again."

"And on what authority do you set yourself forth as judge?"
Odhinn asked.

"Because I have decided that it shall be so," she answered
quietly, as if that was not to be questioned. "Because, being
who and what I am, I am the ultimate authority, the only
authority, over all things that pass within this realm."

"Because you believe that you are the greater power!"
Odhinn declared, and laughed.

"That is so," she replied coldly. "Within this world the
affairs of gods and men may pass as they will, until I decide
otherwise. Right and wrong, good and evil, are beneath me.
The only reality is what I desire . . . or what I will allow."

"And it is your desire that Hreidmar should have this
gold?" Odhinn demanded. "It is a thing of power. It will
destroy him, and anyone who lacks the will to command it."

"That is so," Jordh freely admitted. "It will destroy him.
Others will seek it, and it will destroy them as well. I care
not. They will but hold it, until such a time as a way can be
found to destroy the gold itself. I have the resources to
sacrifice; but at least you will not have it."

There followed a long moment of silence. They each weighed
Jordh's cold and merciless words. The mortals saw true power,
the one whose pawns they really were when their possession
came into question, and the Aesir themselves felt much the
same. But Hreidmar's desire for the gold was not diminished;
nor was Loki's. Nor Odhinn's determination to take it.

Angry now at this interference, he took another step forward. "Why? Why will you not allow me to have the gold?"

"Because you cannot control it any better," Jordh explained. "Once, when you were far greater than you are now,
you saw the gold for what it was and destroyed it yourself.
Mimir has told me so. But now you share the weaknesses of
that mortal form you wear. You are flawed with mortal pride,

and mortal blindness. And if you are no longer able to see the truth for yourself, then I will decide for you.

"The gold is worth far less to you than you believe. It will not serve you as you desire, for it has a will of its own, and everything that you would do with the gold will be perverted into a reflection of its own evil nature. Nor can you take it from this realm, for the world-gates will not allow it to pass."

"And how do you know so much of the gold?" Odhinn asked.

There was a long silence, as if she did not have words to express what she knew to be true. "Because my powers are greater than yours, and always were. This thing radiates with more than just power, but with life. I sense this life and in it I sense things that should not be awakened. Deepest of all there is power. Over that a will, an awareness, and more awake now than ever before. And above that is a shell of something that I cannot identify, except that it is evil, and it discolors with its evil all things that pass into the inner will or radiate out from that core of power.

"Hear me well, Odhinn. Touch this thing and you are cursed with wanting it. Desire it, and that desire will distract you from all else. Use it, and you will create such evil as you will not believe. Loki is already cursed with it; Hreidmar as well. They are doomed, and will do only evil until they bring about their destruction. But you can yet be free of it, if that is your desire. I will do what I can to keep it from you, but I deem that you are cursed as surely as the rest."

Odhinn laughed, arrogant and unconcerned. "And what can you do to stop me from doing what I will?"

There was another long silence, and most of those who watched grew fearful of Jordh in that silence, unable to know what she intended and fearing the worst. They slowly drew back, until only Odhinn dared to stand before her. And Loki and Hreidmar as well, too caught up in their struggle for possession of the Rhinegold to care.

"What can I do?" Jordh asked at length, seemingly amused. "These are my terms. I will close the world-gates into this realm, and all those trapped within who count themselves of Asgardh will suffer destruction. That I will do immediately if you do not surrender the gold. And should you or any who

serve you ever break those terms or meddle in the affairs of
the gold and whoever may bear it, then my punishment will
be as swift. Consider well what will come of your authority if
it is known that you have broken your given word, when that
authority is based upon trust. A distrusted lord is a tyrant, and
that is what you will become if you seek to possess the false
gold.''

Odhinn paused. For beneath all her threats, her final words
held reason and logic, and reminded him too well of his own
fears and concerns. It was not what he wished, but all things
have their price and this one came dear to him. What he
desired above all else lay at hand, and he had to give it away
to keep what was more important still, the loyalty and trust of
those who supported him.

"You argue well, old friend," he said after only a moment
of consideration. "I will surrender the gold to keep what I
already have, and if you can promise that it will not fall into
the hands of those who are the enemies of the three kindreds."

"Such is my intention, and my promise to you."

"Then give me the gold, Loki," he ordered. It was doubtful that Loki would have obeyed, for Odhinn still underestimated the power of the gold over its bearer. But Jordh acted
first. A shaft of light shot out from the glowing sphere to
sting Loki on the hand that held the gold, hurting far more
than it damaged. Loki cried aloud and dropped the gold, and
Hreidmar snatched it up almost before it touched the floor.
Thus was the Rhinegold transferred to its new owner with the
greatest speed.

Odhinn looked surprised at Jordh, as did everyone, but she
replied before he could ask. "He would not have surrendered
the gold willingly, and we have no time for games. Nor
should you have touched it. Even if you truly did not desire
it, it would have been in your possession even for that
moment, and it would have cursed you with overwhelming
desire for it."

"Then you are satisfied?" Odhinn demanded.

"No, far from satisfied," Jordh replied emphatically. "I
will do the best I can, but I fear that this is the beginning of
many dark and terrible days in which we will see the end of
much that has been with us for a very long time, and the

coming of things that we cannot expect or foretell. Much of what will be depends upon you, Odhinn. Choose well.''

And abruptly she was gone, fading away like a bright flame suddenly robbed of its fuel. Everyone stirred and blinked, as if released from a common vision as reality returned. Indeed it might have been a vision that had held them suspended for a moment out of time, except that Hreidmar now held the Rhinegold while Loki held only his numbed hand, and the floorboards where Jordh had stood were reduced to charcoal.

Hreidmar saw that the others were watching him, and quietly, confidently slipped the gold inside his shirt. Then he calmly settled his clothes into place and stood erect, more tall and erect than he had stood in years. And it seemed to Odhinn that he was no longer old and tired, but strong and firm and animated with a new purpose. But an alien purpose, which made him something as cold and hard as it was.

"You have my hospitality for the night," Hreidmar said in a voice that was less than welcoming. "But I prefer that you leave in the morning. I grow weary of the constant trouble that you have brought, nor do I feel entirely safe with Loki under my roof."

His sons looked up in growing alarm, sensing that something was different and very wrong. Odhinn watched him for a moment and nodded gravely. "So it shall be. I think that we should call an end to this night. But if you will excuse us, I think that I should stay up for a time with Loki to speak with him, and remind him of certain promises."

"As well you should," Hreidmar replied contemptuously. "And I trust that you will remember your promises as well, for I can plainly see that you desire the gold for yourself. Let the mighty ones beware, and stay well away from myself and my kin and the place where we dwell, for a mightier one still demands it."

Hreidmar's sons stared in horror and alarm, as dismayed at the words themselves as that the kindly old man they had known could have said it. No other mortal would have dared to say such a thing in the Allfather's presence, but Hreidmar did so with impunity. For his threats bore the weight of truth; there was nothing that Odhinn could do that would not be regarded as interference.

"Fools, do not just stand there!" he snapped. "Move all of this wealth to a safer place. Do you think that I would leave it lying about with thieves under my roof?"

They flinched again, as if expecting the wrath of the Valkyries to descend upon the entire holding. Then they moved quickly to sack up the gold bricks and haul their burdens through the door into the back part of the hall. The Aesir looked upon this quietly, knowing that they were not welcome to as much as approach the gold, which Hreidmar worried over like some small, vicious dragon guarding its hoard. The door slammed behind them as Hreidmar left his guests, forgotten, standing alone in the hall.

CHAPTER SIX

The Forging
of the Ring

The next day Hreidmar began to consider what the Rhinegold might do for him. Since he was one of the very few who had ever been privy to Andvari's secrets, he knew that the dwarf had only used the Rhinegold to seek out true gold and silver that lay in the river's bed, which would glow brightly in response to its hidden powers. But he also knew that this was but a bare beginning of its total powers. Andvari had either never considered delving into the gold's other secrets, or had dared not, or had simply been content with the wealth it had brought him over the years. But there were greater things than mere gold to be had. The Rhinegold was the key to real power, even to the rule of all the Rhinelands or even the mortal realm itself.

At least Andvari did not come about whining for the return of his lost treasures. Hreidmar thought of it all as his now, and especially the Rhinegold. He gave the order that Andvari or any other dwarf was to slain upon sight, whether there at the holding or wherever they might be found. Dwarves did have a magic of their own and Andvari possessed a great measure of his own, and Hreidmar was fearful of his tricks. But it was also very obvious that the dwarf was wise enough to know that he would get nothing out of his neighbor but trouble. He locked the gate of River Hall and did not venture forth.

The Rhinegold also represented to Hreidmar a new life, a second life, young again and without pain, and he meant to make the most of that. He was done with quietly waiting out his final years, for by the power of the gold he meant to live a very long time. There were so many things that he planned to do, and so many things that he planned to have. And above all he wanted the respect he was due as the Lord of the Rhinegold. He possessed power now. The powers of a god, and he meant to be treated accordingly.

He paused in his thoughts, and lifted up the gold to look upon it. And, in some vague way, he was dissatisfied. A cold, unworked lump of gold was good enough for a thieving dwarf who swam as a fish to steal funeral treasures. But somehow it was beneath his dignity, unfitting as a source of the great powers that he could command through it. He imagined something grander, a symbol of his heightened authority. It occurred to him that he should have it made into a ring.

The task was not so easily done, for this was no ordinary lump of gold; he was aware of that from the start. What it could do for him was more important than its appearance. He did not want it harmed in any way, so that its special powers might be lost or even lessened. He was encouraged by the fact that Andvari had been able to pierce it to attach the chain. But melting it down, or even forging it cold, was something altogether very different, and something that he did not care to try without due caution.

It seemed to him that he could warm the gold gradually, using his ability to command it to test for damage to its powers. He guessed, based upon what he had heard of such magic, that heating it was far less likely to damage it than hammering it cold. He began there in the fireplace of the great hall, heating it cautiously and testing it often to see how it responded to his will. There was no change that he could tell, and when he took it from the fire it was still as cold as before he had placed it into the flames. It drank in heat unlike any ordinary metal.

And so he took it that night to the hold's forge, alone and in secret. He heated the forge to a fierce glow, but again he warmed the gold cautiously so that he might test it from time to time. When he had heated it to the point that even iron would have been soft and easily worked, he set it upon the anvil and pierced it through the center with a metal rod, sharply pointed, forming it into the basic shape of a ring. But when he drew it from the rod, he discovered an amazing thing. For the gold immediately began to draw in upon itself, so that within minutes it had returned to a featureless lump. So it seemed that the gold would hold no shape other than the one that was basic to it.

He heated the gold again, this time until it glowed not with power but from the flaming coals of the forge. Iron would have long since melted when it was only just beginning to glow, and it took many hours to get it to that shape. When at last he thought it was ready, he drew it out and took it quickly to the anvil. Again he pierced it with the rod and hammered it into the shape he wanted. But it cooled to the touch as soon as he had finished, and his hopes sank. And indeed it returned to its former shape within the hour.

The next morning he sat down and began to reconsider his plans. If he did not know how to forge the gold into a new shape, then he might find one who could. Andvari had been able to pierce the gold, so it could be done. And what better smith could there be but one trained by the dwarf, except the dwarf himself? Reginn was a second son, without prospects of a holding of his own and not a very able warrior either. But he had trained long at Andvari's forge and knew most of the secrets of the dwarvish smiths. Reginn, it seemed, was his only hope. But he did not wish to have to go to anyone for help, least of all one of his own sons.

That night Hreidmar sat alone in his hall with just his sons. Even the servants were gone, so Hreidmar saw his chance to speak privately. He called Reginn over and had him pull up a chair close beside him. Reginn came with some reluctance, for he no longer understood or entirely trusted his father because of the evil thing that had possessed him. But he hid his nervousness as best he could.

"You have studied long with the dwarf Andvari," Hreidmar began hesitantly, still very reluctant to share his plans with anyone. "I suppose that he has taught you well?"

"I must admit, modesty aside, that I am a far better smith

than any you will find in the mortal lands," Reginn replied, equally hesitant. "But compared to the great smiths of Nidhavellir, I am but a crude novice. He taught me a great many of the dwarvish secrets, but I cannot even say how much more there might be that I have not learned."

"But he did teach you of the making and working of . . . magical things?"

Reginn nodded slowly. "Some. Those were the secrets that interested me the most, and I used to hound Andvari until he would finally teach me something to be rid of me."

"Could you . . . perhaps . . . make the gold into a ring," Hreidmar asked almost painfully, then quickly explained his own attempts and what little he had learned from those.

"I must agree that it is unlike anything that I have ever heard tell of," Reginn said. "But perhaps I could tell more if you will allow me to inspect the gold."

Hreidmar paused, as if in reaction to some threat, and looked more cold and suspicious than ever. He wanted no one to touch the gold save himself, for fear that they might seize its powers and take it from him, even command it against him. But he forced down his fears and brought out the gold, holding it up for Reginn to see. Although he kept a firm hold on the chain, as if to jerk it back.

Reginn reached out and slowly took it from his hand, although the chain prevented him from taking it far. At first it was cold and lifeless, heavier than gold and harder as well. Then it seemed to him that he heard a distant voice, as if borne on the wind that rustled through the trees outside, and before his eyes he saw dim and distant visions. For a long moment he sat and stared aimlessly. Hreidmar immediately recognized it for what it was and jerked the gold back to him by its chain. Reginn stirred and blinked uncertainly.

"What did you hear?" Hreidmar demanded in a low voice.

"I do not know," Reginn replied hesitantly, still bemused by the gold's spell. "Everything was distant and confused. But it seemed to me that it searched my mind and judged my skills and learning. It spoke to me. I believe that it agrees with what you have in mind, and it told me how that might be done."

"How?" Hreidmar demanded harshly. "How can it be done, and are you able to do it?"

"I have seen it done. And Andvari taught me how to do it myself. But I have never actually done it. It is, perhaps, the most dangerous thing the dwarvish smiths ever attempt."

"But you can do it?" Hreidmar insisted.

"I can try," Reginn said. Then he seemed to break from the spell at last, and sat up with renewed energy. "But I would prefer not, if I could help it at all. Andvari pierced that lump somehow. He found the secret for making that gold hold form, or even that small hole would have closed."

He sat and thought about it for a long time. Hreidmar watched him with growing impatience, for it seemed to him that Reginn was more preoccupied with thoughts of how he might avoid this task than how it could be done. He slowly, unobtrusively closed his hand about the Rhinegold and silently summoned its powers, forcing his will over that of his son. After a moment Reginn stirred uneasily.

"I see no hope for it," he admitted. "I fear that we must do what the gold suggested to me in its visions."

"When?" Hreidmar demanded.

"Tomorrow night, perhaps," Reginn answered. "There are a great many preparations to be made."

During the next day Reginn had the contents of the foundry moved high into the peaks that bordered the Rhine along the length of Andvari's Force. It was not easy, for there were no established trails into the rugged, treacherous heights. Fortunately all he needed, besides a case of tools that he had carefully selected, was the main anvil, a massive block of iron as heavy as a large man. The forge itself did not interest him, and he left all parts of it behind. When Hreidmar at last asked why he did not need it, he replied only that it had already failed them.

The site he selected was a large, flat shelf of rock well up into the heights. It faced north, and they could stand there and look out across the river's narrow, twisting path through Andvari's Force and well beyond into the rolling hills of the lowlands. The open shelf of rock was very wide and deep, but was also well sheltered to the back and east side by the mountain itself. Near the back were several large boulders and flat slabs of stone that had broken off the towering rock face. Among these Reginn had them build a shelter, squeezed between two of the largest boulders so that it had walls of stone on three sides. The roof and remaining wall they built of heavy timbers. He obviously expected the need for such protection, for it was too solidly built for a place meant only for a single night's stay.

He set up the anvil and his tools out in the open, within only a single long stride of the shelf's jagged edge. Again he went to great lengths to see that everything was secure, dragging out a thick slab of rock to serve as the base for the anvil, which he fastened down with long spikes. Hreidmar watched it all intently, almost suspiciously.

Last of all Reginn had all others withdraw, with the instructions that they should take even the horses and not return until dawn. With this Hreidmar's suspicions were fully aroused, beyond what he was willing to accept. It seemed to him that Reginn might be trying to trap him in this deserted place all alone, with no chance of escape.

"Why would you send everyone away?" he demanded.

"Because this is no safe place for them, with what will happen here tonight," Reginn replied.

"And that secure little hut?"

"For our own protection."

Night came swiftly, cold and clear and bright with the wan radiance of a moon just past full. They could stand at the edge of the rocky shelf and still see many miles across the moon-washed land. But Reginn had no time for that view. As soon as it was fully dark, he went to stand ready at the anvil, his tools at hand.

"What I will do is no power of my own," he explained. "I will call forth the spirits of sky and wind, and if they hear me they will come swiftly to my call. But I do not know if I can do this alone. You must help me."

"How?" Hreidmar asked.

"Bring forth the gold and take it from its chain," Reginn instructed. "Call upon its powers and think only upon lending that magic to me, strengthening my call. When all is ready, then you must be prepared to give it to me without hesitation or question."

Hreidmar nodded gravely, beginning to suspect what his son was about to attempt. "I understand. Proceed when you are ready."

Reginn stood for a moment in silence, then took up the hammer and struck it three times upon the anvil. The clear, ringing notes shattered the cold night air and echoed between the peaks and ridges. He stood for a moment longer as the sound died away, as if listening for some answer. And it came, unseen and unexpected, a blast of frigid winter wind that swept past the two who stood together at the anvil. Then it returned, curling swiftly about them as if they stood at the center of a whirlwind, or as if some invisible being, summoned by that call, awaited some message.

"By the power of wind and sky, I invoke your aid," Reginn called aloud to the wind. "Grant me the fury of a storm, to serve as the hearth of my forge!"

"You know the risk . . ." the wind called back.

"I know the risk," Reginn agreed.

"Then so it shall be. . . ."

The wind whipped around them a final time and shot back toward the north. For a long moment all was silent. Then a gentle wind began to stir throughout the broken land, sweeping down from the north like an unbroken wave. And in the far north they saw a flash of light, and in the golden glow of the moonlight they could see a massive cloud explode upward into the heights, billowing rapidly outward, and as it grew it began to move toward them at a tremendous speed. So quickly did it grow and sweep south across the lowlands that they could well guess that the winds which drove it were of terrible, even unearthly force and speed.

Reginn quickly pulled on a pair of heavy gloves, then took up a pair of tongs whose handles were as long as his arms, especially made for holding objects over a hot fire.

"I have made a bargain with certain forces of this world," he explained. "The storm that you see will lend its full power to our task, but we must be done and in safety before it reaches us or we will not survive its fury. No one can say if the spirits of wind and sky actually seek our destruction, or if those forces, once gathered and unleashed, simply cannot be stopped."

"How long will we have?" Hreidmar asked.

Reginn shrugged. "When the storm reaches the base of the mountains that border Andvari's Force then it will be close enough to serve us. But it will also be slowed by that barrier, and give us perhaps twice as long. Still, ten minutes is the most that we can count on.''

Then he turned back to the north to watch the progress of the thing that he had summoned. In only a few short minutes it hurtled across the lowland plains and hills, a writhing, boiling mass of dark clouds, bolts of lightning rippling across its surface but never lancing down into the lands below. As it reached the true foothills below Andvari's Force it seemed almost to run up against some invisible barrier. It was slowed considerably in its progress, and at the same time it grew rapidly into the towering, menacing shape of a true thunderstorm.

"Do you see?" Reginn demanded. "It assumes the shape of the great anvil, the symbol of the dwarvish smiths. That is the sign that the spirits of the wind will serve us. Quickly now, place the gold in the teeth of the tongs."

Hreidmar did as he was directed, holding out the gold in a shaking hand. Reginn carefully positioned the teeth so that it was held securely exactly where he wanted it, then held the handles tightly together so that the teeth closed upon it firmly.

"Now you must get to whatever safety you can find," he ordered. "Only I can stand forth and be protected from the energy that is to be unleashed."

Hreidmar nodded and retreated into the barricade of rock and boulders at the back of the shelf, choosing a large slab of rock behind which he could watch in safety. Reginn turned to face the vast and threatening storm. A sudden, fierce blast of icy wind struck the ledge like a physical blow aimed by the storm at its tiny adversary. In response, Reginn lifted the gold high above his head, holding it as far away as the long handles of the tongs would allow.

For an instant it seemed as if the storm paused, its winds stilled and the furious display of lightning tamed, as it looked down to consider him. Then a single, slender bolt of lightning shot down from that rolling mass, striking upon the center of the Rhinegold. Reginn closed his eyes and lowered his head, but did not dare to move his arms as that single, sustained bolt continued to play across the surface of the gold. Hreidmar watched from hiding, so fearful of what it would do to his gold that he was unable to turn away his tormented eyes.

The bolt retreated after what seemed a very long time, but the ledge remained bathed in the light of the gold, glowing now not golden but fiery red with heat so great that the tongs which held it were beginning to melt. Reginn quickly laid it on the anvil, where it hissed and spit as it ate into the cold iron. He threw aside the ruined tool and took up a pair of short-handled tongs to hold the gold as he beat it out with a hammer.

He moved with quick efficiency, knowing that time was very short. Each fall of the hammer brought not a shower of sparks but a flash of brilliant light. He worked swiftly, switching from tool to tool as he shaped that core of fiery light into a ring. He held it up at last, still glowing brightly orange with its remaining heat. A cold wind, this time bearing a trace of sleet, whipped down from the storm to cool it.

When Hreidmar saw it he could wait no longer, but scrambled from his hiding place. Reginn, still admiring his work, did not see him until it was too late. Hreidmar snatched the ring from the grasp of the thongs, but quickly dropped it with a sharp cry of pain. He searched for it among the rocks until a lightning flash showed it to him, and when he picked it up again it was quite cool.

"The forging is complete," Reginn shouted above the rising wind. "This is now its true shape. Even if it is damaged or bent, it will return to this shape. Now let us get to shelter, before the full fury of this storm strikes."

Hreidmar did not seem to hear. He looked upon the ring a moment longer, then slowly slipped it on. Lightning arched down from the dark clouds to play across the slopes and ridges, dislodging massive falls and slides of rock. The wind whipped with hurricane force, carrying before it an edge of light sleet.

"We must get to shelter!" Reginn insisted, shaking him.

Hreidmar glanced up at the storm and laughed.

"Shelter from what?" he asked, and held aloft the ring. It glowed now with a cold, golden light. "Spirits of wind and sky, do you dare to stand before me, Master of the Rhinegold? Begone!"

The sky itself was split with a blinding sheet of lightning. Reginn ducked his head, guarding his eyes, then looked up to see that his father still stood at the edge of the shelf, the ring aloft. The storm seemed for a moment to gather in upon itself before blasting outward in all directions as if the terrible winds that drove it raced away in fear. Hreidmar stood and laughed, that insane, arrogant laugh.

"Do you see who is the master?" he demanded of the world. "Behold the new god, the Lord of the Ring!"

CHAPTER SEVEN

The Theft
of the Ring

That night Hreidmar sat alone in his hall and wondered what he might do with the ring now that it was his. From the moment when he had first come to possess the gold, he had held some vague plan of becoming a great lord through the power it could grant him. But the power of the gold did not manifest immediately, turning his half-thought desires into tangible results. He needed to know what he desired, and how he might go about obtaining it. Then the gold would work to fulfill those plans, granting him the means to take what he wanted.

What he wanted—that was simple enough. He wanted to be a far greater lord than the one he was. The gold promised that there was no limit to how far his influence might spread, but he saw now that it would not be so easy. He would begin slowly, taking the holds of his neighbors one by one until he was by far the most powerful lord in Midhgardh and immune to any attack, and could take what he wanted.

To accomplish that, he would need the obvious instruments of war: men, weapons and ships. Ships, now. He had been considering the construction of a new ship, a winter's work for idle craftsmen. Let them build him a sleek new ship to add to his small fleet. And a new, fortified keep to replace his simple hall. Those were his desires, and so the next morning he called his master craftsmen before him. They came quickly enough, confused and somewhat fearful, and it pleased him to see that they were afraid of him. Let them distrust him, and they would work all the harder to avoid his displeasure.

Then he told them what he expected, and by the power of the ring he drove his people like slaves by the irresistible compulsion he set in their minds. The craftsmen were set to building the ship and the new keep, while all others, even the women and children, were set to the task of cutting stone and timber. Hreidmar was relentless in his impatience, forcing his people to work from the first light of day until well after sunset, regardless of the weather, even as the days grew shorter and harsher before the coming winter. And so the weeks passed.

Reginn retired quickly to his room late one cold night in early winter, fearful of being sent back to the forge if he lingered about. He had discovered, to his surprise and regret, that he was now the hold's master-smith, for he alone knew the secret of making the dwarves' rust-free steel. And Hreidmar wanted it for his new ship, if it was to be the very best warship that they could build.

Not even his own sons were free from Hreidmar's oppressive will. Fafnir fared better, for he was a warrior, possessing no special skills but those with sword and spear, suitable perhaps for the backbreaking work of cutting and lifting stone but spared so that his strength and quickness would be true and his health good when he was called upon to fight. But Reginn did not envy him. Women and old men now did the heavy work that younger men could do best, and their strength failed as that relentless compulsion grew and they sweated and toiled away their lives. But Fafnir and the warriors would all die in a moment when their lord saw fit to use them in his plans of conquest.

Reginn's first and only thought was to find an end to this misery. And for that there was only one answer. Hreidmar must be separated from the ring and its power, however it could be done. For Reginn it was now a matter of survival, for he did not believe that he could survive a year of such unceasing toil. One would have to be destroyed, either the ring itself or the will behind it. And as the gold had already withstood the searing touch of raw lightning, it was essentially invulnerable. The weak link was Hreidmar.

But winter was nearly past before he finally found the courage born of desperation to act. And so he went secretly to his older brother and spoke of his plans, and Fafnir was quick to agree. Unlike Reginn, Fafnir's concerns were not so much for himself but for his people, and also for freeing his father from the curse of the Rhinegold, whatever the cost. They were agreed that their father must be slain, the only way that he could be separated from the ring. Then they would seize the ring for themselves and use it to set right all the damage that had already been done.

Hreidmar was hesitant to answer the soft but insistent knock at the hall's outer door. He was suspicious of everyone those days, not yet completely secure in his command of the ring. His one haunting fear was that the power that supported his will would slip and fail, and that one of the people he treated as less than slaves would come with a mind for dire revenge. Still, it did not occur to him that assassins would knock softly at the door.

He opened it to find Reginn and Fafnir standing outside, staring like the pair of fools they were.

"So what do you want?" he demanded impatiently, then drew back in alarm when he saw Fafnir holding a bared sword.

"It is about the sword, sir," Fafnir explained. "It is about all the swords that Reginn is making. A question of quality."

"Oh, come in, then!" Hreidmar snapped, wanting to close the door against the cold wind. He snatched the sword away, looked at it closely, and flexed it. He handed it back, shrugging. "What do you imagine to be wrong with it?"

"It is too brittle," Fafnir said. "He thinks that a sword should feel firm. But this one has no play."

"And he believes that a sword should wiggle like a willow-wand, " Reginn said, snatching away the sword. "It should feel solid or you cannot trust it."

He began thrusting and swinging the narrow-bladed sword, while Hreidmar watched impatiently, arms crossed. Then, gaining more confidence, he began to swing it with increasing speed, twirling it in an intricate pattern. Suddenly he swung it out horizontally, arms straight. Hreidmar's head rolled backward over his shoulder and fell behind him to the floor. His body collapsed over it a moment later.

There had been no other way. Hreidmar had been secure against more direct attacks, for by the power of the ring he could have stopped the hand of any assassin or even command arrows in flight. Catching him by surprise had been their only hope. Fafnir, who had never set hand to the ring, looked away, but Reginn seemed little concerned for that act. Indeed, he seemed almost pleased with himself.

When Fafnir glanced back a moment later, he saw that his brother had already retrieved the ring and seemed likely to claim it for himself, although their agreement had been clear that neither of them should actually wear the thing. And in a moment that seemed suspended out of time he heard a soft, persistent voice speaking to him alone, telling him that he should be the only master of the ring, that Reginn wanted the thing only for his own selfish ends. He watched as Reginn claimed the ring and set it upon his own hand, and he was filled with a furious rage and loathing unlike anything he had ever known. He launched himself into battle with a cry of fury and desperation. They met in an impact that sent both rolling several paces across the floor.

But the battle did not last long. A moment later Fafnir came up on top, both hands locked about his brother's throat, choking the life from him. But Reginn was himself as near to victory. He lay on his back, seemingly helpless. But he calmly reached with his right hand around Fafnir's back and laid hand to the hilt of the dagger belted at his left side. A moment more and he would have drawn the knife to slip its sharp blade into Fafnir's back, and so he would have likely won after all. But it was not to be.

"Stop it, both of you!" a voice barked above them. "You have already shown us how to deal with someone under the full curse of the ring."

Surprised even in the act of mutual murder, Reginn and Fafnir looked up to see Ingolf, the captain of their father's guard, standing over them. A score of drawn longbows ringed them.

Ingolf purposefully walked over and kicked the fallen ring to one side, even as Reginn had been about to reach for it. Then he took out a small, narrow-bladed knife and drove its point deep into the floor through the center of the ring, pinning it to the boards. As an added measure he covered it with a piece of heavy fur, so that no one could look upon it. He still did not seem satisfied as he walked over to the sons of Hreidmar.

"You might as well let him go," he told Fafnir, who still held Reginn's neck loosely in both hands. "Although I dare say that he does deserve it."

Fafnir did let go, but they both just sat and stared, too stunned to move.

"You have done us a great service," Ingolf continued. "Especially you, Reginn. Your desire for the ring was even stronger than the will that held us all. But you would have done us a far greater disservice in taking it yourself."

"I would have used it only for good!" Fafnir declared. "Give it to me, and I will undo all the evil that has been done."

Ingolf looked at him in surprise. "So it owns you as well, my friend. And I cannot believe that it did when you entered here earlier."

Reginn had been watching him shrewdly. "Are you in command here? Perhaps you meant to take this prize for yourself."

Ingolf shook his head sadly, although his regret was not for the ring but for the evil that it had done to people who had once been only good. "No one can safely touch the ring, and we have had enough of tyrants. And if we cannot destroy it, at least we can do something to insure that it is never used for evil again."

And so the sons of Hreidmar were imprisoned in a back room in the hall, and the ring was set that very night inside a massive block of iron, so heavy that two strong men could barely lift it. Ingolf's intention was to have it taken down the Rhine that very next morning, carried far out into the open sea and sunk in the great depths between Hafvang and distant Thule. And so the block containing the ring was set within the newly completed warship, and everything was made ready to sail with first light.

But that same night, less than an hour before dawn, the sons of Hreidmar escaped their prison by secret means which only Fafnir had known, taught to him by his father should the hall ever be besieged. With possession of the ring beyond them at that time, they could only flee. Thus they stole the ship which bore the iron block containing the ring, and taking also the ottergild they set sail in the darkness down the length of the Rhine toward the open sea.

Their one advantage was that their small, swift ship was carried along on the river's swift current with the spring's first gentle wind from the south filling their sail. The two of them together could not have rowed even that small vessel to any effect and there was no place along the river where they might hide, while any ship in pursuit would have the advantage of a full team of rowers. For three days and nights they raced down the length of the river, sleeping and tending the ship it turn, until they came at last to the sea.

"What now?" Fafnir asked as they left land behind.

"For now I believe that we should take the ring and our treasure and flee to some distant place far away from all men. And after a time, when we are completely secure in our plans and in the use of the ring, then we will begin the foundations of our empire. Our father had the right idea but he was too impatient, too uncaring for the lives that he could use and throw away. Imagine how our authority would be if we could command loyalty and respect of our own people as well as the minds and wills of our enemies."

"Where?" Fafnir asked eagerly. Reginn explained everything so well and made it sound so simple, he was beginning to believe it in spite of his prior suspicions.

Reginn thought about that for a moment. "Straight north, to the land of mountains and fjords beyond Hafvang, to Vikfjallaland, where hardly anyone dwells. There we would be undisturbed in our preparations."

The journey northward up the coast proved to be even harder than they had anticipated. In spite of their best efforts, they could barely keep the little ship on course and moving. Neither had sailed the open sea, and tacking was seldom possible in the Rhine. That proved to be a formidable task even though the dragonship had all the elvish improvements that Andvari had taught their father's father years before: a steering oar that was fixed like a rudder and a retractable centerboard. These two things did allow the inexperienced seamen to fight their way up the coast of Hafvang and across the straits to Vikfjallaland, but it was a journey of three weeks.

But even here they found a land that was hardly less populated than their own, for a tiny holding seemed to be hidden in the back of every bay and fjord. Also this was the land of pirates, from small bands of luckless thieves to the great sea raiders whose fleets preyed upon whole towns and holdings. And so they proceeded cautiously up the coast, first west and then northward, until they came to a land that was rent and broken by towering peaks and ridges that rose above deep fjords. And when it had been two days since they had passed the last small holding, they put to shore at last in the back of a massive fjord that cut nearly fifty miles inland.

Fafnir drove the ship well up on a gravel beach, timbers creaking and groaning as they scraped over hidden rocks. They did not even pause to pull in the sail as they tumbled over the bow and sat there on the beach, exhausted after weeks of fighting the wind and the sea. Snow still lay knee-deep over the land about them, but the beach where they sat was exposed by a low tide and bare.

"Now what?" Reginn asked. "Shelter?"

Fafnir nodded. "Yes, and soon. I have quite forgotten what it would be like to be warm again. We can build a fire some place out of the wind, and tomorrow we will see where we can build our new hall. The treasure can stay where it is until we are ready for it."

"I think not!" Reginn exclaimed, looking up in alarm. "Our ship is sinking. She spit us up on the shore and died, I think."

Fafnir looked, and leaped up in alarm. "By Thor's beard, she is going down! Her timbers must have cracked when we slid up on the beach."

They leaped on board and began unloading their treasure and supplies as quickly as they could. The little ship had indeed cracked its timbers just behind the bow, but they had also driven up to shore with the centerboard still locked out, and when that ripped loose on the bottom it also cracked the keel. They quickly lifted out their treasures and dwindling packs of supplies, piling everything on the beach.

Then Fafnir went aboard a final time and began to rip out every board and length of rope that he could find, and even pulled up one of the large wooden platforms that sat between the ribs to form a level deck. Last of all he took down the spars and sail and even the block and tackle and threw it all overboard. He leaped out after it, and he had no sooner landed heavily on the beach when the little ship suddenly lifted up to stand on end, a third of its length out of the water, pausing for a moment before sliding backward into the depths.

"Well, I never expected that!" Fafnir remarked. "She must have been lying across a sunken ledge, and slid off as she sank. You were nearly rid of me that time."

"It would have been your own fault," Reginn said. "What do you want with all of this stuff anyway?"

"Why, to make a sled. The gold alone is as heavy as a small horse, and that block of iron would make a pack for it. You want to carry all that?"

Reginn understood immediately, and put his skills as a smith to some use in converting the salvaged parts into a serviceable sled. It was light enough that, working together, they could pull it easily over the snow, and the block and tackle could be used for difficult slopes. Driven by some indefinable need to hide themselves, they set out the next morning for the snowy heights.

Two more days found them well up into the rolling foot-hills and ridges, heavily wooded and rocky, but still far from the towering mass of bare stone and ice that they had selected for their goal. They had come barely twenty miles, slowed as they were by the burden of the sled. It was an endless torment of cold and backbreaking labor unlike either of them had known even under the domination of Hreidmar.

Fafnir knew that Reginn was near the limit of his endurance. Long weeks at the forge had been followed by weeks more at sea, fighting a reluctant steering oar and unruly sail. He was half-frozen, and half-starved from poor rations. Fafnir himself, stronger to begin with and without the burden of weeks of harsh labor behind him, was heartily tired, so he knew that his younger brother must be enduring an unrelenting torture of physical torment.

But that was just as well, for Fafnir knew that the gold was talking to Reginn, torturing him further with promises of what it would give him if he would only set it free. Reginn had been desperate to have it free of the iron block since the day they had landed, and early the previous night it had begun to drive him to distraction with its demands. Fafnir knew also that Reginn must not have it; for now, in his present state, there was nothing he would not do.

And if Reginn died of the cold and exhaustion, that was all the better.

Fafnir paused in his task of hauling the heavy sled to look up at the path ahead. Suddenly he brightened. "There it is! A cave, not a hundred paces ahead. Pull now, and in a very short time you will have dry shelter and a warm fire."

They bent to the ropes a final time, but one of the runners fell into a hidden depression beneath the snow. The entire sled was shaken, and the block of iron tumbled off the top into the deep snow to one side. Reginn dropped his rope and, muttering curses, hurried to retrieve it.

"Come on, now," Fafnir urged. "We are almost there."

"No!" Reginn insisted. "I must have the ring! I have to have it out now."

Then, taking the heavy block in his arms, he half-ran laboriously through the deep snow off the path to one side, to where a group of boulders poked through the white blanket. He brushed the snow off the rounded top of the largest and set the block on the very top.

Fafnir, marveling at his sudden strength, ran up behind. "Reginn, please come. What do you think you can do?"

He had his answer soon enough. Reginn crouched to stare at the block, and Fafnir could feel him calling upon powers such as only Hreidmar had been able to command. So he had been in exchange with the ring, hidden as it was, strengthening his link as he learned its powers. The seams burst and the steel plates of the outer shell fell away, and a moment later the block of solid iron melted like a lump of butter that had fallen on the hot bricks of the hearth. Liquid iron ran down the rounded sides of the boulder to hiss and steam as it flowed into the snow. The ring, lying upon the center of the stone, glowed fiery red for a moment, burning away the remaining coat of iron. Then it shown forth in golden light, a light that slowly died away. Reginn snatched up the ring, already cold, and put it on.

"No!" Fafnir roared in fury and dread. "You shall not have it! You are a murderer and a thief, and it belongs to me. Give it to me!"

"Fool!" Reginn said as he gloated over his prize. "The ring belongs to me. It has for a very long time now, and the only will it serves is mine. Behold your new master!"

He turned slowly and held up the ring, meaning to use its power to command his brother's will. But before he could, Fafnir's sword arched up and severed the hand from its wrist. The hand was hurtled away to land in the deep snow, carrying the ring with it. Reginn cried out in frustration and despair and lunged at Fafnir, piercing his chest with the short knife he held in his other hand. It was a deep blow, but not deep enough. Fafnir staggered back and brought up his sword a final time, and a moment later Reginn lay dead.

Fafnir stood for a moment over the scene of battle, shaking and panting harshly from the pain in his chest, leaning heavily upon his sword. Then he dropped his weapon and staggered over to retrieve the ring from Reginn's hand. It was his now. All of it was his, and his only thought was to get his treasure into hiding, into the shelter of the cave. Then he could rest, and call upon the power of the ring to repair his wound.

He laid out the block and tackle and by its aid drew the sled up to the entrance of the cave. He pushed the sled inside that wide, dark opening, then paused as he felt a breath of searing cold reach out to him. And he knew in despair that this was an ice cave, and no shelter for him. Suddenly the sled began to move away from him, sliding down the inclined surface of the cave floor, which was slick ice. He reached for it with a desperate cry but it was gone, disappearing into the darkness of the cavern's depths. Several long moments later a muffled boom echoed back to him; the sled, hurtling down that dark passage, had crashed into some distant barrier.

Fafnir cut a torch from one of the trees outside, and by its light he followed the icy tunnel nearly a mile into the heart of the mountain. At last he came to a place where the tunnel curved sharply to one side, and beyond that lay a short passage that ended in a large, rounded chamber carved of ice. The sled had come up against the wall with force enough to burst the chests and scatter small bars and coins of gold across the cold floor. With his remaining strength Fafnir gathered up the gold into a pile. Then he sat down beside it, and a short time later the cold and his wound claimed his life.

Jordh watched all that had passed, and was satisfied. She would have preferred that the gold had been sunk into the ocean's depths as Ingolf had intended. Reginn and Fafnir's escape was something that even she had not anticipated, but she had carefully shaped events to this end. Now the gold was lost, in mostly uninhabited lands, in the bowels of a wandering ice cave. An age hence that ice would join with a great frozen river that would slide and creak down to the sea. And she would shape the currents to carry that ice far out over the trackless depths, where it would melt and release the ring to sink at last into the lightless deep, and she would bury it over with a slow accumulation of silt.

But until that time the ring needed a guardian, one that would never leave it unprotected, and never be tempted by its dark promises. Through Mimir, whose being was infused with the world-tree and all its roots throughout the nine worlds, she bespoke Queen Hel, who was the embodiment of her counterpart in the lowest realm, the spirit of Nifheim itself.

And Hel had the solution. For often she sent back the spirits of greedy kings and lordlings to endure a second, unending life in the form of a lesser dragon, brooding for all time over their funeral treasures. Thus when the death-maidens bore Fafnir's spirit to her, she bid them take it back.

Deep within the ice cave the walls began to glow with a pale, cold light. And in the chamber, over the mound of gold, a misty shape began to form and take on substance to become a lesser icedrake, larger than a horse and nearly as formidable as its larger kindred. Fafnir looked about, then turned to nose his former body with disdain. With his great armored claws he slipped the ring from the cold hand, to place it on the smallest claw of his right forepaw. Then he turned away and settled himself on his golden bed, curled up with his long tail

wrapped about him. And he seemed to sleep, except that his
eyes were open and glittered attentively. The gold was his
again, and simply the having of it was all that was important
to him. The ring's powers and brave promises meant nothing
to him and went unheard.

And Jordh was satisfied with the guardian she had found.

Here ends the *Song of the Dwarves*. The story
continues in *The Valkyrie*, which tells of Odhinn's
attempt to win the ring through the warrior Sig-
mund, and of the disobedience of the Valkyrie
Brynhild.